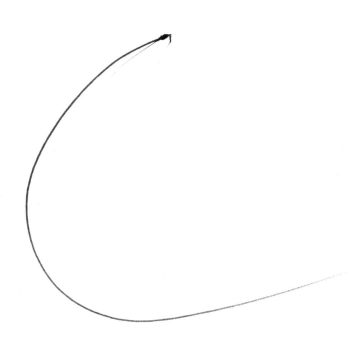

Pel and the Butchers' Blades

The 'Pel' novels by Mark Hebden

Death Set to Music
(Reissued as Pel and the Parked Car)
Pel and the Faceless Corpse
Pel under Pressure
Pel is Puzzled
Pel and the Staghound
Pel and the Bombers
Pel and the Predators
Pel and the Pirates
Pel and the Prowler
Pel and the Paris Mob
Pel among the Pueblos
Pel and the Touch of Pitch
Pel and the Picture of Innocence
Pel and the Party Spirit
Pel and the Missing Persons
Pel and the Promised Land
Pel and the Sepulchre Job

By Juliet Hebden

Pel Picks up the Pieces
Pel and the Perfect Partner
Pel the Patriarch
Pel and the Precious Parcel
Pel is Provoked
Pel and the Death of the Detective

PEL AND THE BUTCHERS' BLADES

Juliet Hebden

Constable · London

First published in Great Britain 2001
by Constable, an imprint of Constable & Robinson Ltd
3 The Lanchesters, 162 Fulham Palace Road,
London, W6 9ER
www.constablerobinson.com

Copyright © Juliet Hebden 2001

ISBN 1-84119-319-4

Printed and bound in Great Britain

A CIP catalogue record for this book is available from the
British Library

Though the city in these pages does exist
it is however intended to be fictitious
as are the characters.
Any resemblance to any actual living
person is purely coincidental.

Pour le colosse de Rô
taillé en pierre.

1

Friday, 29th October
Kids all over France came home with their satchels bulging,
looking forward to a week's holiday and celebrating that wonderful Celtic tradition, Hallowe'en. Pumpkins were hollowed
out, candles added. Garlands of ghosts and woollen spiders'
webs were hung in children's windows to fool the witches when
they came.
And Evariste Clovis Désiré Pel was very kindly bullied by his
wife into ordering a brand new car. He was told there would be
a three-week delay.

Saturday, 30th October
A bright sunny day: which was a great relief to all the Dads
on their day off. They pushed their arguing offspring out into
the chilly autumn air, shouting at them it was their turn with the
telly.
Les Bleus, France's rugby XV, beat the All Blacks in the semi-
final of the World Cup at Twickenham. It was an amazing match
and the millions of spectating French, wild with excitement,
could hardly believe their eyes. Quite a few of them got drunk
afterwards. *Les sacrés Bleus!*
And Fabrice Presot beat Béatrice Presot to a pulp in their semi-
detached house at Fontenay, then put the barrel of his twelve-
bore in his mouth and blew his brains out. It was a sickening
sight and the dozen police, cautious as they entered, could
hardly believe their eyes. One or two of them threw up afterwards. *Une sacrée merde.*

Sunday, 31st October
The clocks went back, or forward – whatever – and everyone
had one more hour in bed, which meant they missed the witches
on the rampage at midnight, twice.

7

At 0830, doctors Edouard Georges Cham and Jean-Louis Boudet, the city's pathologists, scrubbed up and started the autopsy on Fabrice Presot. When they'd finished him they got to work on Béatrice. Commissaire Pel of the Police Judiciaire de la République de France was pretty sure of the outcome but he had to have scientific confirmation of the events prior to their deaths, before closing the case and releasing the bodies for burial.

Monday, 1st November
Mountains of chrysanthemums were faithfully carried into the graveyards to mark the French respect – or obsession – for their dead. For the most part it was the only time in the year they were remembered.

Friday, 5th November
Guy Fawkes? Forget it, the French have never heard of him.

Saturday, 6th November
In Cardiff, capital of Wales, the French were beaten in the rugby World Cup final. It was a great disappointment. Enough said – we'll have to try harder next time.

In Dijon, capital of Burgundy, Marianna Roquetas had the hell beaten out of her before her attacker took out a pocket knife and had a go at dissection. It wasn't really his forte. Not a man who'd excelled himself at school, he had largely forgotten the lessons in the biology lab. However, he set to all the same. The first thing he did, quite sensibly really, was to slit the poor girl's throat, from ear to ear, opening her neck in a vivid crimson smile – just to make sure she was dead. A surprisingly humane action, considering he was such a monster. The blood flowed on to his hands; he looked as if he was wearing scarlet gloves. He was, in fact, wearing the rubber gloves Marianna had used to do the washing-up. He sat back to study his progress and, satisfied that with the end of her life he could do whatever he liked, he proceeded to posthumously penetrate her. Well, that was what

8

she'd invited him there for and it wasn't worth wasting such a lovely erection, was it? The killing had made him perspire, he was panting with warped lust and excitement. Having got that gruesome little act over and done with, he went back to the mutilation, more important than ever now – after all, the evidence of sexual intercourse had to be confused, covered up, cut out.

Satisfied that what remained of her genitalia looked more like minced meat than a tasty little snack, he hacked off both breasts, enjoying the feel of her soft flesh, still warm, in his fingers, weighing them each in his hands. After that it got a bit difficult; a pocket knife, large and sharp though it was, isn't really the right tool for the job when you want to joint a carcass. Searching round the scruffy kitchen, now awash with blood, he found what he was looking for, a pair of poultry shears, not ideal but better than nothing.

Exhausted by his exertions, he took a swig of sweet white wine – why did women always have to drink muck? A full-bodied red – he giggled at the thought, looking down on what he'd done – or whisky, or pastis, would have been worthier of his consumption. He'd resisted touching the half-empty bottle until the carving was completed, he didn't want inebriation to hamper the task he'd undertaken; however, all he had to do now was load the remains into the plastic bags and lob them into the river. He was sure no one would ever discover them. Not for a very long time anyway.

The butcher was called Jo-Jo – a shortened form of his given name but that's how he introduced himself to most women.

Sunday, 7th November
Jo-Jo slept most of the day, his evil need for blood temporarily satiated. It had been a surprise to find the killing so satisfying. It was the first time, you see – well, except for a couple of cats from time to time but that didn't really count. He killed the cats for fun, then masturbated over their lifeless little bodies, but he'd never considered killing a human, knowing it was punishable by imprisonment – he had a deep-rooted fear of being locked up, it was one of the reasons he'd never excelled at school and

why now he could never contemplate working in an office. The anger and frustration had started bubbling as the argument with Marianna grew more animated, but it was only when he was accused of being a twisted pervert – he'd wanted to indulge in a short bout of anal intercourse – that something had snapped inside and the beating had begun. Once that started he couldn't stop, it released all the pent-up emotion he'd been feeling for months. Now he felt better, and slept peacefully, renewing his energy, knowing he'd have to be up early the next morning for work. He had a Louis-Philippe wardrobe to restore and he'd promised his clients it would be finished by the end of the week. Jo-Jo liked to keep his promises. He'd promised Marianna she'd regret it if she didn't agree to being buggered.

Monday, 8th November
Schoolchildren groaned and went back to school. Mothers gave a deep sigh of relief and went back to what they were doing before the holiday.

Commissaire Pel walked into his overheated office at 0740. As he stripped off the heavy overcoat, woollen scarf and leather gloves, he had a scowl deeply engraved on his face – it wasn't unusual, he practised in private – and a half-smoked Gauloise hanging from his lips. Shaking the overcoat out, he hung it on its hook, crossed to his desk and sat down, thinking, Who needs November?

September had been hot and sunny. He'd seen the twisting crocodiles of schoolchildren winding their way along the pavements of the city to enjoy their last few sessions in the open-air swimming pool. On his way home from work once, he'd even joined the city's rheumy-eyed elders, stacked like frayed playing cards on the benches under the shading trees, to wistfully watch the children chalking hop-scotch grids in the small squares and play until supper at seven. And listen to the boys teasing, shouting mild obscenities at the girls, who skipped in intimate groups, plaits and ribbons flying like small colourful banners, chanting breathlessly as they jumped, tripped and started again. It had made him feel very old.

October had been deliciously mild and sunny too. He and his

10

wife had often eaten outside at midday – when he was home, which wasn't often.

But November, dark and grey and soggy, when dawn doesn't come until eight and then not with force or clarity . . . November, slashed with penetrating rain, and a chilling wind . . . November, full of mud and muck . . . Nasty November. Who needs it? Pel certainly didn't. In November there was far too much weather, the sort of weather that made him want to curl up and hibernate for the rest of the winter. Unfortunately for him, as a senior member of la Brigade Criminelle, come rain or shine, he was out in it. Or in it up to the neck because boring Chief Lambert was taking him to task over his tactics and disregard for police regulations, mild though it was. Sod it, Lambert was a pain in the arse. He was such a pain in the arse that Pel was seriously considering leaving the police force. It wasn't the only reason but fortunately it was the only recurring one. The death of one of his best officers earlier that year had hurt Pel. It had made him feel vulnerable, realising that he was actually quite fond of the rest of the team, even though they'd never suspect it while he bellowed daily at every one of them. Darcy's death had made him realise how fragile the thread of life was – he intended enjoying the rest of his, what was left of it, and Lambert didn't make it easy.

Getting to know the computer on his desk wasn't easy either.

Lambert had insisted on modernising Pel, and being a difficult little bugger, he hadn't taken kindly to the suggestion. Stubbing out his cigarette savagely, he switched the damn thing on and watched it come to life. Bloody silly contraption, he'd never get the hang of it.

There was a knock at the door, '*Entrez!*' as Pel scanned through his e-mail messages – what was wrong with snail mail, or the plain old-fashioned phone?

Blond Alex Jourdain, the only woman left on his team, and nicknamed the Punk due to her extraordinary hairstyle, pushed her way in, carrying a bundle of envelopes and a mug of coffee. 'Good morning.'

'I'm glad you think so. Personally, I think it's a rotten one. How the hell am I supposed to reply to this idiot if the message I'm writing obliterates the address every time?'

'Easy.' Jourdain clicked on *Répondre à l'auteur*. 'That way the sender gets his original message back, you don't have to repeat the references, and you simply add your answer.'

'Aren't you the clever one?' he said sarcastically.

She picked up an untidy pile of papers from his out-tray, smiling to herself at his deepening frown. Pel wasn't an easy man to work for, but oddly she was glad he was her commanding officer: he was cantankerous but clever, explosive but fair, and he'd been surprisingly kind after she'd been kidnapped and beaten to within an inch of her life. Not only that, she'd met his wife, Geneviève, an attractive and intelligent woman, who'd put up with Pel, apparently very happily, for more than eleven years, which had also surprised her; there was obviously more to her boss than met the eye.

She met his eye now as he lifted his head, pulled a face behind his specs and looked down again. 'Can't read what I've written! It's too small, you need a magnifying glass!'

Jourdain once more came to the rescue.

'Oh,' Pel said. 'Thank you. I mean, sod off, surely you've got better things to do than hover like a bloody buzzard waiting for breakfast to appear.'

She sodded off, grinning broadly.

Nosjean, Pel's newly appointed second-in-command, entered without knocking. 'How's it going?'

'How's what going?'

'Your initiation with modern technology.'

'It keeps answering me back, telling me I can't do what I want to do.'

'What are you trying to do?'

'Send a blooming message.'

'Are you connected?'

'Of course I am, or the damn thing wouldn't be all lit up.'

Nosjean moved round behind the desk and peered at the screen. 'But you've cut the connection with France Télécom,' he said.

'What have they got to do with it?'

'You can't send messages unless you're plugged into the phone.'

'Now there's an idea, I'll ring the bugger.' Pel pushed the

keyboard away and gave a long sigh of relief. 'I wish this thing was one of you lot, then I could throttle it. Nothing but a time-waster. Bit like Misset. Is he in yet? I feel like shouting at someone.'

The oldest member of the team, Misset was sluggish, foolish and enjoyed investigations that involved being out and about town, where he could delay in one of the many bars over a glass of beer. Pel thought of him as the village idiot, and told him so regularly, although once in a while Misset did switch his brain on and come up trumps. Once in a while he was brave and behaved with intelligence. It was, unfortunately, a rare occurrence. Misset the sloth was, for the most part, pleased to take on any surveillance, content to write lengthy reports, and willing to do late duty every evening, giving him the perfect excuse for not going home. According to him, his wife was an ex-SS officer, his children – far too many – circus clowns, 'if you didn't laugh you'd cry,' and his mother-in-law, in residence permanently now, a reincarnation of Attila the Hun.

Nosjean placed a sheet of paper on the desk. 'He's in, everyone else too, ready for the morning meeting when you are, *patron*. Here's the duty roster.'

'How are the new men doing?'

'Morrison's all right, a bit young, he blushes every time I speak to him.'

'So did you, until recently.'

'A lot's changed recently.'

Pel tapped out a Gauloise and lit up. 'Hmm, four of my team have disappeared, one to play on the computers downstairs, one to procreate, one to prance about in front of a camera, and one to police headquarters in heaven. And they were all good men, even Annie was a good man, and they've been replaced with an inadequate and an intolerable. These proposed cutbacks aren't doing police morale much good. I've heard echoes concerning Gilbert – what's the latest?'

'I don't want to talk about it.'

'I gather you don't like him?'

'That's the understatement of the year, and I'm not the only one. Pujol nearly thumped him.'

'Little Pujol?'

'He's a martial arts expert, *patron*. Luckily de Troq' was around and talked him out of it.'

'Always the aristocrat.'

'And Misset got the giggles after Cheriff left the room.'

'What was the argument about?'

'Cheriff being an Arab.'

'Cheriff is French, born and brought up in Burgundy, you can't get much Frencher than that.'

'Gilbert was goading him, saying he didn't like working with dirty immigrants. Cheriff ignored him, Pujol didn't.'

'Who's he partnered with?'

'Le 'Ulk, Bardolle, he's big enough to keep an elephant out of trouble.'

'Gilbert came from the CRS, not the same sort of outfit as ours. Give him time to settle – he may just be asserting himself in new surroundings. If there's any more trouble, though, I want to know immediately.'

'If he's an example of la Compagnie Républicaine de Sécurité, no wonder peaceful demonstrations turn into riots.'

'He may be a pain in the arse, Nosjean, but he's a pain in the arse we're going to have to get used to. Lambert selected him personally, he's here to stay.'

'Like modern technology?'

'Do as I do, try and ignore it.'

Slamming back the door to the sergeants room, causing the collection of cups on the filing cabinets to rattle, Pel made his entrance. His squad weren't surprised, it happened every Monday morning – as well as Tuesday, Wednesday and Thursday, not forgetting Friday. Only young Morrison was startled and dropped a wad of papers, which cascaded on to the floor like outsize confetti. Pel stared as he picked them up and Morrison blushed deeply, turning from red to purple, the colour of beetroot. He'd been with them only a few days and hadn't yet got the hang of the daily hullabaloo. Gilbert, who'd been with them a few weeks, looked up from a magazine he was reading and yawned. Misset stifled his silly satisfaction at Gilbert's insubordination and adjusted his dark glasses, worn to make him look dashing.

14

Not only was he slow-moving and mostly stupid, he also fancied himself as an ageing James Bond.

'All right, you lot! Pay attention.'

Nosjean slipped in beside Pel, sharply alert. They had hundreds of cases on file – breaking and entering, petty thieving, sale of alcoholic drinks to minors, sale of drugs to anyone, drunken driving, bar-room brawls, vandalism, hooliganism, fraud, arson, smoking in a public place, dogs chewing holes in postmen, cows chewing holes in the neighbour's hedge, the list was endless – all important, none of them dramatic, not like murder – ah, but they didn't know about Marianna yet – and all of them needing immediate attention.

'Let's get one or two of these cases wrapped up, shall we? Lambert is hassling for better statistics and for once I'm inclined to agree with him. You're getting sloppy! This one, for instance; the block of flats in avenue Général Leclerc. Five apartments broken into and the burglar is still at large. It happened two months ago! Three more flats were done last month in Talant and you haven't got a single suspect.'

'We've hauled all the usuals in for questioning,' Nosjean pointed out quietly.

'Then haul in a few unusuals! Use a bit of intelligence and initiative. And this one – who the hell is selling marijuana to the kids at the college? It's been going on since the beginning of September!'

After listening to his team's reports on the previous day's activities, and discussing the small problems that had arisen, Pel gave them one last blast of his voice and turned on his heel. On the whole, he reflected, making his way back to his own office, things were ticking over nicely. Steady progress was being made, the statistics weren't as bad as he'd implied, definitely not as bad as Lambert was making out when he whined to Pel about it. The trouble was, as fast as they cleared up one misdemeanour, two more were reported. August and September had been relatively quiet – the end of the summer holidays – but now the local villains were back in business with a vengeance, and although there was nothing really serious on the books, he had a feeling that any minute there would be.

He was right.

Friday, 12th November

It started raining around ten o'clock in the morning. It looked as if it would rain all day.

It did.

Big Bardolle knocked on Nosjean's door late that evening, walked in and crossed to the desk. 'Don't put me with that pig again, please.'

Nosjean looked up. 'Which pig?'

'Gilbert. I'll take young Morrison on if you like, for months on end, but no more Gilbert. I swear you'll have to arrest me for grievous bodily harm if I spend one more day listening to why all Arabs should be expelled from France. He's still going on about Cheriff, says it shouldn't be allowed.'

'Cheriff s French.'

'I told him that. Gilbert replied he looked like a bleeding *bougnoul*. I tell you, I nearly sloshed him one right then and there.'

'Why didn't you?'

'The traffic lights changed, I was driving.'

Saturday, 13th November

The driving rain continued all night.

France woke up in a state of shock. In the south-western region more than a year's rain had fallen in less than twenty-four hours. The Montagne Noire area, a triangle between Albi, Carcassonne and Narbonne, was declared a disaster area. The River Aude had risen out of its bed, swept over the embankments and flooded the countryside for miles around, devastating villages and leaving hundreds of families homeless, seventeen dead and ten missing. That was the first count. But it wasn't only the river to do untold damage; one poor sod, on his way to get help, watched impotently as part of the hill behind his home detached itself in a rumbling muddy landslide. Within seconds the small bungalow was buried, along with his wife and three small children.

It was nothing compared to the earthquake in Turkey, or the war in Chechnya, but because it was just down the road, where friends or family lived, it was far more shocking.

16

Fortunately, further north, the rain had been constant but not as violent. The Saône grew angry and dark, its turbulent waters swirling and crashing into bridges. Fields filled with water and a number of trees were wrenched from the banks. One or two incautiously parked vehicles were overturned and dumped further down the road, wrapped round a convenient lamp-post. A campsite at Larroque was flooded, but only three empty caravans were swept away. Burgundy got off lightly. Burgundians woke to extraordinary blue skies, with only the hint of the storm smudging the horizon; it gave the fire brigade time to pump out cellars and for the local police to erect barriers round the collapsed edges of country roads before someone got hurt.

And Jo-Jo the Butcher finally finished the wardrobe he'd been restoring. He rang his clients, announced the good news and waited for them to call and collect it. He hoped for payment in cash – that way he could go out on the town tonight, pick up a *pute*, make a meal of her, or meat, depending on whether she co-operated or not.

Sunday, 14th November
As the Saône slipped back between its banks, and continued rushing south to join the Rhône at Lyon, tons of filthy debris were left dumped in the surrounding fields. By midday, the farmers were out, doing what they could to remove tree trunks and mountains of mud, going out with tractors and trailers, shovels and chainsaws, in order to salvage what they could of their crops.

As twilight crept over the cold grey countryside, a large mongrel left his housing estate and trotted along the edge of the river, on his way to visit the bitch on heat at a farm not far away. Stopping to lift his leg, he smelt something inviting in the air, and putting his nose to the ground, set out to discover what exactly it was.

The black plastic package, buffeted by waves of angry water, had caught on an immersed tree stump and been ripped open, so he had no difficulty extracting the contents. More interested in a free meal than the bitch, which was usually locked up anyway, he retraced his tracks proudly and headed home. Tired by the kilometres he'd covered, carrying his prize, he finally settled down on the outskirts of town, to devour what he could.

And in the Montagne Noire region, they announced the flood had claimed not seventeen, but twenty-seven lives. They were searching for the remaining three, still missing, and we all know what that means.

Monday, 15th November

Having listened, as was his habit, to the seven o'clock news, and sighing sympathetically at the latest figures – now thirty-one dead, four missing – the caretaker of Collège Albert Camus, Bèze, went to open its doors for the director, Monsieur Léon Sarman, who usually arrived around seven thirty. The students, between the ages of eleven and fifteen, weren't allowed in until ten minutes later, stumbling over the threshold, only half awake, to prepare for the day's work due to start at eight sharp.

By seven forty, the sun was climbing over the horizon, gilding the corners of the college, giving the ugly modern, yet out of date, building a short-lived face-lift. There was still only a trickle of resentful youngsters, ejected from revving cars driven by parents who were hard pushed to keep the family together and hold down a decent job. With heavy satchels being carried, kicked or dragged, the early birds nodded *bonjour* to one another, sleepily shook hands, and shuffled off grumbling.

A couple of bright sparks, who considered that at the ripe old age of fourteen they were men, practically men, old enough anyway to talk dirty to women – well, make the eleven-year-olds blush at least – certainly old enough to drink beer – diluted discreetly with lemonade of course – and for heaven's sake, definitely old enough to smoke – they'd been doing that properly, inhaling and everything, for years – ducked behind a handy bush on the edge of the car park. Taking a couple of bent cigarettes from a crumpled packet, they shoved them hungrily between their lips and surreptitiously lit up.

'Nothing like a fag to start the day, eh?'

'Too right, feel depressed if I don't get mine.'

The trickle of arrivals had turned into a steady flow, voices were growing louder, the crowd was thickening outside the main doors. A car drew up not far from their bush and the two bright sparks shrank back.

'Shove over, you'll get me seen!'

'Shut your face, you'll get us heard!'

'Shove over!'

He shoved over and went sprawling. 'Shit! What's that?'

'*Ta gueule*! It's the old cow, Madame Maffre.'

Madame Maffre climbed tiredly out of her car, pulled a full briefcase after her, slammed and locked the door carefully – she knew what the kids were capable of, she didn't trust them further than she could see them, sometimes not even that far – and, sighing deeply at the prospect of another bloody day trying to drum up a bit of interest into the little bastards for her English lessons, walked towards the main entrance.

When she was out of earshot, one bright spark said to the other, 'Give us the lighter, Florian, I've trodden in something rotten.'

A moment later the fourteen-year-old, who was old enough to talk dirty, drink beer and smoke himself cross-eyed, was screaming his head off. Shortly afterwards he was violently sick, and ten minutes after that he was crying his eyes out in the arms of the old cow Madame Maffre. Not a very mature reaction but understandable, considering he'd just stepped in the bloated remains of Marianna Roquetas's torso. His friend, Florian, the other bright spark, had fainted.

2

As the insipid dawn dissolved rapidly into the growing daylight, colour seeped back into the countryside, turning the fields green and the sky blue, where small cotton wool clouds scudded about playfully, raising everyone's hopes for a pleasant day. In the director's office, however, things were far from pleasant; Monsieur Sarman was telling Capitaine Baron Charles Victor de Troquereau what had been found and by whom, while the two bright sparks – Florian revived, Bastien still nauseous – sobbed in the background. De Troq' understood why the boys were crying, the human torso was enough to make anyone weep. Already ghastly enough when it was lobbed into the river, its eight-day immersion, plus the big mongrel's teeth, had not improved it.

Standing to the right of de Troq', Lieutenant Morrison, blushing uncontrollably, was making copious notes, and Lieutenant Alexandra Jourdain, the Punk, was listening to the old cow Madame Maffre.

'God, it was foul! Can you imagine doing that to someone?'

'Personally, no.'

'Look, I know I shouldn't suggest this but do you think I could offer these poor boys a cigarette? They look as if they need it.'

'Is it allowed?'

'Only in the staff room. What about a drop of brandy? Jesus, I know I need one.'

Outside, the technicians were working methodically; Boudet, the assistant pathologist, completed his preliminary examination of the human remains before indicating they could be removed to his lab for autopsy – after, of course, the examining magistrate, Maître Brisard, had been, seen and given his permission. The forensic scientists, spread out across the car park and grass, were meticulously searching for anything, any minute scrap of anything, that might help them establish when, why and by whom the mutilation had been caused. Sweet papers, cigarette ends, scraps of torn paper, a broken pencil, chewed chewing-gum, a split condom, even a sample of canine excrement, was collected, labelled and added to the growing collection for analysis.

Tuesday, 16th November

Thirty-four dead in the Montagnes Noires.

One in Burgundy.

It was more than enough.

Death is not nice.

It's not nice when surrounded by fresh spring flowers. It's not nice adorned with the lavish blooms of summer. Nor decorated with the gold and copper leaves of autumn. Even the glittering silver frosts of winter don't make any difference.

Death is definitely not nice. Sometimes it's very ugly.

It was at its ugliest lying on one of the cold metal tables in the path lab. The skin, where it was unbroken, was as pale as paper; the livid slash marks in the bloated flesh, and the gnawed edges, stood out in vivid purple. The pathologists, Boudet and Cham, scrubbed up, tied each other's gowns, pushed their clinically clean hands into latex gloves and started work on the torso. The autopsy had been delayed by a car accident – both occupants badly burnt after their Renault Mégane plunged on to the railway line and burst into flames, the driver with 3.23 grams of alcohol in his blood, as pissed as a newt; by a baby of six weeks – reported as a cot death, but had to be proved not to be wilful suffocation by a parent; and by journalistic interference – newspapermen, local and from Paris, excited by the story that had broken the day before, had been jostling to get the scoop first. The police could tell them nothing, so they'd gone to pester the pathologists, who also told them nothing.

By midday, they'd finished their examination of the torso and turned their attention to analysing particles removed from it: the contents of the opened stomach, large and small intestine, together with the swabs taken from all the ragged edges and what was left of the vaginal and anal cavities. From the growth, size and length of the bones, they had so far established that the victim was a woman, aged between twenty and twenty-five,

21

1m50 to 1m55 tall, slim, weighing approximately 43 kilos (about the size of an average young teenager), of Southern European origins, possibly Spanish or Portuguese. She had been killed between 3rd and 10th November; they couldn't be any more accurate given what they had to work with, which wasn't much.

Boudet rang Pel that evening to give him the relevant details, confirming he would be sending it through to his e-mail address as soon as it was written in full.

Pel stared at the notes he'd made, wondering who the poor unfortunate woman was, then as there was nothing more he could do that evening he decided to go home. It was 2020. He unlocked his front door at 2050, just in time to miss every item of the news, about the only programme he bothered to watch with regularity.

As it happened the technicians at TF1 were on strike in answer to the newly imposed thirty-five hour week – reduced from forty – and as a consequence, instead of American series about Barbie dolls and unbelievable cop movies, that evening they broadcast repeats of *Mr Bean* and *Benny Hill*. It was a definite improvement.

Wednesday, 17th November

It started raining again. Although it wasn't as heavy as the previous weekend, it was enough to hamper the clearing-up operation after the floods. The cost of the catastrophe was becoming clearer. South-western France supplied 65% of all France's lettuces; the whole lot had been destroyed, and prices were already soaring. Prize-winning vineyards had been wiped out, the ancient gnarled trunks sucked from the saturated earth, then the earth had followed, flowing in a gushing landslide into the river, leaving bare sterile rock – the vines that had provided wine fit for gods for many generations would never be planted again. Factories had been ruined; the tops of machinery poked out of the mud, looking like drowned dinosaurs staring blindly up at the torn tree trunks rammed into the overhead rafters. Roads, bridges, homes and herds of sheep had been simply washed away. The insurers, instead of sitting comfortably in their centrally heated offices, sipping coffee and adding up how much the premiums would bring in today, were for once out and about, swathed in woollies, scarves, hats, gloves and boots, assessing the devastation. It was a depressing sight, even the hard-hearted experts found it so. Crates of clothing destined for Kosovo were rerouted and distributed to the homeless families, still sheltering in the local schools. And the Red Cross did what they could to feed the hundreds of hungry inhabitants who no longer had kitchens to cook in.

In the Hôtel de Police in the capital of Burgundy, Pel lit a Gauloise and puffed patiently while his computer played its opening tune, clicked efficiently on Outlook Express, clicked on Connection, inhaled deeply, and watched his mail arrive. He was at last getting the hang of one aspect of modern technology. The message he'd been waiting for was of course from Doc Cham, enclosing the completed pathologists' report. But Pel couldn't find it. All he could see was a small paperclip sitting by the title of the message. *Putain de merde*, how he longed to go back to the days when paperclips weren't virtual but metal, and held real folding paper.

As Jourdain came into the office with his early morning coffee and an assortment of envelopes, he smiled angelically, making him look more like Quasimodo than a Chief Inspector. She smiled back. 'Anything I can do to help?'

Thirty seconds later he had page one of the report in his hand; the other fourteen were still being printed out. He read from start to finish, snatching the paper from the printer as it emerged. It told him very little, until he got to the last page which was where the doctors noted their conclusions.

Stapling the pages together, Pel lifted the phone, lit another cigarette and tapped in the lab's number. Boudet answered on the third ring.

'Morning, Pel.'

'Is Cham there?'

'He is, but he's busy, up to his elbows inside an old boy who snuffed it last night.'

'You're repulsive.'

'No, he is; very smelly. I think he'd started rotting before he died, his lungs were filled with green bile and –'

'Boudet!'

'Sorry. What did you want?'

Page: 15/15 (ref: QC/EGC/99.2082376538756.5)

Participating Pathologists: E G Cham, J L Boudet
Date: 16th November
Name of victim (if known): unknown female, possibly Spanish or Portuguese
Age: estimated between 20–25 (para 3/9)
Location: south-eastern side of car park, Collège Albert Camus, Bèze.
Investigating officer (if applicable): Capitaine CV de Troquereau
(commanding officer: Commissaire ECD Pel, Police Judiciaire, Dijon)

Conclusions:
Death is presumed to have resulted from the multiple stab wounds mentioned above (para 8/3) caused by a sharp blade (8/5). The mutilation (para 21/1) and dissection (21/15) of the body appears to have been carried out by a person with little knowledge of anatomy using a sharp knife (para 21/7 + 8/5) and another utensil, very probably poultry shears (21/9). The torso had been wrapped in black plastic (para 30/1) and immersed in muddy river water for more than one week (30/5), possibly as much as ten days. During this time extensive damage occurred consistent with having come into contact with large solid immobile objects, one of them the broken branch of a tree (para 21/19). Further mutilation (para 21/29) took place after it was removed from the water. Canine saliva has been identified, therefore we suggest a large dog (para 21/31) moved then mauled – or vice versa – the remains and left them where they were found (para 33/3 – see Leguyder report on location). The question of rape has arisen; unfortunately due to the comprehensive mutilation, plus the lengthy immersion in water, we are unable to give an opinion.
Estimated time of death: between 3 Nov and 10 Nov (para 31/1).

Dept de
Pathologie

DIJON
16/11/99

EGCham

JLBoudet

24

'A translation.'

'Which report? Give me the reference, I'll get it on the screen.'

'What, all of it?'

'The last four figures'll do.'

'*Sept cents cinquante-six, point, cinq.*'

'Okay, hang on . . .'

Pel inhaled, drawing the soothing nicotine down to his toes, and exhaled impatiently.

'Got it. Which paragraph?'

'I'm looking at the conclusion.'

'Okay, fire away.'

'Why poultry shears?'

'It was the only thing we found that would cut through human joints leaving the marks observed.'

'You mean you tried it!'

'We have our methods – and our reference library.'

'What about secateurs?'

'They're not serrated.'

'*D'accord*. You say muddy river water, why not a muddy pond, or canal?'

'The algae, grit and particles of earth are consistent with turbulent, running water, not a stagnant or partly stagnant pond. Canals have locks to stop turbulence; even in a storm, although the surface is rippled, the water underneath remains calm. Plus the fact that one of the wounds we examined had particles of bark and newly broken wood in it, suggesting the branch of a tree. Hence we concluded that the torso had been put in a dustbin bag for disposal and thrown in the river.'

'Dustbin bag?'

'The black plastic we referred to. There was a small strip of it caught on a broken rib. Check with Leguyder, but I'm pretty sure he'll find that's what it is.'

He did.

'A large dustbin bag,' he confirmed. 'The smaller ones are flimsier, and either blue or green. This was the 50 litre size.'

'What else have you discovered?'

'We're still working on it!' the scientist snapped. 'I'll mail you my report as soon as we're finished.'

25

'Please,' Pel begged, 'tell me what you've found so far.'

'So far we can prove the children at the college smoke too many cigarettes. Someone ought to tell them of the dangers involved.'

'I'm sure they have.'

'It certainly wasn't you! Your tobacco habit puts the whole of Dijon in danger.'

'I gave up for more than a month in the summer.'

'Only *just* more than a month, since then you've made up for lost time.'

'It was Darcy's fault! After he, he . . .' Pel stuttered to a stop. Remembering the sight of the detective's bloody body being removed from the farmhouse where he'd died didn't make him want to weep any more but he still didn't enjoy it. 'Sod it, Leguyder, you know why I started smoking again.'

There was an odd silence from the other end of the phone. Then, 'My findings so far indicate that the human remains found at Collège Albert Camus were brought there by an unknown person or persons.'

'Or dog?'

'It's possible. There is no evidence surrounding the location that murder was committed there. Nor is there any evidence of the murderer having been there. We lifted a lot of footprints, all of which, so far, coincide with the footwear of the students from the college, although, as I'm sure you understand, some of them have big feet and weigh as much as a man. The students are still co-operating with my technicians to eliminate the prints we've taken. We have yet to identify three. Apart from that, I can tell you there *was* a large dog present some time before the torso was found; it's got worms.'

'Which has nothing to do with anything.'

'Precisely, but you did ask . . .'

'Yes, Leguyder, I did. I'll look forward to reading your 300 page novel when you've finished. In the meantime, I may just smoke myself to death.'

'Pel?'

'What!'

'Forget it!'

So, now Pel knew. The victim could have come from any-where. She'd been killed, chopped up and lobbed into the River Saône. She could have come from as far north as Bains les Bains, although he doubted it, the river was only a stream at its source. She could even have come from Germany and been transported in pieces over the border – stranger things had happened. She could, on that premise, have come from Paris; there were plenty of Spanish and Portuguese women living there. She could have come from anywhere, although considering the flow of the Saône, he was pretty sure she'd come from a little further north and not too far from the river as that was where her murderer had decided to dispose of her. Well, it narrowed things down a bit. At a rough guess it narrowed it down to approximately 600 square kilometres covering a good part of two counties. The police in both counties, together with the counties through which the Saône ran – another seven, including those after it became the Rhône – would be alerted, and henceforth would be on the lookout for more grizzly parcels, in the hope that on finding one, containing say her head or her hands, they might be able to finally identify their victim. Or perhaps they'd get lucky, perhaps she'd be on a missing persons list.

She wasn't.

They were going to have to do it the hard way.

They did it the hard way for the rest of the week, and they still didn't know who the poor woman was. Pel's team wore their legs down to stumps, smoked themselves silly, and one or two of their children wondered who the stranger was who came to eat with Maman occasionally – Papa looked younger, didn't bite their heads off and smiled when he walked in through the door. One or two wives were asking themselves the same questions. They hadn't finished yet.

And Chief Lambert was complaining loudly that they hadn't made an arrest. What did the bloody man expect? A miracle?

Pel sighed: it would be nice once in a while.

Instead, he got another murder, but he didn't know that for another few days.

27

Thursday, 18th November
It rained on and off all day. Pel's team, tramping the streets and the countryside, in search of information and inspiration on any one of their many cases, got wet.

Lionel Jospin, the French Prime Minister, visited the L'Aude region. It had already been declared a *catastrophe naturelle*, which meant the insurers would be paying up more rapidly than usual – on the properties and items therein that were covered, a lot weren't – and Jospin promised the devastated communities financial support from the government – in the region of 10,000,000 francs to rebuild schools and other council property so essential for a return to normal life, and to re-establish electricity and water, equally essential. For all that, no one knew what to say to the middle-aged tool-maker whose machinery, working perfectly before being engulfed in mud, had been 'written off' over five years and who would therefore receive no compensation from the insurance company; he was facing total bankruptcy.

Friday, 19th November
The rain had a bite in it. The storm that had raged all night, lifting tiles off roofs and whipping branches from the trees, had calmed, but the wind was still bitter, making noses drip and pinching fingers.

Nosjean and young Morrison were about town following up the investigation into a cat-burglar who was blighting flat-dwellers' lives.

De Troq' and Jourdain arrested a lad of sixteen for shoplifting, having caught him red-handed as he tried to make a run for it after snatching a mobile telephone from the display in the hyper-market, Géant. He said he'd wanted to phone home and tell his Mum he'd be late. They handed him the phone in the police interview room and told him he'd better do it now.

Cheriff and Misset did a house-to-house around Collège Albert Camus just in case someone had seen something suspicious. Cheriff asked the questions, Misset wrote down the answers and in between complained non-stop about the number of children he had. 'Children,' he said, 'are a drain on humanity. No sooner are they born than they start shouting their demands. First it's only a breast or a bottle, but you wait, very soon it'll be Action Man or Barbie, after that it's the GameBoy or GameGear, all of which, you'll point out, are fairly accessible. But you wait, when they're fifteen it'll be the Playstation or worse. Then you'll be paying for driving lessons which will lead to the need for a car. And just when you think the worst is over, off they go into the army for a year.'

'Conscription's been abolished.'

'Damn good thing too. When my sons came out, they were men, there's no doubt about it, men who wanted, felt they deserved, women, motorbikes and money.'

'They could work.'

'With unemployment as it is? You're joking. What a wonderful world, Christophe just lies in front of the telly fondling his girlfriend's tits, waiting for Dad to bring home the bacon. I was born in the wrong generation, Cheriff.'

'Talk to him, explain, and if he doesn't want to listen, throw the sod out.'

'And have my wife throw me out?'

'I thought you didn't get on?'

'Yeah, well, once a week we manage to tie and gag the mother-in-law, grease the palms of our offspring so they disappear to the cinema, and retire to bed early. It's the only time I wouldn't rather be at the office.'

While Cheriff and Misset were discussing the ups and downs of life, Bardolle and Pujol were asking questions about arson, and Gilbert, who no one wanted to work with, picked his nose, clipped his fingernails and would have taken off his shoes and socks to attend to his toenails if Pel hadn't caught him, one sock on, one sock off, so to speak, and given him a dressing down, slamming an armful of documents on to his desk and telling him to do something useful, 'like filing the buggers!' As the phone started ringing he added, 'Well, sitting looking at it won't tell you what the caller wants, answer the damn thing!' That was just before Pel joined the head of Forensics, Leyguyder – something he wasn't looking forward to – and half a dozen gendarmes, to edge their way along the river bank in the hope of finding a clue to the torso's identity. They found twenty-seven plastic bags, all with the name of the local supermarkets on them, none of them containing anything but mud, twigs, and in one case a rusty tin of Cassoulet au Cuisses de Canard. They also found a collection of rags various sizes, colours and stages of decay – five shoes and two socks – one grey, one brown; they were all bagged and added to Leguyder's sample boxes. The rusting red and yellow toddler's wheelbarrow was also loaded up. The rest was left where they found it: a broken and very old pram, a metal bed frame, four fridges, three mattresses, two empty oil drums and a partridge in a pear tree.

At five to two they'd finally finished and Pel hurried back into the city centre, stopping at the Bar Transvaal across the road for a tray of food as soon as he arrived.

'Sorry, mate, the kitchens closed half an hour ago. All I can offer you is our selection of hot snacks: croque-monsieur, hamburger, hamburger with cheese, hamburger with onions, or hot dog.'

Pel knew the hot snacks only too well; they were deep frozen and encased in a polystyrene box, brought to a consumable temperature, and the consistency of rubber, by a quick trip round the inside of a microwave – *non merci*.

'What about a sandwich then? Ham, dried sausage, garlic sausage, pepper sausage, cheese or pâté.'

Pel sighed at his rumbling stomach; he would have liked to take the legally allotted two hours to eat a decent meal like every other inhabitant of his beloved Burgundy. As it was he asked about the pâté.

'Duck,' he was told and agreed to try it.

It would have been more appetising if he'd eaten it there and then, but being a conscientious policeman with a lot on his mind, he made the mistake of carrying the plastic-wrapped food, and a bottle of beer, back to his office.

Before he'd forced entry into the hermetically sealed package, Chief Lambert called him in for a conference. He was worried, he said, about Pel's team. He was worried, he added, that with so many changes, and too few replacements, efficiency and therefore statistics might suffer.

Pel suffered for a long twenty minutes while his lunch perspired and, to all intents and purposes, expired on his desk. Lambert had a lot to answer for, he thought bitterly as he at last bit into half a flaccid baguette, a limp lettuce leaf and something masquerading as *pâté de canard*; it looked and tasted more like tinned catfood. He chewed and swallowed all the same, driven by a gnawing hunger that felt as if it was drilling holes in the walls of his stomach, and washed it down with the now tepid beer.

After he'd finished, he trotted across the road again, hoping a short burst of physical exercise might help the digestion of such an evil meal, and treated himself to an espresso at the bar, noting with satisfaction that not one of his team was propping it up, not even Misset. Then, leaving 6 francs on the counter, he made his way more slowly back up to his office to read reports, write reports, make phone calls, receive phone calls, and sit for another long hour listening to Lambert's monotonous voice, expounding on the subject of overall discipline and updating the whole police force. By the time he went home at 2100, he was ready to resign.

His wife met him in the hall and hung his coat on its hook, then, following him into the sitting-room, handed him a glass of his favourite whisky. 'Did you ring about the new car?'

'It hasn't arrived yet. They say next week.'

'How disappointing. Supper'll be ready in a few minutes.'

'If it's batwing soup, I don't want any.'

'I'll tell Madame Routy.'

'If you sack her, it'll be fine by me.'

'Not tonight, you'll need her to feed you tomorrow, I'm going to Paris first thing.'

The perfect end to a perfectly bloody day.

Saturday, 20th November

Overcast and cold, it started raining by nine o'clock – not that that made any difference to anything.

Jo-Jo, the Butcher, woke shivering, pulled the duck's-down duvet up to his chin and, as it was the weekend, decided he was feeling randy.

Pel's wife left the house quietly at six o'clock, while it was still dark, and drove herself to the station in her turquoise Twingo. Not only was she attractive and intelligent, she was also an

31

astute businesswoman and much to Pel's delight made a lot of money from her high-class clothes shop, not far from her high-class hair and beauty salon. Unfortunately, being an astute businesswoman involved going to Paris occasionally to see the winter fashion collections during the summer months, and the summer collections in winter, which meant Pel was left in the claws of his fire-breathing housekeeper, Madame Routy, who, if she ran out of bats' wings, stirred toads' tails into her cauldron before serving them to long-suffering Pel for supper. She only did it when his wife was away. When she was at home, Madame Routy was an angel. Not only was she a witch, she was schizophrenic, a frightening prospect to come down to first thing in the morning.

'Your coffee's on the table!'

Pel winced at the grating voice, shrieking from his kitchen – he'd have winced anyway but this morning he had a headache which made it worse. 'What did you make it with, iron filings?' He heard her hobnail boots goose-stepping across the *carrelage* floor and rapidly slipped into his seat, shook out his serviette and, adding one sugar, started stirring.

'Not iron filings, I ran out, I had to improvise with black beetles and spiders' eggs. Here's your croissant, I heated it up for you in the microwave.'

'You're sacked!'

She saluted, did a military about-turn and marched off muttering, 'For the first time today.'

The croissant appeared to be made of rubber, either that or chewing-gum, and he gave it up as a bad job, preferring instead to butter a *biscotte*. The hard-baked square of bread was brittle and, as he applied the butter, it exploded into a thousand pieces, most of which landed in his coffee. Fishing them out with a spoon, watching the greasy blobs float and spread unappetisingly across his bowl, he fed the soggy remains into his mouth, then picking up the bowl he drained it of coffee, pulling a face as he swallowed. 'Disgusting as usual, even worse than iron filings.'

It didn't help his mood, which was already far from convivial – he was convinced he had a cold coming on.

Driving into the city didn't improve it. While he was trying to light up, he accidentally tipped half the packet of Gauloises into his lap, almost collided with the back end of a lorry while collecting them together, and in dismay, when he finally got one between his lips and applied his lighter, discovered it was broken. Swiping it on to the floor, he nearly set light to the car and had to stop to extinguish the fire. By the time he arrived outside the Hôtel de Police, there was a stream of angry motorists shaking their fists in his wake. Pel was not a particularly good driver, always having so many more important things on his mind. One of which was murder: the torso found at Collège Albert Camus and still not identified, which didn't help the investigation at all.

Nosjean met him at the top of the stairs; he, on the other hand, looked pleased with himself.

Pel sneezed loudly and scowled at him. Jollity at this time on a Saturday morning should be discouraged. 'What's up with you? Got yourself a new girlfriend?'

'I haven't even got the old one. I think Anna's father told her to drop me for good.' Nosjean followed Pel down the corridor and into his office.

Pel struggled out of his coat and threw it at its peg. While Nosjean picked it up off the floor, shook it out and put it in its place, Pel sneezed again, lit a cigarette, then in an unexpected show of generosity, held out the packet to Nosjean. 'Hard luck. It's one of the handicaps of being a policeman – a lot of fathers disapprove of their daughters frequenting gun-slinging detectives, specially if the man's got something to hide.'

'I don't think this one has, he's a judge.'

A lighter twitched and both men lit up. 'All the more reason for him to disapprove, he knows what your work involves. There are too many police widows nowadays.'

Nosjean's expression changed, he exhaled noisily. 'Have you seen Kate recently?'

'My wife had lunch with her last week, took her to a posh restaurant to cheer her up. She says she's thinking of moving back to the Tarn to be closer to her parents. Understandable, I suppose – it was Darcy that made her move here, now there's no one to make her stay. She's being brave but feels very vulnerable in that huge house in the middle of the forest. No neighbours for miles.'

33

'Last night that huge house in the middle of the forest was broken into.'

Pel spun round to face his second-in-command. 'Was she in it? Was she hurt?'

'Fortunately, no. She'd taken the children to have supper with Cheriff and Annie, didn't get back until close to midnight. It was only when all four kids were settled in bed that she noticed something odd: two silver candlesticks were missing from the big beam over the fireplace. At first she thought she must have moved them, or mislaid them. It hasn't been easy adjusting to life without Darcy, she says sometimes she does things automatically and can't recall them afterwards. Anyway, when she went up to bed, she found the room in a mess, all her underwear strewn across the carpet, her clothes and shoes chucked out of the wardrobe, and the dressing-table drawer empty. That's when she called the police.'

'Who's handling it?'

'Commissaire Klein, his team was picking up the calls.'

Pel sneezed and blew his nose. 'Get it transferred. Explain why, he'll understand.'

'He's already been on to me and offered to hand over, that's how I know and why I rang her. Leguyder's report, as soon as it's finished, will come direct to us. Klein's file, such as it is, has already been mailed through to my terminal. I'll let you have the paper file when it arrives.'

'Good. Work with Pujol on it – in fact, get him out there to see her.'

'He'll be embarrassed.'

'Don't be fooled by his thick specs and his irritating habit of licking his lips – he's a very competent detective with a knack for noticing things the rest of you don't, he'll cope.' Pel sat down and, switching on his computer, waited for it to come alive. 'And she doesn't know him, which will be less embarrassing for her. So, what were you looking so pleased about?'

'We got the drug dealer outside the college.'

'At last. Tell me.'

'It was the Punk actually. After that gruesome parcel was found there, she got quite chummy with the two lads who discovered it. She and the teacher, Madame Maffre, took them off for hot chocolate and a fag in the canteen. To keep their minds off what they'd just seen, she chatted with them about life in general at the school, working her way very neatly round to the drug problem. They weren't prepared to name names, but they did say it might be worth hanging about by the bus shelters one Friday evening. They did, and two *lycéens* were subsequently arrested – mind you, de Troq' had to knock the bigger one out cold, he was the one with more than 1000 francs in his pocket. Leguyder's just confirmed his jacket pocket showed traces of marijuana. The same marijuana Jourdain took off a twelve-year-old boy at the bus stop.'

'Have they been charged?'

'Brisard came out last night for the interview and for once he wasn't obstreperous, he agreed to sign the charge sheet immediately.'

'Wonders will never cease.'

'Well, it's one less in the casebook.'

'Follow it up, Nosjean, we still have to have the facts and figures to get a conviction. We need witnesses and proof of frequent dealing, simply smoking the stuff isn't enough any more.' Pel sighed. 'When will they make it legal? It would simplify matters enormously, the kids could then grow it in their back gardens for their own consumption and the dealers would be out of business. As far as I can see marijuana is no more dangerous than having a couple of beers.'

'Until someone gets knifed for not paying up.'

'Or the resin is mixed with another substance to pad it out.'

'In other words, smoke what you grow.'

'When it's made legal.'

'*If* it's made legal. The politicians are still debating the issue.'

'Considering the huge pension they look forward to, you'd have thought they'd be a bit more snappy about making simple decisions, but no, they waffle and argue. Sometimes I think they see the law as a convenient pastime before a rich retirement.' Pel stubbed out his cigarette and changed gear. 'We're wasting time! You're wasting mine! Get out of my office and let me do some work. I want the report on the arrest on my desk ten minutes ago.'

'Yes, sir!'

Pel sighed. 'And don't call me sir! That's Lambert's name.'

Opening his e-mail he read, *'De Lambert – Objet: nouveax règlements!* Commissaire Pel, as this is the only sure way of making you pay attention, I'm ordering you into my office NOW!'

The Chief, a smile of self-satisfaction on his horrible face, was sitting solidly behind his desk looking like a snow-capped mountain, the thick waves of white hair combed carefully into place. Without thinking, Pel ran a hand through his own thinning thatch as he crossed the room and realised he had even less than he thought.

'No salute?'

'Give it a rest, Chief.'

'You should salute on entrance.'

'I forgot.'

'You always forget!'

'What did you want to see me about?'

'What did you want to see me about, *sir*?'

'I didn't call you, you called me.'

'*Sir!*'

'I'm very flattered but with all due respect, I'd rather you called me Pel.'

'*Pel!*'

'I'm glad we got that sorted out.' Pel folded his legs wearily under a wooden chair and pulled out his handkerchief.

'I didn't tell you to sit!'

'My legs did, they ache.'

'That is no excuse for insubordination!'

As he sneezed, something snapped inside Pel's brain. 'Oh for Christ's sake, sir! Wrap up, will you? Either say what you've got to say or my legs will tell me to march smartly away again. Have you got some information you've been keeping to yourself? Or what?'

Lambert's eyes flashed angrily but he said nothing, he knew only too well what Pel was referring to. Lambert had jealously, or inadvertently, withheld a file that should have been available for the team; as a result Daniel Darcy had gone rushing into an apparently empty farmhouse and had his guts, and his breakfast, splattered all over the wall behind. Although one journalist picked up on the story, Pel had refused to expose Lambert's

36

error, believing that implying to Kate that her husband's death could have been avoided would be unnecessarily cruel.

Pel knew he'd hit a raw nerve and was satisfied by the effect. 'Well, it's been nice having a little chat, we must do it more often.' He stood up, flipped a perfect salute in Lambert's direction and made for the door. 'In the meantime, mail me anything urgent.'

As he disappeared, Lambert reached for the phone. One of these days, one day soon, he was going to teach the disrespectful little devil a lesson. 'Brisard! Lambert here! I want to talk to you about that bugger Pel!'

'Lunch on Monday?'

'Why not today?'

'If you insist. Twelve thirty at La Marmite.'

While Lambert and the *juge d'instruction* tucked into a slap-up meal of fine food, washing it down with a bottle of Château Cantemerle 1993, a *grand cru* from Haut-Médoc, and costing nearly 200 francs for three-quarters of a litre, in the well-known restaurant La Marmite, Pel was tucking into sausage and mash with a glass of *vin de table* in the Bar Transvaal, across the road from the Hôtel de Police. And Nosjean had been tucking into a stale sandwich with a bottle of beer in his small dull office. Now, he grinned as he replaced the phone in its cradle: Anna was arriving that evening. Apparently Anna, while loving her father dearly, had decided to go against his advice and was on her way for a weekend with Nosjean. By the sound of her voice she was champing at the bit to get at him. That was fine by Nosjean.

He stood up, lit a cigarette thoughtfully, and wondered where he would take her for dinner, whether he should buy flowers to welcome her, and croissants for Sunday morning breakfast. *Merde*! He'd have to hurry home and clean the flat. The beer cans were piled up under the window, where he sat meditating life and love, and sometimes sex – since his divorce he didn't think he was getting enough; his entire stock of crockery was stacked in the sink – he only did the washing-up when he ran out of unused plates; and the bathroom . . . no self-respecting woman would consent to a seductive *douche à deux* in that pigsty! Only

37

one problem: he was on duty until six, Anna's train was due in at half-past, no time to shovel out his domestic mess.

Crossing to the window, he stared down into the street. Still raining; the pavements glistened black. There were very few people about for a Saturday afternoon. The gutters ran energetically towards the gratings and the trees opposite were swaying ominously in the strong wind that tore the turning leaves from their branches, swirling them momentarily up the avenue before dumping them in soggy dark piles, clustered into every available corner. Even the cars looked fed up, advancing cautiously up the avenue, headlights blazing, wipers swishing back and forth in irritation.

At least things are reasonably quiet, he thought foolishly. At least, for once, he thought even more foolishly, I'll be able to leave on time.

Had Anna let him know earlier she was intending to visit, he'd have swapped Saturday's duty with someone else, Misset for instance – he was always willing to avoid his family.

It would have saved him a lot of trouble.

Nosjean turned away from the window and went back to his desk still deep in thought. That was the only good thing about the filthy weather, it seemed to calm the criminal mind. Maybe it wasn't so exhilarating mugging old ladies when water was trickling down the back of your neck while you lay in wait behind a stripped and dripping hedge. Maybe rape in the park lost its excitement when you knew you were not going to simply lift a flimsy skirt and have your wicked way, after stuffing the victim's knickers in her mouth of course, but battle your way through stiff jeans, tights and possibly long-johns and that was after laboriously rolling up the thick overcoat to get at the struggling garments underneath. Robbery wasn't so much fun either – as he was about to find out.

While the cathedral of Ste Bénigne chimed, announcing five o'clock, the cat-burglar who'd been relieving the city's wealthier inhabitants of their more precious belongings made his way carefully across the roof-tops to a fire escape and his future happiness, and slipped on the metal steps. He somersaulted the first flight, cascading, as he fell, silver teaspoons and an assortment of jewellery on to the pavement below. He landed awkwardly, with his full weight behind him, his head bent anxiously, his hands flapping like flippers, trying to catch the escaping booty; he consequently broke his neck.

Seeing the treasures falling from above, and hearing the distant rumble of something soft but heavy bouncing about above him, Pierre Lapitte looked up, saw the twisted form of a man come to an abrupt halt, wedged into the corner of the fire escape, and went up to see if he could do anything to help. Non-assistance of a person in danger is punishable by up to eighteen months in prison. Non-assistance of a person in danger resulting in death, in certain circumstances can be considered as accidental manslaughter, punishable by up to five years. Pierre Lapitte was therefore quick to do his duty. As quick as his seventy-six-year-old legs would allow him, that is.

Ten minutes later, his phone call alerted the ambulance service and the police. He was getting on in years but he knew a dead man when he saw one; he'd survived the occupation of France during the Second World War, and was in no doubt at all that what he'd discovered should be put in professional hands.

Nosjean sighed deeply, glanced at his watch, 1713, and sincerely hoped it wouldn't take too long to clear up the body in rue Gambetta.

It took until 2100 hours.

When three occupants came home to find their flats had been broken into, they thought it was frightfully fortunate the police were already outside their prestigious building, and one by one demanded attention.

Throughout the scuffle between the forensic scientists, the fingerprint experts, the medical team, the pathologist, the local gendarmes who'd also somehow become involved and the traffic police brought in to keep the evening rush hour on the move in the pouring rain, and interviewing a lonely old man, Pierre Lapitte, who didn't often get the chance of talking to anyone, plus of course the inhabitants of the flats who'd lost their belongings and the *concierge* of the building who had to be woken from his place in front of the shrieking telly, with young Morrison tripping over his feet and blushing apologetically, Nosjean became more and more frustrated. And very wet. As the light failed and six-thirty came and went, he forced down the anger simmering inside him, sadly said goodbye to his romantic evening with Anna, and fighting his way through the crowd, quietly pressed his front door key into the cool hand of a uniformed officer. He confidentially begged him to collect and escort the young lady who looked remarkably like Julia Roberts from the station to his personal address and ask her very kindly to wait there. It was only after the uniformed officer had disappeared on his errand of mercy that Nosjean sighed unhappily and decided there was no point hurrying to her side when circumstances permitted. The moment she saw the state of his home, she'd do a smart about-turn, march straight back to the Gare SNCF to board the very next train to Paris and report to Daddy that he was, after all, right.

Au revoir, Anna.

3

Au revoir, Renée Clavier.

That afternoon, Renée Clavier, peering out through the tatty curtains, smiled to herself, then pulling the waterproofs tighter round her youthful body, clipping her helmet carefully over long pale hair, she straddled the old moped and pedalled off down the rutted drive, splashing through the murky puddles, praying the tiny engine would fire and take her where she'd been longing to go all week. Poor Renée, so young and pretty, so full of life and love, just a few days away from turning eighteen, from being legally classed an adult. Just a few short days from telling her Mum and Dad she was leaving home to live with her lover, whether they liked it or not. Renée Clavier, looking forward to the future, looking forward to her birthday and the freedom it represented. She found freedom all right, the ultimate freedom.

Poor Renée didn't die immediately, her heart went on tragically pumping her life juices through her veins. Outside, the rain, oblivious to the tragedy, poured relentlessly from the heavy charcoal clouds, tapping at the windows as if trying to attract attention, and drumming monotonously on the thin roof, a flimsy barrier between heaven and hell.

Her attacker loosened the hands round her neck and withdrew them, then, planting them firmly on Renée's shoulders, shook her violently, screaming at her. No response.

Dragging her out on to the stony ground, the killer worked quickly, then ran from the car into the house, stripped and redressed and, snatching up the first weapon available, gripping it tightly in rubber-gloved hands, returned to the now sodden limp figure and plunged it into her belly, tearing the skin, savagely working it into her flesh. The sight of blood spurting from the wounds, spreading rapidly and flowing on to the drenched driveway, diluting, dispersing, was disgusting but also an intense relief. However, not yet satisfied the job was properly done, the killer drove the scissors under the girl's ribs, wanting to be sure.

Renée's mouth opened in a pathetic plea, blood came bubbling up from her punctured lungs. She lifted a pale hand, fluttering weakly, as if to beg forgiveness or fend off the blades, dripping crimson.

Sunday, 21st November

During the night it had snowed enough to close the motorway between Montelimar (not the capital of nougat) and Valence (where, in 1755, Mandrin, 'le bandit bien-aimé' was caught and killed, all because he'd been a little less than hospitable to the local tax collectors – but that's history). When dawn crept hesitantly over the desolate white landscape, the children in the South of France looked out and clapped their hands with glee. The motorists who'd spent the night stuck in their cars clapped their hands too, but not with glee, with cold, and climbed out into the freezing morning, hoping to be rescued now daylight had come. They weren't the only ones; along the A7 more than 500 lorries were parked. The emergency services had done what they could to help the thousands of stranded travellers; a centre d'exposition had opened its doors to be filled with camp-beds and blankets for the more fortunate – those who'd made it through the drifts to the doors. The fire brigade provided hot snacks and coffee. Thousands of inhabitants of remote villages were without electricity. Just outside Orange, Provence, the Red Cross handed out food and blankets where another 300 lorries had been forced to shut off their engines and settle down for the night.

400 kilometres further north, yesterday's rain had turned into stinging sleet. The countryside was grey and uninviting, and, staring dolefully through the windscreen, the two detectives couldn't see much further than the edge of the muddy track a few metres away. They'd been in the sergeants' room drinking coffee when the call came through at eight thirty. This being Sunday and a day of rest, the rest of the squad were doing precisely that, resting; it was Cheriff and Bardolle's turn to be the skeleton staff in case of an important squeal. Now they were

cursing their luck. Klein's team were out investigating a disco-theque that had gone up in flames – no casualties, a bit of luck for everyone – during the early hours, and they had no other choice but to leave their coffee to go cold, climb inside their raincoats and head for the country.

When they arrived, they could make out the dull flashing of blue on top of the gendarmerie's break. They could also discern movement between the trees that lined the stream on their right. Neither of them wanted to look at a dead body. Least of all, Capitaine Cheriff Kamel. His wife was in hospital and he was desperately worried.

He and Lieutenant Bardolle, a massive man, nicknamed affec-tionately 'the Hulk', stood up out of the car and turned up their collars while the freezing rain hissed round their ears. It rattled through the swaying branches, catching the leaves with a clatter and drenching the ground beneath. Already rivulets were rush-ing past them down the slight incline towards a shallow valley. The pathologist's large-wheeled vehicle was parked in front of a small shrine; the Virgin Mary was looking more miserable than usual, cemented forever into her cheerless stone abode with only a bunch of faded fake flowers to keep her company.

As the detectives, two powerfully built men, made their way towards the distant voices, Cheriff was frowning. Faced with public violence, terrorism and murder; faced with a stranger whose steaming entrails were hanging from a massive hole in his gut; faced with a drug addict who'd overdosed and died a horrible death, vomiting the contents of his stomach and finally drowning in them; faced with a child who'd been savagely raped, discarded unconscious and torn, Cheriff remained calm. Horrified, sad, revolted, but always calm. Dealing with Darcy's death, he'd wept openly; faced with Annie's blood, however, he'd been ready to panic.

With the freezing rain stinging their faces, turning their cheeks pink, Bardolle and Cheriff shook hands with the uniformed policemen attending the incident, i.e. one unidentified corpse. To the right and left, men from Forensics, all dressed in black water-proofs with 'Police Forensics' painted white on their shoulders, silently ferreted, picked, bagged, labelled and marked. It struck Bardolle that they looked like a flock of crows after the early worm and he nearly smiled. Below them, the assistant pathologist, Boudet, was bent double, the green oiled jacket shining wet on his rounded back, the tweed cap on his head dark with moisture. His sleeves were rolled back, revealing a pair of pale latex-covered hands attached to tanned forearms, the hair on them glistening as he reached down into the muddy water of the Rin. The swollen stream was gurgling round his gumboots, and round the lifeless body of what had once been a pretty young woman.

Cheriff hoped with all his heart that Annie was all right, that the haemorrhaging wasn't serious. He'd ring the hospital as soon as they'd wrapped up this little lot. 'Who found it?' he asked a ruddy-faced gendarme, wrapped cosily in his cape.

'Tafelski,' the képi nodded towards a pair of dripping peasants, 'and Marsonet.'

'Out shooting,' Tafelski said. 'Me and 'im, we took the same route we always take, only this time as we jumped across the stream, I saw something round and white down 'ere. Caught my eye, see, thought it was an old chamber pot, or something. Anyways, just out of curiosity, I stroll over and try to lift it with me foot. Got the shock of me bloomin' life. 'Orrible it was.'

''Orrible,' Marsonet confirmed.

'Stark naked! It was her bum that caught me eye, see, well 'alf her arse, if you know what I mean. One bloomin' bright white buttock.'

'Bright white buttock,' Marsonet echoed.

Cheriff wished Boudet would hurry up and finish his preliminary examination. He wanted to get to a phone.

As if in telepathic response, the doctor's back straightened and he started peeling off the latex gloves. 'Can't do any more here,' he shouted. 'Let's get her back to the lab.'

'Once bloody Brisard turns up.'

Bardolle offered his hand and heaved the dripping doctor up the bank on to the saturated grass. 'Any idea about cause of death?'

'It looks pretty obvious, she's been stabbed at least twice, but I'll let you know definitely once we've completed the post-mortem.'

'Mutilated?'

44

Boudet sighed. 'I'm afraid so.'

'Oh Jesus, don't say we've got a serial killer on our hands.'

'So far you've got two dead women. I hope to be able to tell you if the murderer is the same person when I've had a chance to examine the wounds more closely. Which is worse, two murderers, or just one who's after a lot of blood?'

Cheriff didn't answer, both were equally tiresome. He walked with the doctor towards his car. 'Talking of blood, Annie lost a lot.'

'When?'

'Late yesterday evening. I called the SAMU.'

'Which hospital?'

'Sacré Cœur, they said this might be a sign that the end's in sight.'

'Then what the hell are you doing here?'

'I'm a criminal detective on duty. We didn't expect anything like this to happen.'

'The body?'

'No, the bleeding. I was with her half the night, she had a lot of pain. They said she was exhausted and gave her something to help her sleep. They sent me home. It was only then I remembered I was on duty today; too late to swap.'

Opening the car door and pulling himself up into the empty seat, Boudet removed his cap, ran a damp hand through his flattened hair and stared down into Cheriff's anxious face, then without another word he picked up the mobile on the passenger seat and started tapping in numbers. A moment later, he announced himself and asked for news of Annie Saxe-Kamel. He disconnected abruptly. 'If you hurry, you might just get there before it's too late. Come on, I'll take you.'

'Just a moment.' The examining magistrate had at last appeared and by the look on his plump face was anxious to prove his importance. 'No one's to leave the site without my permission.'

'He's right,' Cheriff sighed, 'I can't, I've got to sort this lot out.'

Boudet slid out of his seat and landed between them. Not being a policeman he wasn't answerable to the pompous *juge d'instruction* and didn't care for his interference. 'Then you'd better look sharp and give your ruddy permission, this man has an emergency on his hands. Non-assistance of a person in danger, as you well know, is an offence in this Republic and punishable –'

His quotation of the law was interrupted by Bardolle, splashing through the puddles to join them. 'I'll cope with the necessary,' he said. 'For Christ's sake get going!'

They all turned to Brisard who, in the middle of the expanding hostile group, drew himself up to his full height. He was now under the scrutinising eyes of not only the belligerent pathologist and a pair of imposing detectives, but also two scowling peasants and half a dozen drenched gendarmes: they'd all wandered over and none of them were looking pleased. 'I repeat, no one –'

'Brisard! You want the newspapers to know about your inhumanity?'

The *juge d'instruction* stared at Boudet; the last time the journalists had been informed of his stubbornness they'd followed him to a restaurant where he'd been having an intimate evening with his mistress – it had taken quite a lot of explaining away to his wife. Angrily, he pushed through the crowd of dripping men and almost whispered, 'Permission granted.'

A moment later, the doctor's car was reversing urgently down the track looking for a place to turn. As Boudet swung the steering wheel and stamped on the brakes, the back tyres slid through the mud. He punched the large vehicle into four-wheel drive and carefully accelerated away.

Cheriff sat back, trying to relax, but still very apprehensive. 'Who's the person in danger? Annie?'

'No. That fathead back there. I think I might've bopped him one if he hadn't let you go.'

'*Accouche!*' Pel bellowed as Bardolle's clothes leaked gently on to his office's thin carpet. His head still ached and his throat felt as if someone had been at it with a metal rasp.

'That's just what Annie's doing, *patron.*'

'Never mind about Annie, give me your verbal on the *cadavre!*' He scowled at the outsize lieutenant, lowered his eyes to the

46

puddle forming round Bardolle's feet, then flicked them up again, a smile twitching round the edges of his mouth. It never got much further, Pel preferred scowling. 'Oh,' he said, pushing his specs into his sparse hair, 'is she? Where's Cheriff? Call for a car, lights flashing, order an escort, the lot – he ought to be there!'

'He's on his way, *patron*. Boudet did the honours once he'd finished with our body.'

'That's all right then.' Pel's specs dropped neatly back on his nose. 'Now, the verbal!'

Annie Saxe, once a member of Pel's team, delivered a fine baby boy weighing 3.4 kilos at 1005 that morning. Cheriff arrived just in time to see his son born. They decided to call him Daniel.

Boudet, the pathologist, delivered his preliminary post-mortem report at 2005. He arrived just in time to ruin Pel's evening. Pel called him a number of names then sat down to discuss the grim details of Renée Clavier's death.

'She drowned.'

Pel fingered the wad of papers in front of him. 'All this to say the girl drowned!'

'She drowned because she was too weak to crawl out of the stream. The wounds were deep, done by some double-bladed implement, possibly large scissors. I'll spare you the anatomical terms. Basically one was under her left breast, missing her heart but piercing a lung. The other was lower, near her navel. By the time I got to her, the large intestine was hanging in loops from the massive cut.'

'Is that all?' Pel asked, hoping it was while wondering where he'd left his indigestion tablets.

'I'm afraid not.'

'Then let me find my Rennies before you go on.' His desk drawers banged open and closed, and not finding what he wanted, he opened the packet of Strepsils and placed one on his tongue. It was better than nothing.

Knowing Pel's distaste for blood and guts, Boudet waited a moment before continuing. 'Her vagina was ripped through to the anus, her thighs were cut to ribbons. But no main artery was

47

severed. If she hadn't drowned she'd have died through loss of blood.'

'There was very little near where she was found. Admittedly the sodding rain didn't help, but even so . . .'

'There would have been litres of it where she was attacked, Leguyder will have found traces if it was on the banks of the Rin.'

'And if it was actually in the stream?'

'There would've been splashes.'

'Rape?'

'Her body was in such a position, it's impossible to tell. She was lying on her front, her head downstream. Her legs were splayed so the current of the stream, pretty strong after all this rain, simply washed her clean. Who was she anyway?'

'We don't know.'

'If it's any help she was about eighteen, long sandy-coloured hair, 1m67 and thin.'

'Distinguishing marks?'

'Not really, except a small gold ring, like a sleeper ear-ring, just above her navel. She'd been opened like a book but the ring was still in place.'

'I think I'll read the rest, thank you.'

Sunday, bloody Sunday.

Now they had two dead women, neither of them identified, both of them mutilated. It looked like being a long winter.

And Jo-Jo the Butcher went to bed early. It had been a tiring weekend what with one thing and another.

Monday, 22nd November

The snow reached Burgundy. Large flakes of it tumbled from the sky, punctuating the dull grey daylight with fluffy white full-stops. The temperature had dropped again, making excited children yelp as it nipped their fingers on the way to school, but making their parents irritable and impatient.

Nosjean couldn't believe it. Turning from the window, he grinned wickedly at Anna. Not only had she waited for him, she'd also tidied the flat, not in that homely 'I want to mould my man' way, just in a 'let's make space to have fun' way, and she hadn't even flinched at the state of the bathroom. She had Monday off. So did Nosjean. Purely by chance he'd taken the day off, thinking he really ought to make the effort to see his three adoring sisters and their parents, fill his stomach with good home cooking, and perhaps have his clothes washed – he was running out of clean shirts. If his dear departed wife had done nothing else, she had at least done the laundry.

Now he couldn't believe his luck. Anna, while waiting for him, had filled two pillowcases with sheets and what was lying on the floor in the bedroom and bathroom and taken them to the laundrette. Today they looked forward to another clean, but dirty day in bed. Sunday had been a dream. Eating snacks, drinking champagne – always a bottle ready in the fridge – snoozing, waking, turning over and doing it again. He definitely couldn't believe it, although he knew he'd feel a total wreck on Tuesday, but right then, smiling down at Anna, he felt totally reckless. Going to the phone, he plugged it back into the wall and rang his favourite restaurant, Chez Lucette, to reserve a table for two at midday – well, a man can't live on love alone. He'd just replaced the receiver and was bending to unplug it again when it sprang into life and vibrated on the scratched coffee table. Without thinking, reacting spontaneously, being a conscientious policeman, he answered it, and regretted it immediately.

'Be here in half an hour!'

'*Patron*, it's my day off, you signed the request form.'

'And yesterday was my day off, not that my wife noticed, I was in the office. We've got another unidentified mutilated corpse and I've got flu. You are my second-in-command! I repeat, be here in half an hour!' The line clicked and Nosjean studied it silently for a moment. There were times when he just couldn't believe it.

Boudet was doing his best to sew the corpse back together again prior to burial. Although the girl's body in front of him had suffered severe laceration by its attacker, to complete his anatomical examinations, beyond the visible wounds, he'd had to open her further, making a vertical incision from the sternum to the pubis. Then, with clamps to hold back the flaps of flesh, he'd removed the internal organs to establish exactly how she died – which was essential to the police investigation. A pathologist's report could also often, but not always, indicate why a death was caused. For instance: was she pregnant? It could be a case of the father not wanting to assume responsibility for one reason or another. Drug addict? If affirmative it could point the homicide research in a particular direction. Drunk? Hepatitis? AIDS? Already, Boudet had been able to tell Pel what she'd eaten – roast chicken, boiled potatoes and cabbage, a plain yoghurt and an apple – and at what time – approximately midday, four to five hours before she died judging by the well-established digestion. All these things helped them build a picture of what she'd been doing during her last twenty-four hours, giving them an idea of her movements and the people she may have been with. It would also, incidentally, after an arrest had been made, add scientific weight to the court case, proving a suspect's guilt or, of course, innocence. Hence, having spent a long time digging about inside the body, he now had to repair it, close the 30 centimetre incision, so when a member of the public came to identify the victim, there weren't gaping, horrific holes staring up at them – even though the whole of the corpse would be covered by a sheet until the moment of truth.

Boudet was anxious to finish stitching the skin back together. De Troq' was bringing in a woman whose daughter hadn't come home on Sunday morning; the girl's description fitted the dead girl's. Although they wouldn't have wished tragedy on any family, they certainly hoped Madame Clavier would make an identification. It was invaluable to know who'd been butchered and left to die, stark naked in the bottom of an overgrown stream. With that knowledge they could interview her family and friends, her workmates, if she had them, or teachers, if she was still at school. They'd be given permission to go through her belongings, finding out more about her life: what sort of person she was, where she went, how often, with whom. Odd though it may seem, they needed to know if she was happy, comfortable, loved; or obstinate, quarrelsome, lonely. It was one of the steps they had to take in the hope that it may just lead them, eventually, to the killer. And possibly the killer of the other corpse, or more precisely, part of a corpse, found by those two bright young sparks at the college.

The phone trilled. Cham, whose hands were clean – he'd been busy catching up with the paperwork – lifted the receiver to his ear.

'*Pel à l'appareil, comment allez-vous?*'

'*Ça va, et vous?*'

'Bloody awful, my nose is streaming and my head feels like it was hit with a hatchet.'

'How's the throat?'

'Fighting off the honey and eucalyptus pastilles.'

Cham chuckled. 'I'll look forward to doing your post-mortem personally.'

'Cut the clever remarks, will you, I'm in need of enlightenment. I've got Leguyder's report in front of me. The fibres you removed from the girl's neck come from a pair of brown woollen gloves . . .'

'That corresponds with the bruising.'

'. . . which doesn't help us much. From their search of the site, he's able to tell me an unidentified car had been parked there recently, probably a modern hatchback plus there are tyre marks from a child's three-wheeler, although they'd been almost obliterated by the car. Here's the interesting bit; the rider of the trike weighed approximately 50 kilos. Is it possible for a kid to weigh that much?'

'Depends on the kid. What sort of three-wheeler? What age group?'

'The tyre's width suggests it was made of solid rubber, no inner tube, and not more than 30 centimetres in diameter, which means the kid was between the age of three and six.'

'Then no, I've never come across a case of such enormous obesity. The normal average weight of a girl between three and six is 10 to 20 kilos, for a boy it's slightly more, I had a patient of eight years old who weighed nearly 40 but he was an exception and was under treatment.'

'That's what I thought, it wasn't a kid. Okay, there were also footprints, some belonging to the two peasants who found the body and others, which incidentally don't match anything at the college near where the unknown torso was found. One was fairly good, it belongs to a size 39 walking boot. What size did our body take?'

'Hang on, I'll have a look. You got the reference?'

'Yes,' Pel sighed, 'stark naked, Sunday morning, face down in the Rin.'

'I don't like numbers either,' Cham smiled. 'Unfortunately we're forced to work with them. Come on, Pel, give me the last four or five numbers.'

'*Zero neuf, quatre-vingt treize, point, trois.*'

'Hold on, I'm searching.'

Pel blew his nose and wiped it carefully, it was already sore.

'Got it, scanning down the page. Size 39, the same.'

'How much did she weigh?'

'55 kilos.'

'Leguyder says the boot was worn by someone weighing 58. Could she have gained 3 kilos between life and death?'

'If she was wearing hiking boots, they'd have weighed a bit, plus other clothes and maybe a heavy coat, it's been damn cold recently. Mm, but no, not 3 kilos – unless of course she was carrying something when she made the footprint.'

'That may explain it. Bugger, it could easily be her boot. I was hoping it wasn't and we'd got something to work with. On the other hand, it could have been her sitting on the child's bike.'

'Why?'

'To have her photo taken? Search me.'

'Did they find her clothes, or evidence of them?'

'Not even a pair of briefs.'

'Then why was she wearing boots?'

'Cham, she could have got out of the car for a pee or something, before her clothes were removed.'

'Carrying 3 kilos?'

'It could've been the bike.'

'Surely that would weigh more?'

'I don't know. I'll have to get back to Leguyder.' Pel scribbled a note, muttering to himself, 'If not, what could it have been?'

'My daughter's handbag weighs a ton, I'm convinced she carries a couple of house bricks around in it.'

'Ah, that could be it, youngsters nowadays have their bags strapped to their fronts or backs, to avoid pickpockets. Young girl with heavy bag, accompanied by killer and tricycle, parked well away from the road.'

'Did Leguyder find blood on the banks of the Rin?'

'None.'

'So she can't have been murdered there.'

'She could have been murdered in the car and carried to the stream.'

'She'd have dripped.'

'Not if she was wrapped in a blanket.'

'It would've had to have been a thick one.'

'It's possible. Leave that for the moment, I've another question. You can't prove rape, or even that intercourse had taken place, but is it reasonable to think it's likely?'

'In view of the way she was positioned in the stream, yes, it's possible.'

'Which would also explain why she was undressed, although I'm not counting on any of it. Until we know who she is and what her movements were during the hours preceding her death, unfortunately we're dealing with hypotheses, something I don't like, but we can't afford to just sit around patiently twiddling our thumbs. The Butcher case at the college has come to a dead end – we're going round in circles, going over and over the same tracks. I was hoping this one might nudge it into action again.'

'I can't confirm it was the same murderer, nothing indicates it.'

'And nothing proves it wasn't. You know our statistics for crime in Burgundy, the chances of having two different murderers on the loose at the same time is very slim.'

'But not impossible.'

'Indeed. Okay, Cham, thanks anyway. We'll go back to our circles – you never know, we might have missed an important detail, or come up with one soon.'

Cham replaced the receiver and tried to find his place in the report he was checking. The phone rang and, hearing the nasal cold-encumbered voice, he knew it was Pel again.

'Almost forgot, de Troq's bringing you a woman whose daughter's been missing since Saturday evening.'

'I know, he rang through an hour ago, we're expecting him any minute.'

'Ah, glad to see someone's being efficient.'

'*Ciao*, Pel.' Cham looked up from his desk, studying Boudet's progress. 'Your time's nearly up, couple of minutes?'

A nod came in reply which was just as well, because the doorman announced the detectives' arrival with Madame Clavier.

When Boudet, scrubbed and clean, and wearing a jacket and tie instead of a blood stained overall, pulled the trolley into the visitors' room, the corpse was completely covered. He waited while de Troq' prepared the woman for what she was about to see, but was ready to lift one corner of the white sheet, revealing the carefully washed face, the matted untidy hair, and part of a bruised shoulder. If it *wasn't* her daughter, why show a woman, not connected with the crime, the horrors they had to deal with? If it *was*, why let her see more than she had to? Her imagination could drive her mad, wondering how all those wounds were inflicted on her child's tortured body – not forgetting the puckered zipper from sternum to pubis; post-mortems weren't particularly pretty either.

Madame Clavier stood nervously between de Troq' and Alex Jourdain. Boudet thought she looked too old to have a daughter of eighteen. Her cheeks were thin and haggard, there were deep wrinkles round her mouth, her eyes and engraved in her forehead – from working outside all her life perhaps; if anyone knew what weather could do to skin, a pathologist did. Even so, he still thought she looked too old to have a daughter of eighteen – menopausal pregnancy? It happened.

On her head she wore a faded cotton scarf, knotted under a bristly chin; her nose was red from the wind outside. She carried a large plastic handbag and was worrying a handkerchief between bony fingers. As de Troq' finished speaking, she murmured, '*D'accord*.' De Troq' looked up at Boudet and nodded.

The doctor took the corner of the sheet between his fingers, folding it back gently. Madame Clavier gasped, her fist rushing to her mouth. For a moment Jourdain thought the woman might

54

faint and put out a hand to steady her but she just went on staring.

'Is this your daughter, Madame?'

'It can't be,' she whispered.

'What do you mean?'

'I mean I know what our Renée looks like and it's not like that!'

'So this is not your daughter?'

She shook her head.

'Have you ever seen her before?'

'And I don't want to see her again, she's disgusting!'

Boudet understood the woman's shock; all the same he tried to clarify the situation. 'Madame, did your daughter wear a small gold ring in her navel?'

'Certainly not!'

De Troq' watched from the window as she left the building, her head bent, her nose buried in the handkerchief. 'I think she was lying,' he said to no one in particular.

Jourdain joined him as Madame Clavier walked out of the car park and turned left into the street. 'About the piercing?'

'No, that was the only straight answer she gave, but she may not have known – it's the sort of thing a shy girl might not exhibit willingly to an out-of-date mother. No, I think she was lying about recognising her. Did you notice the way she avoided replying directly to the other questions? And when she shook her head, it was almost in disbelief, not confirmation of a negative reply.'

'So it is Renée?'

'That's what we've got to find out.'

When they arrived at the Hôtel de Police, most of the offices were empty, their occupants either still out, or across the road in the Bar Transvaal eating lunch. Pel was about and, when they clattered up the stairway and walked towards the sergeants' room, he called them in. Nosjean was already seated in front of the desk. Closing the door, they both pulled up a chair while a session of nose-blowing and coughing was completed. Pel looked at them from red-rimmed eyes.

'Identification?'

'No, but Madame Clavier's reaction was odd.'

'Go on.'

'I think she recognised the dead girl and didn't want to say so.'

'Jourdain?'

'I'm not sure, but yes, it was rather peculiar. There was something missing; when she implied it wasn't her daughter there was no real relief.'

'Because Renée's still missing,' Nosjean suggested. 'Being faced with a dead girl of the same age would have put ideas into her head, ideas that may not have occurred to her before.'

'Did she talk at all on the way home?'

'She marched off into town, said she had some shopping to do and would catch a bus home.'

Like de Troq', Pel wasn't satisfied. 'Drop in on her later, check Renée hasn't turned up, find out more about her, ask for a photo. It'll give you a chance to make a better assessment of Madame Clavier. It isn't unheard of for teenage daughters to be cruelly dispatched by their mothers. Or fathers, or brothers, uncles or aunts, for that matter – maybe she's protecting someone.'

'But what about the torso at the college?'

'The two are not necessarily connected.'

'They could be.'

'God help us if they are. It means we've got a psychotic monster on the loose out there.'

4

When de Troq' and Jourdain stopped in front of the scruffy farmhouse that evening, it was raining again, the snow had turned back into slicing, biting rain. As they got out of the car, a collection of thin cats leapt from the windowsill where they'd been huddled and slipped out of sight. A couple of grey sheets slapped noisily, snapping open as the wind folded and unfolded them, tearing at them like sails. A couple of bald chickens peered out from a ramshackle shelter between a tumbling pile of wooden crates and cut branches. There were bent saucepans discarded in the mud and a miserable dog, chained to the wall, sat trembling outside its kennel. And, somewhere, someone was singing. It reminded de Troq' of his mother standing beside him at morning mass every Sunday when he was a child. She'd had a lovely voice, this was too, and it seemed incongruous in the squalid farmyard.

'*Alouette, gentille alouette,*
Alouette, je te plumerai.
Je te plumerai le dos,
Je te plumerai le dos,
Et la queue, et la queue,
Et les pattes, et les pattes,
Et les ailes, et les ailes,
Et le cou, et le cou
Et les yeux, et les yeux,
Et le bec, et le bec,
Et la tête, et la tête,
O, alouette, gentille alouette,
Alouette, je te plumerai.'

The two detectives glanced at each other: it was a macabre song to hear when they were dealing with two grizzly murders. The poor little lark in the song had had its back, tail, feet, wings, neck, eyes, beak and head plucked. The assassin responsible for

57

the dissected trunk at the college had gone one stage further, hacking off the head, arms and legs as well, and although the girl in the stream hadn't been plucked or chopped up, she had been stabbed, torn and gouged.

Jourdain shivered. 'This is a weird one'. Her words were barely audible against the sudden howling wind, sweeping up the valley and tearing at their clothes.

They knocked at the wooden door and had to wait some time under the dripping eaves before it opened a crack.

'I'm sorry to bother you again but we've one or two more questions.'

Madame Clavier frowned, obviously puzzled, perhaps not remembering who they were. It was possible; she'd paid very little attention to them that morning, averting her eyes when she'd spoken.

As de Troq' held up his wallet, showing the unmistakable red, white and blue stripe announcing the *flics*, she poked her nose out and examined it, then, stepping back, allowed them to enter. She was wearing a stained apron over an old dress, and woollen stockings rolled down over thin ankles. Her steps were muffled by a pair of worn men's bedroom slippers and, although she was trying to hide it, her prematurely aged face was sorrowful. Waving to them to follow, she shuffled into the kitchen where a cauldron was bubbling in the fireplace, spitting on to the embers beneath and making them hiss. 'Cooking my husband's supper, aren't I?' she said miserably.

'Will he be home soon?'

'Home soon! He's home the whole ruddy time – in there, he is.' She pointed to a closed door and briefly Jourdain wondered if she kept him in a cupboard. 'I'll introduce you if you like, not that it'll do no good.'

She pulled open the battered door, which screeched as it caught on the uneven tiled floor. The heat behind it was stiflingly unhealthy. Blinking through dim electric light, they could see an elderly man lying on a bed, propped up by a heap of pillows. Although a towel covered his genitalia, he was otherwise naked from the waist down, until his bony legs ended in thick socks. The filthy room stank.

'Shat meself, mother,' the toothless mouth said.

58

'Reckon you pissed yerself too. I'll sort you out in a minute. Say good evening to our visitors. They've come about Renée.'

'Evenin'. Have they found 'er then? Change the sheet, will you, it's all oozing an' chilly underneaf.'

'Shouldn't shit yerself, should you. I'll do it when they've gone.'

'You rotten old cow . . .!'

She pushed them hurriedly back into the kitchen and slammed the door. 'No good, that's what he is, no good. Never has been. Used to have a vineyard, trouble was he drank every drop he produced. Now it's me that works to make ends meet, it's not easy I can tell you. Him an invalid, Renée needing money for her . . . Is there any news? Is that why you're here?' She lifted her eyes in pathetic supplication, pleading with them to tell her that her daughter was safe and sound.

'Do you have any other children, madame?'

'Nearly didn't have her. I prayed every Sunday for a child and after twenty-odd years I gave up. Then just when I thought it was too late, there she was.'

'Tell us about Renée. Was she still at school?'

'Nah, left when she was sixteen, worked in a shop for a while, didn't last long. Then she got a job as a waitress in a restaurant, that didn't last long either, a year, maybe a bit less, it was too far away, see. Recent like, she's been on a course, learning how to type and things, wanted to work in an office.'

'Wanted?'

The woman's face flushed. 'Still wants to, as far as I know. You can ask her when you find her.'

'She lived at home, did she?'

'Only seventeen, well, she'd have been eighteen this week. I was paying for her to do a sec'etarial training, took every penny I earned, but I reckon she deserved it, give her a chance in life, see.' She paused, sighing. 'All down the drain for nothing.'

'Why do you say that, Madame?'

'Well, she's disappeared, hasn't she?'

'When you saw the dead girl this morning, what did you think?'

'I thought it shouldn't be allowed! I wanted to get out of that room as quick as I could.'

59

'You're sure it wasn't Renée?'

'I told you, my girl don't look like that.'

Although they talked gently round the subject, and in the end a little more harshly, Madame Clavier still refused to admit the dead girl was her daughter. She did, however, agree to give them a photo of her. They stared in dismay at a six-year-old child wearing dirty dungarees and mud on her happy face, holding a kitten.

'Haven't you got a more recent one?' Jourdain enquired patiently.

'Might have.'

It was of an eleven-year-old child wearing a white dress and ribbons in her hair. 'It was taken at her confirmation,' Madame Clavier told them proudly.

'Do you go to church often?' de Troq' asked.

'What's that got to do with it?'

'With what?'

'Anything.'

'I just wondered.'

'I go every week, like a good Catholic should. We're honest moral people, you ask the priest, he'll tell you.'

'What about the school photographer?' Jourdain suggested, still studying the snapshots. 'Didn't Renée ever want to keep a record of her classmates?'

'Couldn't afford it.'

'Why were you singing "Alouette" when we arrived?'

'She used to sing it when she was skipping in the yard. There's no law against it, is there?'

'Why were you singing it today?'

'What's wrong with you? I can sing whenever I want. As it happens, it was that little girl this morning, she reminded me.'

'The corpse reminded you of Renée?'

'No,' she snapped. 'It reminded me of the song.'

They left disappointed, convinced now she'd been lying in the path lab. They hoped Debray, or Rigal, newly transferred to the computer room and proving to be a whiz with the manipulation of technology, would be able to prove it.

*   *   *

60

Lieutenant Pujol found it was proving more difficult than he'd thought plucking up the courage to introduce himself to Commandant Darcy's widow. He hesitated a long time before continuing up the forest track that led to her house. He hesitated again by the front door.

Kate opened it, frowning slightly, holding on to the collar of Rasputin, the snarling Bauceron. Pujol wasn't sure how to start; this wasn't an ordinary enquiry, Kate wasn't an ordinary victim of robbery. He showed her his identification card.

'Oh, sorry, l didn't recognise you! Razz, get back, you idiot, it's a friend, a policeman.' The huge dog shrank back, still snarling, still suspicious. 'Ever since Darcy stopped coming home, he's become terribly possessive. Sorry,' she said again, '*entre, entre.*'

Pujol licked his lips and tripped over the door jamb, almost dancing into the kitchen, all the time eyeing the dog lying not more than a metre away. 'I, er . . . well, Commissaire Klein came to see you about a burglary, I believe.'

'That's right. Want a drink?'

'Well, I'm not sure I should.'

'Is this official business, or a social call?'

'Half and half, I suppose.'

'Then have half a drink. I need one and I don't like drinking alone.'

'Okay, just a small one.'

As she poured white wine into two glasses, her twin sons, now eighteen months old, came at a lopsided gallop to see who was there. They pointed at Pujol, and grinned. The two older boys, Patrick and Jack, appeared, solemnly shook hands, scooped up the babies and returned to the sitting-room, closing the door on a television set going full blast.

'Thank God I've got them,' Kate said, handing Pujol a glass. 'I think I'd go crazy alone.'

'It can't be easy.'

Kate swallowed and sat opposite him at the table. 'That's not what you came to talk about, I'm sure, and don't tempt me. Being the only adult in this house tends to make me pounce on any visitor and talk them cross-eyed, but I'm getting better. Now why are you here?'

'Pel – well, Nosjean – both of them actually – wanted me to

find out more, minor details and things, you know. The case has been handed over to us, because of our connection with the family, and we are all anxious to catch the bastards.'

Kate grinned at his short speech and for the first time Pujol realised she was as beautiful as he'd been told. He licked his lips. 'I've read the report Klein made and seen the list of missing property. I think it may be kids – well, young adolescents in need of ready money. They took small articles that would be easy to carry and sell afterwards.'

'Klein thought it was someone with a warped mind, trying to get his own back on Daniel for arresting them.'

'Obviously we'll be investigating all possibilities, Debray is making up a list of likely candidates, but in our experience reprisals happen when a policeman is still alive, not after his death.' He licked his lips once again. 'I'm sorry, I didn't mean . . .'

'Don't worry about it, Pujol, it's actually a nice surprise to hear someone talk about Darcy's death in a normal voice – so far everyone tends to still whisper about it. I try and speak normally, but after a bit my voice gets a bit wobbly, then it dries up completely, I sort of get gagged, if you know what I mean.'

Pujol smiled at her. 'I do, I've been suffering from that ever since I met Pel!'

She laughed. 'An old bugger to work for, isn't he?'

'A brainy old bugger, who's bad-tempered, stubborn, bloody-minded and sometimes a bully. He's not easy to work for but I wouldn't want to work for anyone else. Funnily enough, I like him.'

'So do I and so did Daniel, they were good friends.'

'It's hard to imagine Pel being friends with anyone.'

'I know, but he often came to share a nursery supper with us, when his wife was away and there was only Madame Routy to look after him. We were his safety valve, I think.'

'So he's human after all?'

'Very much so. You should have seen him at the funeral. I think he was closer to tears than I was, although I must confess I'd taken a mild sedative.'

'I wish he would sometimes.'

'Oh, come on, he's not that bad.'

'He was better when Darcy was around, he knew how to handle him. Nosjean's still learning, and Lambert just rubs him up the wrong way.'

'Daniel was . . . oh dear, here we go!' She swiped at her eyes, swallowed hard and reached for the bottle, standing up to serve him. 'How about another half-glass? Being mildly sozzled might help me sleep.'

Pujol stood up too and, taking the bottle out of her hand, placed it gently on the table. 'Drinking too much won't bring him back, you know.'

'No,' she replied tearfully, 'but it helps the hurt.'

Pujol didn't know what to do. He wanted to reach out and comfort her, and in the absence of any other idea, feeling foolish doing nothing, that's what he did. She collapsed against his warm chest and sobbed her heart out.

Tuesday, 23rd November

Pel was reading the newspapers. Beside him was a box of tissues, a new packet of Strepsils, a packet of Doliprane and a large bottle of cough mixture. None of them made him feel any better. The end of his nose was on fire, his throat raw, his temperature only just under control, and added to that every so often he coughed himself purple in the face. The only thing that cheered him up was his wife, mercifully back from Paris, who'd supplied the selection of medication he now had at his elbow.

At breakfast that morning she'd pointed out an article on sexual harassment. 'Equality of rights is all very well but someone ought to tell the employers. This woman was ostracised for weeks. In the end she couldn't stand it any longer and walked out. She's no right to dole money for six months because she didn't give any notice, and now she can't find another job.'

'She's probably a foul old bat who makes life a misery for everyone.'

'Pel'.

By the look on his wife's face, he knew he'd made a mistake and humbly apologised. Now, rereading the article in the office, he wondered if Lambert could be had up for detective derangement;

from what he'd understood, the Chief's behaviour was worse than that of the employer who was about to go to trial. In fact, if Lambert didn't talk to him again for a month – for a year – forever – he'd be a much happier man.

Thinking of happy men, he completed a quick coughing fit, gasped, lifted the phone and tapped in ten numbers. Cheriff's sleepy voice replied.

'How's fatherhood?'

'Everything Darcy made it out to be. Annie's radiant and the baby's doing fine, a couple more days and they'll be home safe and sound. You don't sound too good though.'

'*La grippe.* I think my sell by date's expired. Families pleased?'

'Both the Catholics and the Muslims, although it was touch and go at first.'

'Is she up to a visit from her irritable ex-boss?'

'I'm sure she'd be delighted.'

'I'll try and call in tonight.'

'Your wife away?'

'Only going to be late this evening, having dinner with a designer or something. Thought I'd make Madame Routy wait before serving me her gruel.'

The Punk, blonde hair standing on end as usual, a warm smile on her face, pushed her way into his office and placed a cup of hot black coffee on his desk together with five packets of Gauloises and the morning mail.

'A blonde alien has just materialised on my carpet. She looks like she's had her fingers in a faulty plug.'

'Jourdain?'

Without thinking, Pel nodded to the phone. 'Business calls. Make the most of your time off, the files are already piling up for you. Maybe see you this evening.' He disconnected. 'Anything interesting, Alex?'

'Not a lot. Clavier still insists it's not her daughter lying in the morgue.'

'She should know.'

'I think she does but she won't admit it.'

Pel looked up. 'Why?'

'That's what we've got to find out. De Troq's with Rigal at the moment, working on photographs of Renée as a little girl – he's hoping to age her, virtually speaking, see if we can get an identification that way.'

'Virtually speaking, let me know when you have the results. Anything else?'

'I stopped off at the maternity clinic last night to see Annie. Cheriff's done his stuff and declared the baby as his son at the Mairie. I like what they've called him.'

'Mohammed?' Pel suggested. 'Bashir? Ahmed?'

'No. Hakim is his second name in keeping with Cheriff's Arab origins, but his first chosen name is Daniel.'

'Daniel,' Pel repeated sadly.

The Punk nodded equally sadly. 'They asked Kate's permission. She was a bit shaky, she was talking to Pujol about the robbery, but said it was a lovely idea, as long as they really liked the name.'

'Well, it's a fine French name, better than all the American rubbish kids seem to be labelled nowadays. How can any child grow up normally in the Republic of France being called Kevin? Or Clint?'

Alex grinned unexpectedly. 'Or Evariste, or Clovis, or Désiré?'

'Point taken,' he said, frowning at the string of absurd names his parents had given him. 'And if you ever mention them again, I'll have you suspended!'

'By my guts or my garters?'

'Both if you don't get out. Talk about sexual harassment. Those women ought to try being in my shoes.'

'Be a bit difficult, *patron*, they'd fall flat on their faces. For a woman you've got big feet.'

'*Exit now!*'

Rigal clicked on Enter. 'According to the data you've given me,' he said to de Troq', 'the dead girl and this little girl could be the same. The colours don't match exactly but skin changes with age and the sun, hair too, however the eyes don't. Let's have a go.' He enlarged the eleven-year-old face in front of him, keeping the same shape although removing the plump childish cheeks. 'How long was the dead girl's hair?'

'Shoulder-length,' de Troq' replied.

The child on the screen still looked no more than eleven years old.

Not for long.

Nosjean had spent a long time staring down into the street from his own office, a cigarette hanging limply from his lips. Well-wrapped pedestrians hurried along the pavements, their rapid strides making each one look as if he was late for a meeting of grave importance, huddled inside thick clothes, heads bent, hands in pockets, shoulders hunched, their breath preceding them in puffing clouds. Grubby patches of snow still hugged the corners of buildings, the scene was chilled, dismal – depressing. It suited his mood. He pulled hard on the end of his cigarette, inhaling the smoke deep into his lungs, snatched the stub from his mouth and ground it out in the ashtray behind him. Since being promoted to Commandant, he'd been smoking more than ever. This morning, the added responsibility sat heavily on his shoulders.

He studied the duty roster, staring at the two names he was getting to know: Morrison and Gilbert. Partnering the new men off wasn't simple; no one wanted them.

Morrison was an over-enthusiastic redhead, too tall for his own good and about as well built as a pencil. He had to bend his knees to get through the sergeants' room door and constantly collided with the metal lampshade in the middle of the ceiling. He wasn't much safer sitting down; he was unable to fold his legs under the desk in the normal way, and his protruding feet created a dangerous obstacle to anyone passing. Inevitably every one of the team had, at some time, tripped over them and cursed his existence. As a consequence, he blushed even more, and apologised continually. And he was more of a handicap than a help out on the streets, stuttering and dithering in the background.

As for Gilbert, the only person who liked the bully was slow-moving Misset with his brain in neutral, and they couldn't be allowed to work together again – the last time had been a near disaster. The pair of them had spent most of the day propping up various bars with the excuse of interrogating the customers and had come in reeking of beer with no useful information except that the girl in the green dress had jolly nice knockers and Misset thought he was going to be sick. Gilbert had been confined to answering phones after Bardolle refused to work with him any longer. Now Cheriff was on paternity leave for the rest of the week, which left Misset once more without a partner. Perhaps if he put de Troq' with Gilbert and Jourdain with Misset . . . No, that wouldn't do, Jourdain might break Misset's neck if he made a snide remark about working with a girl, last year she'd almost dislocated his jaw. Bardolle and Jourdain would work well together, which left Pujol to cope with Misset. Bright he might be, but not a strong enough character to keep Misset's mind on the job. Oh hell!

'Eeny, meeny, miney, mo . . .' Nosjean's finger hovered over the names of the team members. The phone rang and gratefully his hesitating hand changed direction to lift the receiver.

'What's keeping you!'

'On my way, *patron*!'

Scribbling names onto the chart, he snatched up the paper and hurried into the corridor, turned left, left again and handed it to Pel who, between coughs, considered the odd pairs of policemen listed in front of him. He lifted an eyebrow and grunted. 'Did this with your eyes closed, did you?'

'Someone's got to have the sods. Gilbert's a real problem,' Nosjean retorted. 'I've got Misset!'

'We'll see how it works. Morning meeting!'

Gilbert was sitting slouched at the back of the room with Misset; the two men were pawing the centre page spread of *Lui*. The rest of the team, although they didn't jump to attention when Pel crashed his way in, did look alert and intelligent. He waited for a few seconds hoping for a reaction – he got none – and, walking calmly through the tunnel of desks, quietly removed the erotic magazine from Gilbert's hands.

'Here! I paid for that.'

'And the city of Dijon pays for your time. You are wasting it. You are also wasting Misset's time, and although he doesn't achieve a great deal even when he's concentrating, it's better than nothing. Gilbert, get back to your own desk.'

'When I was with the CRS –'

'Is irrelevant,' Pel interrupted. 'You are no longer.'

'Lambert said –'

'What Lambert says and what Lambert does are two entirely different things. You're on *my* team. Lambert may be the Chief but I'm your commanding officer. Now.' He turned back towards his men and blew his nose, flinching at the stinging. 'Let's have it. What's new?'

De Troq' handed him two photographs. 'The police photographer took that one after the dead girl had been cleaned up for identification. This one is a figment of Rigal's imagination, built from a picture of Renée Clavier aged eleven.'

'It could be the same girl. Has her mother seen this?'

'Not yet. I'd like to try it on her teachers, she was doing a typing course at the Chambre de Métier. If I get a positive ID, I want to question one or two of the students.'

'While you're at it, find out if she had a small Spanish or Portuguese friend. It could be our two corpses knew each other. Next?'

'We've got all the details on the forest robbery,' Pujol offered. 'Klein's paperwork together with Forensics' report came through this morning. I saw Madame Darcy yesterday evening. She wasn't able to add anything, her original statement was comprehensive.'

'How is she?'

'Being brave.'

'Any leads?'

'None so far. I'll be doing the round of touts and bars – someone may have seen the stolen items changing hands. In the meantime the descriptions have been put into the electronic file.'

'Stick with it, the perpetrators must be put away. Police widows shouldn't be made to suffer any more than they have to. Next?'

'The fire at Fabres et Fabres pharmaceuticals,' Bardolle offered. 'I think I may have a possible suspect; they sacked a packer, Serge Millet, a few weeks ago for pilfering. He worked at a small factory on the industrial estate before Fabres and was involved in a heated argument about overtime, after which a large wastepaper container mysteriously went up in smoke. No one actually accused Millet but he handed in his notice the same day, and the manager's always wondered.'

'Hmm, it's a bit thin. Prepare a search warrant for his home if you think Brisard'll sign it, but make sure you have reasonable grounds for the request. Dig deeper into his background if necessary, see if you can't come up with something more positive.'

The phone rang; Pujol snatched it up. As he replaced it, he was licking his lips. Pel knew something interesting had happened. 'Gendarmerie in Pontailler requests assistance. A caravan was washed up on a farmer's land, he went to haul it off this morning. Once he'd got it back on its wheels, he tried the door and went inside, then called the local cops. They don't like the look of it, say it smells like someone's skinned a pig in there, then left it to rot.'

'This could be the College Cadavre. Nosjean, Misset, get your coats on. De Troq', finish up here. Pujol, call Leguyder, give him the address, tell him it's urgent, we'll wait for him there. And de Troq',' he called, as he disappeared through the door, 'if you're all out, get a man from downstairs to field the phone calls.'

For a change it wasn't snowing or raining, but a heavy mist shortened their vision, drawing the horizon in, closing the countryside into a fuzzy bubble. It lay like a thick damp blanket over the dull, grey fields as they left the city's bypass. Misset was slumped wearily in the back seat. Pel checked his bag of medication then his seat-belt and told Nosjean to go easy on the accelerator, then, once they were out on the D70, heading north-east, he lit up, coughed richly, and opened the window a fraction.

'So Anna turned up after all?'

It never ceased to amaze Nosjean how the *patron* knew exactly what every one of them was up to. When Cheriff and Annie were secretly seeing each other years ago, he'd known before anyone else, and he also knew damn well there was something going on between de Troq' and Jourdain although they'd been extremely discreet. How the hell had he found out about Anna? Extrasensory perception? He wouldn't put it past Pel.

'It was a nice surprise.'

'Her father thinks she's mad chasing after a policeman.'

69

'Does he?'

'Tried to put a stop to it. He feels extremely vulnerable as a single parent – his wife died of cancer when Anna was fourteen, and it hasn't been easy bringing her up without a mother. He even tried finding a new wife to help out, but women, he said, were jealous of her, and Anna of them. In the end he gave up. He realised recently he was jealous of you. She does nothing but talk about you when he wanted to talk about himself.'

Approaching a tight corner, Nosjean changed down a gear.

'How do you know?'

'He told me. Nice man, Maître Lugan. Turn right at the next crossroads.'

They followed the D961 for 31 kilometres before turning left into Pontailler, by which time Misset was snoring peacefully and Nosjean was still wondering why Pel had spoken to Anna's father. The only explanation he'd given was, 'I had a question for him.'

Pontailler was a small village through which the road twisted and turned, curving round the old houses. Glancing down at the map he held, Pel indicated a small lane to the left leading to Mas Amat, the property of the farmer who'd found the caravan.

Already parked outside the large square house was a navy blue gendarmerie break, splattered liberally with mud. Inside the kitchen it looked more like a party than a possible murder enquiry. Steaming glasses of coffee decorated the long scrubbed table and in the middle stood a collection of bottles. The two gendarmes were wearing thick Charantais bedroom slippers and, along with the other seven people in the room, were sipping their *eau de vie* cosily while Madame Routaboule dried their socks and boots by the wood-burning stove. When they saw Pel, they offered their hands for shaking and politely said *bonjour*, thinking he was just another inquisitive neighbour.

Nosjean flipped open his identification. 'Commandant Nosjean, Police Judiciaire, answering your request for assistance.'

'At last,' one of the boys in blue said. 'Now we can go home. Who are they? Your lieutenants?'

'One of them is, Lieutenant Misset. This, however, is Commissaire Pel.'

'Oh cripes!' They both shot to their feet and saluted smartly.

Pel waved them down. 'It's a bit late for that, you sloppy pair. Let's hear what you've found.'

Standing in the corner of his kitchen, scratching a bald head under his cap, André Routaboule couldn't believe it; what he'd expected to be a quick job of salvaging a caravan had turned into a blooming nightmare. When he'd discovered it lying on its side on the edge of one of his fields, he'd thought to himself that if he said nothing for long enough, and no one came looking, he might be able to call it his own. If it was no good as a caravan, he could always use it for storage, or, if nothing else, a kennel for the bitch about to pup. However, when he'd lifted it back on to its wheels with the help of the fork on the front of his tractor, he made the mistake of opening the door, and the stench that hit him in the face had sent him reeling. Being a countryman, born and bred, he knew damn well it wasn't mould or mud, or anything natural, that smelt like that, and hurried up the hill, as fast as his tractor would take him, to phone the police. Now the young buggers were wearing his slippers and drinking his illegally made *eau de vie*, and they'd called in a bunch of detectives. And his wife was enjoying herself! The only one that looked as if he might be of use was the bloke with hardly any hair and a bright red nose – what was he called? Pill or something – but Routaboule didn't really like the look of him either. However, he had work to do, he wanted the police off his land and out of his life.

'Washed downstream,' he said. 'Probably from the campsite in Larroque, a coupla kilometres away, they lost three. I took these lads down to look at it, trouble is them floods have left their mark, the field's fulla mud, they didn't have their wellies with them . . .'

A sharp knock at the door interrupted his story. Madame went to answer it and showed Leguyder and one of his technicians into the overheated kitchen. He nodded to everyone, shook Pel's hand, and demanded to be escorted to the site.

After a great deal of scuffling over sorting out socks and shoes, Madame fussing and finding dry ones, Pel hanging on to his patience and Leguyder sighing, clucking his scientific tongue, they trooped off through the puddles and the chilling mist to the

71

bottom of the hill. It took them seven minutes before the caravan came into sight, another five before arriving.

It took Leguyder seconds to sum up the situation. When he poked his head out of the door, everyone turned towards him in anticipation. 'The brown stains,' he said, 'are deceptive, they could be anything from mud to blood, but this,' he went on, holding up a plastic bag, 'is a finger.'

5

While he cautiously continued to film and examine the interior of the trailer, Nosjean noted down any and all relevant details as Pel questioned Routaboule. Misset stood with his hands in his pockets, his brain apparently in neutral. They left him there to watch the scientists at work, while Pel and Nosjean went to find Hubert Hachot, the owner of the campsite from which the caravan had come.

He was sitting with his feet up in front of a log fire watching television when they arrived, but he welcomed them in with enthusiasm. 'Not much doing at this time of year, is there?' he said by way of an apology for his inactivity.

They got the preliminary introductions over and, finally seated comfortably, Pel asked him about the mobile homes that were swept away by the floods. 'The one I'm particularly interested in is a Flipper City, beige with brown stripes. Whose is it?'

Hachot rubbed his chin. 'Don't rightly know no more. Young lad put it there a couple of summers ago, paid rent for six months, then, well, didn't see him no more. I waited all through the winter but he never turned up. When summer come again, I thought, well, bloody hell, I'd rent it out, that way I'd pay off what he owed me.'

'Remember his name?'

'Hang on a minute, it might come back . . . mmm, Boulot! That's it – Giles Boulot, about twenty I reckon he was, nice lad.'

'Who did you rent it out to?'

'Anyone that wanted it. I guess word got around and soon it was the bonking place for local lovers. Had one or two business-men too, with their fussy little secretaries. Nice it was inside, I always kept it clean.'

'Names?'

'Look in the telephone directory, just about everyone round here under the age of retirement and one or two over!'

'Could you be more precise?'

'Let me see . . . Jean-Luc Loubière when he was still courting the Galy girl, pretty little thing, she got pregnant, they're living with her Mum now, here in the village. Mm, Sebastien Soulié a couple of times. Marc Faure, no, he cancelled and I gave him his money back, and Gabriel Blanc, the rotten devil, he's got ever such a nice wife.'

Nosjean scribbled. Pel waited, handkerchief at the ready, for the sneeze to come.

'Can't think of any more.'

'If you do, please let us know.'

'Hold your horses! That wasn't the end of it. The next winter, it sprang a leak, things got a bit mouldy, see, and well, I couldn't charge what I'd been charging, but there was still the kids, wanting a place to screw each other silly.'

Pel sneezed twice and blew his nose delicately. *'Pardon.* Names?'

'Oh gawd, er, Blanc again, Soulié, Julien Roche, he was a right one, they say it was a different bit of skirt every time, and Urbain, he must be sixty if he's a day. There were others but I can't recall.'

'How much did you charge them?'

'100 francs for the afternoon, or night, whatever – cheaper than a reg'lar hotel, and nice and private, specially out of season, not that we get that many tourists in the summer. Then about three months ago, around September I suppose it was, I gets a phone call; someone saying they'd pay me once a month for sole use of the thing. Well, I could hardly refuse, could I? 450 a month isn't really a proper rent, is it? Anyways, I said okay. Next day the postman brings me a *mandat* for 450 francs, and I puts the keys in the caravan as agreed. Cleaned it up nice, I did too.'

'Have you ever seen your tenant?'

'Only from a distance, at the beginning before the evenings got dark. He was on his moped, chuntering across the field. I gives him a wave, he waves back.'

'Can you describe him?'

'Ordinary, nothing special. He was wearing a crash helmet, couldn't see his face.'

'And you've never seen him since?.

"Ere, I've got better things to do than spy on a reg'lar paying tenant. Got an allotment out back there, takes me all me time to keep up with the weeds.'

'What happened when the van was washed away? Did your tenant come back, to claim on the campsite's insurance, for lost property locked inside?'

'I thought he might, but no, I never saw him again. 'Ere, he wasn't in it, was he?'

'Not when it was found, and the door was closed, so I doubt it. What's his name?'

'Don't know, his rent was paid in cash by the postman.'

'So you didn't see his face, don't know what his name is and have only spoken to him once on the phone.'

Hachot considered this for a moment. 'Yeah, I suppose that's about the size of it.'

'What did he sound like?'

'Like someone wanting to rent a caravan for a bit of hanky-panky.'

'Did he have an accent?'

'Not that I noticed. Mind you, he did sound a bit effeminate. That's right! I wondered at the time if it was a poofter.'

'A homosexual?'

'Well, it could've been, couldn't it?'

As they left, Pel turned tiredly to his second-in-command. His head was aching again and he was sweating, he felt lousy. 'All these people have to be interviewed. One of them could have decided to make the caravan his habitat.'

'Along with the homosexual?'

'A lover's tiff because one of them was seeing a woman as well – that finger didn't look too masculine to me.'

'Being a homosexual could explain the nail varnish.'

'Which would mean it's got nothing to do with the College Cadavre.' Pel put a hand to his hot forehead. 'Or maybe it does. Maybe she was the reason for the lover's . . . *et merde*, it's getting unpleasantly complicated. We'll have the whole team working on the interviews. And the postman that delivered the money-order must be seen. In the meantime, let's check out what else Leguyder's found.'

*   *   *

De Troq' and Gilbert had found someone almost willing to swear the girl who drowned in the Rin was Renée Clavier. Alain Chouillou, her teacher at the Chambre de Métier, studied the photograph taken in the lab and sighed sadly. 'Yup, I think that's her. Poor Renée, she didn't have it easy.'

De Troq' looked at his left eye. Chouillou had a slight squint, it wasn't easy to know which side was focusing. 'What didn't she have easy?'

'Life. I got the impression that it was a bit of a struggle. She came into town by moped, often drenched from the rain, her fingers blue with cold. She sniffed a lot in class, not that that's relevant but she looked permanently hungry.'

The policeman's regard switched to his right eye; it wasn't much better. 'She had a moped?'

'Borrowed it from her mother, I think.'

Making the best of a bad job, de Troq' decided to concentrate on the bridge of his nose. 'Did she get on with the rest of the class?'

'She didn't quarrel with them if that's what you mean, but no, she didn't seem to have any friends, kept herself to herself.' The teacher shrugged. 'Once in a while I saw her talking to one of the others, but usually it was with a work book in her hands – she must have been asking for help with homework or something like that.'

'Who?'

'I'm not sure I can tell you, to be honest. Oh yes, Laetitia Combe was one.'

De Troq' showed him Rigal's computer-constructed portrait and Chouillou smiled. 'That's what she could have been like given a bit of care and attention.'

'Not a bad looker,' Gilbert added unnecessarily.

'Was she a good student?'

'She was willing. What she lacked in intelligence she made up for in determination. She didn't find it easy but she once told me it was the only way she was ever going to be free.'

'Free?'

'I think she meant her parents. She didn't really talk about them but I got the impression she was ashamed of them. They're farm-workers, unsophisticated and scruffy. Her father's bed-

76

ridden, I believe, and her mother scratches a living in the vine-yards or charring for farmers' wives, whatever she can find.'

'Considering she didn't really talk about them, you know a surprising amount.'

'When a student joins us here, forms are filled in. If the student's under eighteen, the parents or a legal guardian have to sign them, having given certain relevant information. You know the sort of thing; name, date of birth, profession, place of work, medical insurance organisation. All I've told you is what was written on the form plus what I gleaned from Renée.'

'Gleaned?'

Chouillou sighed. 'How can I put this without sounding unkind? Renée was, well, she smelt. I therefore understood she didn't have a bathroom at home.'

'Did this cause a problem in class?'

'Well, yes, I suppose it did. You know what youngsters are like, they pulled faces and sat as far away as they could. I felt sorry for her actually. I might as well tell you because no doubt you'll find out, but I invited her home to meet my wife. I thought she might find a way of suggesting she took a shower and washed her hair. I didn't feel able to, being her teacher and, well, I'm a man, I thought she might take offence but I did want to help.'

'You invited her home?'

'For a shower.'

Gilbert snorted. 'And a quick shafting?'

'My wife was there! As a matter of fact, they got on well together. Michelle, my wife that is, often asked after her, kept on at me to bring her home again.'

'Did you?'

'Well, yes. I couldn't see any harm in it, she seemed so grateful.'

'Grateful enough to let you shaft her?' Gilbert again.

'For God's sake! I'm her teacher.'

'How many times did you invite Renée home?'

'Oh, I don't know, maybe half a dozen.'

'I'd like to confirm that with your wife, if you don't mind?'

'No, no, of course not.'

'Perhaps you'd give me your address.'

'Yes, certainly, 15 rue Jean Renoir, it's the estate behind La Clinique Sainte Marthe.'

'Next time,' de Troq' said to his partner, as they left the building, 'keep your damn mouth shut.'

'Only doing my job.'

'Haven't you ever heard of police harassment? You were coming close to it.'

'Look, your highness, Baron bleeding Toffee-nosed de Troquereau, if he was shafting her that's a good motive for murder, isn't it? Specially as he's well and truly married.'

'It's not enough, Gilbert.'

Wary of introducing the unsubtle Gilbert to Chouillou's wife, worried he might do a repeat act of abusive vulgarity, reducing the woman to tears and having them both reported to Lambert or worse, de Troq' climbed back in the car and headed for the Clavier farm. Madame Clavier was at least used to indecent behaviour. Her revolting husband might keep Gilbert quiet while he worked on her.

'Why are we going to see the peasant? I rather fancied a quick trip to rue Jean Renoir, and get a look at the teacher's wife.'

'Think about it, if Clavier still won't co-operate, we may be able to get a definite identification from her doctor or the dentist, if they bothered with them. Without it, we've still got a corpse with no name, plus a kid of eighteen that's disappeared. And,' he added, 'I don't want you near anyone's wife until you've learnt how to behave.'

'*Putain*! You're a right stuck-up bastard.'

'That's where you're wrong, Gilbert,' de Troq' replied patiently. 'My parents were well and truly married when I was conceived.'

'You're still stuck-up. I'm just an ordinary bleeding bloke and I behave like an ordinary bleeding bloke. You've got too used to working with a flat-chested blonde who thinks she's Cynthia Crawford.'

'Cindy.'

'I thought she was called Jourdain.'

'Cindy Crawford, not Cynthia.'

'Whatever, I wouldn't mind a quick one with her. Not Jourdain, she's got nothing to get hold of.'

'You really are an obnoxious squirt. Alex Jourdain is a very good police officer, and, I might add, preferable to you any day.'

'I've seen you looking at her, reckon she's worth a shafting, don't you?'

'Gilbert, wrap up.' But de Troq' did allow himself a private smile: he'd been shafting the Punk for weeks, although personally he'd never have used that particular word to describe the hours of passion and tenderness they shared.

Madame Clavier was spooning watery soup into her mouth when they arrived. She didn't offer them coffee, she didn't ask them to sit down, just went on sucking the soup through the gaps in her teeth and chewing on a lump of hard bread. 'Ain't got time to talk to the likes of you, I've got a living to earn. Out there,' she pointed her dripping spoon towards the window, 'in the vineyards, not swishing about in a posh car.'

Placing the two portraits on the table in front of her, they waited for some kind of reaction. Her eyes fixed on to the dead girl's face and she dropped the spoon with a clatter.

'Is this your daughter, Renée?'

'I've told you before –'

De Troq' uncharacteristically interrupted. 'Yes, I remember,' he said, 'it doesn't look like her. We'd like the name of your doctor and dentist.'

'What for?'

'We've received contradictory information, madame. Renée's teacher thinks this is her'. He put a fingertip lightly on one of the pictures. 'You say it isn't. They'll be able to confirm it one way or another.'

'How'll they do that?'

'The dentist will have an X-ray of the inside of her mouth, that's as good as fingerprints, teeth are unique. The doctor –'

Madame Clavier's sorrowful eyes filled and overflowed. 'My Renée was a pretty little thing, a sweet little girl. She was all I'd got.'

'Then why . . .'

'And he had to go and spoil her!'

'. . . didn't you identify her?'

79

'Because then you'd know who'd done it.'

'Who, madame?'

'That bastard in there!' She jabbed her finger in the direction of her husband's door as the tears coursed down her cheeks.

'Renée's father? He's bedridden.'

'Don't I know it! But he hasn't always been. He did it, I tell you! He took her goodness away!'

'I beg your pardon?'

'I found them! Been cleaning, came back early and found him, that bastard, he was . . .' She screwed up her face as if in pain. '. . . with my little girl. It was her fifteenth birthday!'

'He was engaged in sexual intercourse with her?'

'Don't! Don't say it! We tried to pretend it didn't happen. I sloshed him one, good and proper, gave him a black eye, and told him I'd kill him if he did it again.'

'And Renée?'

'I made her promise never to tell. She changed after that, didn't want to come home, she never said, not a word, but I knew. She didn't want us any more, my little girl. Lost. Because of him!'

'Why didn't you report it?'

'And have her taken away? Are you mad! She's my only child.'

'But your husband, surely you –'

'God knows he earned little enough, but without him we had nothing.'

'You do realise if you don't identify her, if she isn't claimed, she will be buried by the council as soon as her body is released? If you do decide to identify her, she'll come home to you, and you can place her in the family tomb.'

'I can't afford another funeral.'

'Another?'

'My mother died in the summer.'

'If you ask, the council will help.'

'And have everyone know we're too poor to bury our own?'

De Troq' sighed sadly. 'I believe you lent her your moped to go to college?'

'No, it was his, my husband's. Well, he doesn't use it, does he? Not since six months or more. Last time he fell off, they brought him home on the top of a muck-spreader, he was out for the count, peed cheap wine for days he did, and now he can't even walk to the toilet.'

'What kind of moped was it?'

'Grey.'

'What make?'

'Peugeot, I think, nothing special, just like everyone else's really.'

'Have you got the insurance papers?'

'Why?'

'They'll have the make and year on them.'

'What difference will that make? She's . . . she's not going to need it any more.'

'We'd like to find it all the same.'

'It's her own bloody fault,' Gilbert said, as he collapsed into the car. 'All she has to do is ask and the sodding welfare state would give her a handout.'

'She'd have to fill in a thousand forms. I doubt Madame Clavier knows how to read or write beyond her own name.'

'That's her problem – anyway, a social worker would have done it for her.'

'And have everyone know how poor they are? It's a vicious circle.'

'I still say it's her fault. And I reckon it's her fault Renée ended up the way she did. After her Dad shafted her. She was probably begging for a bloke that knew how to use his –'

'Gilbert!'

'I bet she was panting to get her knickers off.'

'If you read any of the articles in the police journal,' de Troq' said between gritted teeth, 'you will notice that after rape, particularly incestuous rape, a girl is usually so traumatised it takes years before she will even consider a normal sexual relationship – if ever.'

'So who says the guy that gutted her was normal?'

De Troq' reversed out of the farmyard, glancing at the dashboard clock as he straightened up. Nearly knocking-off time. All he had to do was drive back into the city with his fingers in his ears – metaphorically speaking of course, he wasn't too good at steering and changing gear with his elbows – dump his partner in the sergeants' room, preferably gagged, report to Pel, requesting a search warrant for the farm, and call it a day. For the first time since he'd joined Pel's team, the Baron Charles Victor de Troquereau de Turenne was pissed off with being a policeman.

He wasn't the only one. Pel was feeling awful, he'd been swallowing various cold remedies all day and they'd done no good at all. Now he was suspiciously eyeing a tiny bottle that Boudet had sent over. Attached to it was a laboratory label, the same, Pel remarked uneasily, that was usually attached to the toe of a deceased: 'Shock treatment – take four today (2+2), three tomorrow (2+1), two the next day (1+1), then one (1/2+1/2), then 1/2 and stop.' He tipped two small tablets into his hand and put them in his mouth.

Five minutes later, when he'd recovered, he had Boudet on the line. 'What are you trying to do? Kill me? Those pill things, I nearly choked to death!'

'You did dissolve them?'

'Dissolve them?'

'In water.'

'You didn't say anything about water!'

'It's written on the bottle, in red.'

'Oh.'

'How many have you taken?'

'Two.'

'Two more before going to bed then.'

'Yes. Thank you, Boudet, I shall not, after all, be arresting you for attempted murder.'

'I appreciate it.'

'We know who the girl in the Rin was too, you can give her a name.'

'I'm delighted.'

'Renée Clavier.'

Replacing the phone, Pel swallowed another half-litre of water, still worried about dissolving the effervescing pills properly, belched quietly behind his fist, and turned back to his screen.

Leguyder, armed with his box full of samples, had confirmed the stains on the caravan ceiling were indeed blood, the same group the College Cadavre, O+ – not that that proved much. 65% of the population shared the same group, it was the most common group in France, if not the world – but fortunately that wasn't his problem.

The grotesque finger he'd found was also O+. Big deal. It could be from the College Cadavre, or another mutilation. Whatever the result, it seemed the caravan had nothing to do with Renée Clavier, due to be released for burial the following morning, and whose blood group was A+.

That was the easy part of his analysis. DNA genetic profiling took rather longer, as Leguyder had enjoyed explaining: 'Now I have a specimen, I shall be able to extract the DNA and mix it with a restriction enzyme that cuts the DNA chain at particular sequences, giving me fragments. These fragments are placed in a gel, to which a high voltage electrical current is applied, sorting the fragments according to size. These are then blotted from the gel by a nylon membrane and incubated, after which it is treated with a radioactive genetic probe. The radioactivity causes the pieces of DNA to be revealed as dark bands, rather like a supermarket code bar actually. As you can see, it's a complicated and lengthy process but does enable me to tell you with certainty whether the College Cadavre was killed in the caravan and whether the finger belongs to it. I'll mail the results as soon as they're ready.'

Pel stared at the blank screen in front of him and wondered if he'd ever make friends with his computer. Clicking on *Démarrer* then on *Arrêter*, OK, he read the machine's familiar message: '*Veuillez patienter pendant l'arrêt de votre ordinateur.*' He patiently waited until the bleeping had stopped and pushed the keyboard away with relief. He had an important meeting to attend to.

Crossing the hospital's large entrance hall, he made his way to the lifts. He knew where he was going, he'd been there before, just once, and as the lift carried him up to the fourth floor, the thought of it saddened him. As the doors whispered themselves open, he shuffled inside his clothes and stepped out, carrying a bunch of flowers as if they'd bite him. Directed by arrows on the walls, he stopped outside room number 323 and knocked. His flu had taken a turn for the better, he was feeling slightly more human, if not slightly light-headed.

'*Entrez*! Pel! How lovely, Cheriff told me you might stop by.'

Annie did look radiant. Perhaps it had something to do with her flame-coloured hair – it had grown down to her shoulders and was shining with health. Motherhood appeared to agree with her.

'Um, I brought you these,' Pel replied, holding out the limp bouquet, 'don't expect they'll last long, and, um, a bottle of champagne, I'm told it's just the thing for restoring the spirit after a mild shock.'

'Come and see the baby. We're calling him Daniel.'

'I know. Yes,' he said, keeping his distance, 'very nice.'

The door to the room burst open, Cheriff marched in with two brown carrier bags. 'Chinese take-away! Darcy said it would be expected if you visited after the birth.'

'I, well, yes, we did when the twins were born.'

'Then we'd better not break with tradition.'

'In that case,' Pel grinned, looking like a dyspeptic gargoyle, 'I suppose I'd better break open the champagne.'

While Pel, Cheriff and Annie made merry in Maternity, floating into the banks of the River Saône – after having been caught in the weir but finally working its way free – not far from Beaune, was a black plastic bag. In it were Marianna Roquetas's arms.

6

Wednesday, 24th November

Beaune gendarmerie were called out to a hysterical woman in Seurre. The moment day began breaking, she'd set off as usual to jog along the river bank. She was an ex-army sergeant and liked to keep fit, although looking at her ugly mug, the answering gendarmes wondered why she bothered.

Regardless of the swirling mists and intense cold – and having left a nicely centrally heated *caserne* where the coffee was hot and the sugar sat invitingly alongside – they were patient while she tried to tell them what she'd stumbled across. Having seen the contents of the black plastic bag, they reported it to Commissaire Camalet and proceeded to take a statement from the still hysterical woman. Commissaire Camalet, au fait with what was going on in Dijon, 38 kilometres to the north, quite rightly phoned through to Pel before leaving his office. His instructions were clear, to instigate a thorough search of the area where the arms were found, then transport them to their pathology department where they were to wait, untouched, for collection by one of Pel's men. This is precisely what he did.

Pujol and Morrison left the Hôtel de Police five minutes after they arrived at 0750. They were back by 1000. Pretty good going considering the distances covered, and the rush-hour traffic in both cities between eight and nine thirty.

Boudet took delivery, scrubbed up, got inside his gown and gloves, put a fresh tape in the recorder and switched it on, then he unwrapped the parcel. The black plastic, together with a blood sample, was sent by internal messenger to Leguyder. Boudet set to work on the arms. By midday he was pretty certain they belonged to the torso at Collège Albert Camus. He was tempted to think this the moment he heard two arms had been found. Even more tempted when he noticed the index finger on the right hand was missing. He resisted the temptation: pathology is not based on presumption. Therefore he worked carefully and methodically, comparing the cuts and the tissue, matching them as far as possible to the trunk he still had in cold storage. The cuts didn't match exactly, which was hardly surprising, a dog had been chewing enthusiastically at the edges of the torso. However, the fat content and thickness of the tissue did correspond. Then he turned to the bones, measuring the humerus, radius and ulna, finally sawing through the humerus to establish the diameter. Now he was pretty certain – the details tallied exactly with the torso. But even that wasn't enough. There are thousands, if not millions, of small women, about 1m55, aged between twenty and twenty-five, of Spanish or Portuguese origin, in France. The chances of two of these women being murdered and chopped into more manageable pieces within days of each other is pretty damn slim, but stranger things had happened and the police had to be sure. He placed the arms in a separate refrigerated drawer, removed his gloves and gown, and went through to the office to write his report from the recording he'd made while undertaking the examination. When he'd finished, he read it through, made one or two corrections and mailed it to Pel's desk. Then, swivelling round on his chair to the coffee machine, he poured himself a plastic beaker of black with one sugar and waited for the phone to ring.

When it did, he chuckled, downed the last mouthful of coffee and snatched it up. 'Bonjour, Commissaire! How are you feeling?'

'How did you know it would be me?'

'Pathologists have ways of working things out.'

'Ah. I'm feeling better, if anything slightly drunk. It's not unpleasant.'

'Have you consumed any alcohol?'

'Two glasses of champagne yesterday evening. Coffee and water today.'

'That would explain it. Stick to water and fruit juice.'

'Fine, jolly good. What's this mess you've sent me? I don't understand a word of it.'

Boudet grinned to himself, it was exactly what he'd expected. 'Go to the conclusion, Pel, that's the interesting bit.'

'That's where I am. What the hell's a head of humerus articulating with glenoid cavity of scapula?'

'Where the arm joins the clavicle and coracoid; in other words, the shoulder. The joint was separated with poultry shears.'

'The same ones?'

'Can't be sure. Certainly the same sort. Leguyder will tell you what you want to know; only he can give you 100% confirmation that the arms belonged to the torso.'

'How sure are you?'

'99%'.

'That'll do for the time being. *Bon appétit!*'

While Boudet had been busy with the post-mortem, Nosjean, accompanied by Misset, his brain stuck in neutral, was re-questioning Hachot, the owner of the campsite where the caravan had been rented, and added another four names to the list of one-night-standers in the caravan. Shortly after that they found the postman who delivered the money-order to Hachot once a month and who was no help at all – 'S'far as I can remember it was sent from Dijon, different post offices every time, s'far as I can remember, couldn't read the si'nature.' Just before midday they tracked down Giles Boulot, coming out of a philosophy class at the university, and who'd originally dragged the caravan on to the site with a view to living there – 'Sure, I remember the van, got bored with living so far out, it wasn't worth anything so I left it there, thinking maybe I'd use it the next summer. By that time, though, I was living with my girlfriend, she's got a good job, and we went to Spain instead. Who knew about the van? Jesus, I don't know, probably everyone, I had mates who came over in the evening, it's a quiet place where you can, well, be private, there were a few tourists but they didn't bother us while we . . . well, you know. Smoke? Well, yeah, you know. Their names? Why, you're not going to do them for possession? It was only a bit of pot.' It was at this point Nosjean raised his voice. 'Right now I don't give a damn what you and your mates smoke, but I would, all the same, like their names. This is a murder enquiry!' To which Boulot replied, 'Hey, none of my mates would kill anyone!'

Nosjean sighed. 'I'm not suggesting they would. We'd like to eliminate them – they may have seen someone else on the site, or know someone who was interested in it.' Boulot finally gave them a list of names. To add to the list of names Hachot had already supplied and added to, and which big Bardolle and Alex Jourdain were busy tracing at that very minute. In total there were twenty-seven.

So far.

That afternoon, Renée Clavier's body was returned to her home. Her mother wept as the body was laid on a clean but grey sheet covering the newly scrubbed table, the only place available. She went on weeping as she pulled another clean but grey sheet up over her daughter's folded hands.

A voice came shouting through to the kitchen: "Ere, mother, I've shat meself!'

If she heard him, she gave no sign; perhaps her grief, finally released, had shut off half her senses. She lit two candles which she placed either side of the putty-coloured head, closed the shutters, and sat down, briefly touching the girl's cold cheek.

As Madame Clavier mourned, de Troq' and Gilbert were sitting in a small but overcrowded sitting-room of a modern bungalow known as 15 rue Jean Renoir. In it there was too much fussy furniture and far too many frills. Madame Chouillou was pouring coffee into tiny cups with rosebuds all over them. 'Poor Renée, poor poor Renée, she shouldn't have died like that, how simply awful.'

'How well did you know her?'

'Oh, not very well really. My husband brought her home first, he'd talked about . . . well, sorry about this . . . but the pretty girl that smelt, and, well, I thought, well, it could do no harm, so I said, yes, invite her over one day, I'll see if I can persuade her to have a shower. Poor love, she did smell, but it wasn't just her, it was her clothes, they reeked of, well, I'm not sure what, my husband said it was cow manure. He should know, his parents have a herd of a hundred Charolais. Well, I showed her round the house, she wanted to see, you see, and when we got to the bathroom, all my anxieties were swept away. She said, how lovely. She said she'd love to have her own bathroom and lie in a hot sudsy bath for hours. So I said, why don't you, now? Well, while she did, I rifled through my cupboards for some clean clothes that might fit, cast-offs, you know. She is . . . sorry . . . she *was* taller but a bit thinner than me. Anyway, I knocked on the door and told her that I'd put a tracksuit outside if she'd like to wear it. Well, I'd put socks and other things with it, and she looked quite different when she came down for supper.'

'What time did she leave?'

'Well, I'm not sure. Oh yes, I *do* know. She looked up at the kitchen clock and said something like, golly is that the time, I've missed my bus. So I said to my husband the least we could do was run her home. It was just after nine.'

'You drove her home?'

'No, I did the washing-up, my husband took her.'

'What time did he get back?'

'About an hour later, there and back, I was in bed.'

'When did she next come to the house?'

'A couple of weeks later, I asked my husband how she was getting on and he said she was smelling again.'

'Did she stay for supper?'

'Oh yes, she did, poor Renée, she always looked so hungry.'

'How often did you entertain her?'

'Well, after that it was once a week, on a Friday.'

'And she always had a bath and stayed for supper?'

'And changed her clothes. I had a real clear-out, she was thrilled, and they were only odds and ends I'd been hanging on to, old-fashioned favourites that I hadn't worn in years. What she left behind I washed and ironed ready for the next time. Oh, she was so grateful.'

Gilbert opened his mouth. 'Grateful enough to –'

De Troq' interrupted rapidly. 'And your husband always drove her home?'

'It was the least we could do.'

'Was he shafting her on the way?' Gilbert had managed it at last.

Madame Chouillou laughed! 'You policemen, you are terrors! No, I don't think my husband would dream of . . . doing that. We love each other. Other men might have thought about it, but not Laurent. Remember, he's used to these young girls, he works with them all day long, there are far prettier girls than Renée at the school, but he has high ideals, after all, they *are* his students.'

'He could've shafted her in the lunch hour.'

'My husband and I meet every day for lunch, I work not far from the school, you see, and I have to tell you, he's never missed a day.'

'Never?'

'Never.'

'What about today?'

'I'm a teacher, monsieur, of five- and six-year-olds, they don't have school on Wednesdays.'

'He could've shafted Renée on Wednesdays,' Gilbert said with satisfaction.

'I doubt that very much.'

'Oh, yeah, why?'

'On Wednesdays, he comes home for lunch.'

'Why isn't he here now?'

'It takes half an hour to get here and it's,' she glanced at a carriage clock ticking on the mantelpiece, 'only just 1230. He'll be here any minute. In fact, I think you'll find that's him now.'

It was.

During the afternoon, they visited Laetitia Combe, the only student Chouillou could name as being friendly to Renée. She was tall and blonde and sitting cross-legged on her parents' sofa watching television, which she continued watching throughout the interview.

'Yeah, sure, I know Renée. Why, what's happened to her?'

'She was murdered.'

'That's rotten.'

'How well did you know her?'

'Only to say "hi" to.'

'We have reason to believe you said a little more than "hi".'

'When was that then?'

'Monsieur Chouillou noticed you talking, he thought you were comparing notes on the lesson he'd just given.'

'No, it was nothing like that. She'd found out I lived in the village not far from her. She wanted my father to give her a lift into town every morning. And home again in the evening!'

'And?'

'No chance! My father loves his car, it's a silver Mercedes. Mum isn't allowed to smoke in it so you can imagine what he'd say if Renée got in. She stank.'

'Recently?'

'What do you mean, recently?'

'Did she smell recently?'

'Sure she did. On Mondays it was okay, but brother, by Friday . . .!'

'What about the other students, were they friendly towards Renée?'

'Not that I noticed.'

'How do you feel about her death?'

'About the same as I felt about her life – irrelevant.'

'You ever been shafted by Chouillou?'

Oh God, Gilbert! Every time he opened his mouth an obscenity dropped out.

'Nope.'

'You like to be?'

'Nope,' she said with a sneer. 'He's far too old, I don't go with wrinklies.'

'Who do you go with?'

'Mind your own fucking business.'

And they still had to talk to the fifteen other students in Renée's class. Not to mention the owner and employees of the restaurant where Renée had worked before going back to college, and the owner and employees of the shop where she'd worked before that, but at least *they* wouldn't be precocious blondes. De Troq' thanked Laetitia for her help, such as it was – 's' okay' – thanked her mother for allowing them to interview her – 'any time' – and bustled bloody Gilbert back into the car, willing himself not to throttle the bugger before the end of the week. Three more days and Gilbert could be someone else's problem. If necessary, he'd walk into Pel's office first thing on Monday morning and change the duty roster himself.

*　　*　　*

91

Leguyder walked into Pel's office at 1845 that evening, a satisfied smile on his face and a thick file in his hands. Pel immediately had a feeling of impending doom. The two men didn't like each other. Leguyder was boring to the nth degree, and he enjoyed using long incomprehensible words just to prove Pel was a dunce. But he never missed a trick and was very valuable to the police force, therefore he had to be tolerated. This was Pel's opinion. Pel was, in Leguyder's opinion, disrespectful and a hazard to his health, smoking incessantly, as he did, those foul cigarettes. But he never missed a trick and was very valuable to the police force, therefore he had to be tolerated.

When the obligatory shaking of hands was concluded, Leguyder shrugged himself out of his coat – it was still cold and foggy outsider – and crossed to the desk, while Pel, without thinking, lit a Gauloise.

Leguyder flapped his arms at the clouds of blue smoke.

Pel was immediately seized by a coughing fit, turning purple and choking on his words. 'You won't learn to fly like that, you know.'

'*Sacré bleu!* And you won't live much longer at this rate. Is it acute or chronic bronchitis that you're suffering from?'

'Whatever it is,' Pel gasped, 'it's under control now.'

'More than can be said for the pollution level in this room. You're more dangerous than a badly tuned pantechnicon.'

'You should know, you're the scientist.'

'Put it out!'

'This is my office!'

'And I'm in it!'

'No one invited you!'

'You'd prefer to know nothing of what I found in the caravan?'

'Is it worth knowing?'

'I wouldn't be here if it wasn't!'

'Fire away.'

'Not until you've extinguished your cancer stick and opened a window.'

'It's cold outside!'

'The fog's worse in here!'

Pel scowled, sighed, stubbed out his cigarette, taking care not to bend it – he intended finishing it later – opened the window a crack and sat down, leaning forward, pencil at the ready, his eyes fixed on Leguyder, hoping for a revelation that would solve at least two enquiries. Two murder enquiries.

'Firstly,' the scientist said, finally satisfied, 'the DNA analysis confirms the arms and the torso belong to the same person.'

'I knew that already.'

'But I can *prove* it.'

'Invaluable, I'm sure. What else?'

'The caravan found at Pontailler, by one André Routaboule, was, as requested, removed from the site and brought into the private car-parking facility behind the laboratories. It arrived at approximately 1735 yesterday evening. I have, however, been working on the samples already removed from the said caravan during the time it took to extricate it from the mud – not an easy assignment – and deliver it to my premises.'

'City premises.'

'I beg your pardon?'

'Granted.'

'Why did you interrupt with the words "city premises"?'

'You said "my premises".'

'As in "the premises where I am employed as a forensic scientist".'

'Ah.'

'Shall I continue?'

'Please do.'

'Where was I?'

'Working on your samples while the caravan was extricated and delivered.'

'Yes, good. The splashes on the ceiling of the said caravan were, as I indicated, blood –'

'You said they were mud and blood.'

'But I'm confirming they were blood.'

'Why didn't you say so at the time?'

'Because my work is not, like yours, based on suspicion. It is based on fact and it is now a *proven* fact that all the splashes are blood. Have I made myself clear?'

'Perfectly.'

'. . . and there were particles of human tissue adhering thereto. I have completed the DNA profile of these particles and of the blood, and can confirm they are also from the torso found at the Collège Albert Camus, at Bèze. None of them match the corpse of the young girl discovered in the Rin on the 21st.'

'Renée Clavier.'

'Sorry?'

'That's okay, I'm still listening.'

'Yes. The finger I found also belongs to the torso.'

'Did the fingernail have anything under it, skin, hair, dirt?'

'Nothing. If there was something, it was soaked off by muddy water.'

Leguyder allowed Pel a moment to digest this information.

'Anything else? Footprints, fingerprints, clothes?'

'As I'm sure even you will understand, as a result of a lengthy immersion in the river, the floors and part of the walls and furniture had undergone a comprehensive washing of sorts and therefore yielded very little information. However, fortunately, and because the caravan's doors and windows were closed, instead of filling entirely with water and sinking, it floated, albeit erratically, before landing in Routaboule's field. There were some areas of the interior, the ceiling for instance, that had remarkably remained untouched.'

'So what did you find?'

'Among other things, a pair of poultry shears, now badly rusted and offering no other useful information except that they exist. A pair of rubber gloves which, although we attempted *very* carefully to lift a fingerprint from the inside, revealed nothing; they too had been filled with water far too long. We did, however, find some good footprints on the panelling above the bunk-bed, size 37. The prints show the toes were bent inwards, the phalanges of the smallest to such an extent it almost disappeared under its neighbour. The phalanges of the largest, the big toe, were also deformed to an angle of 23 degrees.'

'Translate, would you, you've lost me.'

'These deformities, plus the small size, indicate the prints were made by a woman who wore cheap modern shoes that were too tight.'

'What was she doing walking up the wall?'

'The position of the prints suggests she was lying on her back with her legs separated and raised.'

'Ah.'

'Precisely. There were other footprints, most of them smudged, or overlaid with further prints, between the woman's, but we have been able to establish they were of varying sizes, 41 to 45, and were facing downwards.'

'Eh?'

'My conclusion is a number of men lying on their stomachs, probably on top of the woman. On different occasions, of course.'

'Of course. Any traces of spermatozoa on the mattress?'

'None that we could find but it was made of foam rubber, 60 centimetres by 190 and covered in plastic, plus it had slipped into the water. If there had been any, they'd have soaked off.'

'What about the sheets?'

'Same thing – two of them, thin polyester affairs, also in the water, along with a nylon sleeping bag. The only samples we got from them were mud, algae, and a few bugs.'

'Damn.'

'Fingerprints were also found round the window catch. They match the prints taken from the severed limbs Boudet was examining. There were a number of others, as yet unidentified – they are not on file.'

'A pity.'

'Indeed. The clothes found were women's, size 36, and correspond with a girl or woman weighing approximately 42, 43 kilos and measuring between 1m50 and 1m55.'

'That's what Boudet said about the torso.'

'Then you can assume she was the one living in the caravan.'

'*Nom de Dieu!* The effeminate voice! And we've been looking for a bloke!'

'There have been plenty of men in the caravan, we estimate at least seven.'

'Nothing to give us a clue as to their identities?'

'A handkerchief, an empty packet of cigarettes, a disposable lighter, a comb and a watch. They offered nothing more than muddy water, and could have belonged to the woman.'

'Nothing else?'

Leguyder had been waiting for this moment for the last fifteen minutes. He was a methodical man and knew if he'd presented Pel with his *pièce de résistance* at the beginning of his discourse the rest would have been lost in its shadow, and it was important for him to tell Pel *everything* because he also knew Pel didn't read his lengthy, scientific and sometimes – for a dim policeman, you understand – confusing printed analysis, he relied on Leguyder to report it personally, which is exactly what he had done. Now he was going to savour his moment of glory.

'Well?'

'Well, yes.' Opening the file in front of him, he slipped out a small sealed plastic bag; in it was a short, flat, red pencil attached to a piece of string. 'This,' he said importantly, 'is very unlikely to have belonged to a woman.'

'What is it exactly?'

'The stump of a carpenter's pencil.'

'Aha!'

'Don't get too excited, it didn't necessarily belong to the murderer, but it could have. My technicians found it tied to the curtain rail by the bed. Behind the curtain were a number of marks. Four bold strikes with a line through them, plus two more strikes. The marks were made by this pencil –'

'She was keeping count of the number of men she'd had sex with?'

'Let me finish! The strikes were made by this pencil held in the right hand. Correct me if I'm wrong, but I believe the arms found this morning, which belong to the torso, that's to say, the woman living in the caravan, have shown by their muscular development that she was left-handed. Therefore, the pencil was used by one of her lovers, one that visited her frequently.'

'Bingo!'

'Not quite. We couldn't get a single print off it.'

7

Thursday, 25th November

At two thirty that afternoon, Renée Clavier was buried in the council plot in a barren corner of the graveyard not far from where she'd lived. It was a saddening little ceremony. The mist that had covered the countryside for the last forty-eight hours had turned into fog, dressing the day in grey, smothering and diluting autumn's more usual golden robes. It was a damp and penetrating fog, like a fine immobile rain, and the funeral party could barely see from one tombstone to the next. Somewhere in the distance a dog howled, its plaintive call echoing strangely, muffled and weird.

As they entered the graveyard, the priest pushed at the metal gate; it swung back, groaning as it opened. De Troq' looked around, almost expecting the shadow of a horse-drawn hearse to appear on the track with the bits jangling as the horses tossed their heads, their breath snorting out in clouds to hang on the wintry air, the plumes of purple trembling on the corners of the polished black carriage, but all he saw was the plain wooden coffin carried by four council workmen, huffing and puffing with the weight, as they lowered it into the ground. The priest chanted his last short speech, 'dust to dust, ashes to ashes . . .', and Madame Clavier bent stiffly to take a handful of earth. She scattered it, as expected, tapping on the coffin, sounding like impatient fingernails, and in the absence of any other mourners, De Troq' and Gilbert did the same. Although Renée's death had been reported in the paper under the heading of 'TEENAGE GIRL SLAIN', her name had not been given simply because at that time no one knew who she was. When the name did appear days later, it had been squashed in at the bottom of the fourth page, under a speech a county delegate had made on the subject of basically his own importance. Had she been the daughter of the county delegate, she'd have been back on the front page. But

Renée, the only child of a poor and elderly country couple, had, as her mother wanted, gone unnoticed to her grave.

De Troq' and Gilbert had spent all morning interviewing the members of the typing class, with the kind permission of the director of the Chambre de Métier, and, of course, the teacher, Laurent Chouillou – who had high ideals and thought of the girls only as his students and definitely not as possible candidates for a quick shafting, Jesus, Gilbert! Now, with a warning to keep his mouth shut, Gilbert accompanied Madame Clavier back to the unmarked police car while de Troq' spoke to the priest.

'Oh yes,' he confirmed, 'Madame is a devout Catholic. I had hoped Renée would continue coming to confession, but a few years after her confirmation, like a lot of youngsters, she stopped. Although,' he went on thoughtfully, 'it was very sudden with her. The others usually, through some kind of unfortunate guilt, return occasionally. Not Renée, I've never seen her in church since her fifteenth birthday. I tried to talk to her but she refused to respond.'

De Troq' left it at that. He knew only too well why Renée wouldn't or couldn't confess to the priest; she'd promised her mother never to speak about what had happened on her fifteenth birthday.

Sadly he drove the grieving woman home and, leaving her feeding the chickens, led Gilbert upstairs to search Renée's room.

It was pathetically empty and it smelt.

Standing by the door, de Troq' looked in. To his right against the wall, a bed, unmade. Moving round to the left along the next wall, a Formica-topped table and wooden chair. Opposite the bed were a number of nails where some clothes were hanging either side of a cylindrical cast iron chimney coming from below and disappearing through the peeling ceiling. Beyond that, facing the door, was another door, standing ajar. Then on the fourth and final wall, a grimy window, no curtains, a small mirror hanging from the handle.

He moved into the room.

Her bed, metal-framed, cotton-wadding mattress, was covered with two fraying blankets, one brown, one blue, both heavily stained. The sheets were worse – grey to begin with, there was a very clear shadow where the girl had slept, together with a series of what looked like blood spots. The whole lot stank of sweat.

'Bag and label it,' de Troq' said to Gilbert.

'What, all of it?'

'The sheets, blankets and bolster cover.'

De Troq' went to the table and chair: typewritten exercises brought home from her lessons with Chouillou, a red biro with a chewed end, a used paper handkerchief, a leather thong with one colourful glass bead on it and a large card calendar, given free by the post office at Christmas. In one corner it was decorated with misshapen doodled hearts, coloured in with the biro. The entries started one 9th September, with 'Chambre de Métier'; they stopped on 24th November, when she'd marked her eighteenth birthday. Renée had been dead three days by then, found face down in a stream on the 21st.

Taking a large plastic bag from his pocket, he unfolded it and slipped the calendar in, placing it on top of the bagged bundle of dirty linen, then moved to the few clothes hanging limply from the next wall. They too went into plastic bags together with a strong smell of wood smoke. Judging by the black smudges seeping through the bare floorboards, the piping from the stove in the kitchen left a lot to be desired and he was surprised she hadn't been asphyxiated long ago.

In the next corner was what he expected to be a cupboard but he found only another bedroom, just as dreary as the first, just as bare but not quite as smelly. From the dull clothes and scuffed shoes on and under the bed, he realised this was where Madame Clavier slept, and backed out, closing the door behind him – the search warrant Juge Brisard had finally signed, after arguing for hours over the formula, specified 'private quarters of the deceased, Renée Clavier, for personal belongings with a view to establishing . . .' and so on and so forth. Entering Madame Clavier's private quarters would have been trespassing. If the *juge d'instruction*, even more pernickety since Lambert had taken office, got to hear about it there'd be hell to pay. He closed the door and moved on.

The mirror hanging from the window was also bagged, and after getting down on his hands and knees to look under the beds – he found a plastic bucket half full of urine – he took one last look round the room. Then they stepped out on to the chilly landing, closed the door and carried the bags downstairs.

'Didn't touch nothing,' Madame Clavier called miserably from the kitchen, 'left it as it was, just like you ordered.'

De Troq' joined her, placing his bags on the table to write a receipt. 'Thank you. Tell me, did Renée have a boyfriend?'

'Never brought no one home.'

'Did she ever talk about anyone in particular?'

'Only her teacher.'

'Monsieur Chouillou?'

'Mm, that's right. Said he and his wife was ever so nice, she went round there sometimes, I think.'

Gilbert stepped forward, rustling dangerously of plastic. Before he had a chance to put his great vulgar foot in it, de Troq' pushed him towards the door, handed Madame Clavier the receipt, thanked her, and shoved him outside.

'I was only going to –'

'Between now and tomorrow morning,' de Troq' suggested desperately, 'would you be so kind as to think of another question to ask?'

'*Oo la la*, posher than ever, aren't we! What's the matter with you, got your silver spoon stuck in that snotty gob of yours?'

As the team came wearily in, Pel waited impatiently for their verbals. He was perspiring and shivering alternately and his legs felt as limp as the damp handkerchief he was now applying to his raw nose. But his head was clear and the coughing caused less anxiety.

Nosjean and Misset had spent the day in and around Pontailler, interviewing the male inhabitants of the village, in particular the male inhabitants whose names figured on their list of visitors to the blood-splattered caravan. They found all but one, Sebastien Soulié, who commuted to Paris for the week; 'back on Friday evening,' his mother told them. The men they had spoken

100

to did, without exception, when pressed on the subject, discreetly and away from the flapping ears of workmates, secretaries or wives, or mothers for that matter, finally agree that, yes, they had used the mobile bedroom. They also without exception denied having known – in the biblical sense of the word – a small twenty- to twenty-five-year-old woman of Portuguese or Spanish origins. Julien Roche, a nervous mechanic, admitted taking a girl to the love-nest who could have passed for Spanish or Portuguese – note her name, Nosjean – 'but she was seventeen in April, we're going steady now' – cross it out, Commandant. They'd have to wait for tomorrow evening to collar Soulié, not that they expected it would make any difference to anything.

Bardolle and Jourdain had stayed in the centre of the city, following up the other names on the list, the youngsters Giles Boulot had mentioned, mostly students at the university, but also a lad at the Chambre de Métier doing a course in painting – and decorating, you understand, not portrait or landscape or still life. He had a stutter and agreed he'd been to the caravan in the summer, but only once, and 'I'm not g-going back there ag-gain.'

'Who invited you?'

'An old s-school friend, thought I c-could trust him, but they were smoking d-d-drugs.'

'Could you provide me with their names?'

It took half an hour to get them down spelt correctly, by which time both Bardolle and Jourdain were resisting nudging each other, and very hungry. It was 1245.

After a hurriedly eaten plate of steak and chips in the cafeteria, they started tramping the streets between scruffy digs and even scruffier communal apartments.

When they left the last address, the intermittent sun had completely, and it seemed suddenly, disappeared in the space of five minutes, and it felt as if the temperature had dropped at least 10 degrees – it had in fact been dropping steadily since four o'clock and had finally reached zero. Bardolle looked up at the starry sky. 'Bloody hell! Where did the day go?'

Jourdain grinned under her thatch of spiky hair. 'Home to bed, which is where I'd like to be.'

He opened the car doors and they climbed in, their breath following them in like steam from a kettle, then as the vehicle moved away from the kerb, he glanced across at the blonde lieutenant. 'How *do* you get your hair to stand on end like that?'

'I stick my fingers in a faulty plug every morning.'

Bardolle laughed out loud. 'Pel suspected as much.'

'Which is why I have to keep on doing it, he'd be disappointed if I stopped. And anyway, de Troq's Mum finds it shocking.'

'What's the Baroness like?'

'A very grand old lady. Actually we get on pretty well, all things considered.'

'What things?'

'That I'm corrupting her only son and heir.'

'Does it bother her?'

'Not as much as she makes out. Somewhere along the line I think she was a pretty hair-raising gal too.'

When they came in at 1830, they'd crossed off fifteen names, but added twenty-one more – that's the way it goes – and sat down resolutely to weed them out of the *Pages Blanches*, the campus directory and any other directory that was available, ringing anyone listed with the same name until they found a parent, an uncle, a brother, anyone who knew the whereabouts of the elusive students.

Pujol and Morrison, on the other hand, had struck lucky. They'd been to the shop where Renée had worked to speak to the owner and subsequently the five employees. They all remembered the shy young girl who'd come to work in the cut-price store a couple of summers ago and they all remembered why, after a short spell on the till, she'd been moved into the stock room to shift cardboard boxes of cheap goodies up and down off the shelves, alone: 'She smelt.' They'd never seen her since, or so they said – it would have to be checked, together with the two employees who'd left, one to get married, one to a new job in Vichy.

That wasn't when they struck lucky.

They moved on to the restaurant, Relais des Routiers on the N71 heading north-west out of the city. The proprietor was a burly bloke, with a gut that looked as if he was about to give birth to triplets, if not quadruplets, but also very chatty. 'Smelly little kid, all bones and stink. No good serving at table, I get a rowdy lot in here, they like big tits and a bit of leg, and the aroma of a good *pot-au-feu*, not armpits and unwashed bums. Put her in the kitchen loading and unloading the dishwashers but the chef complained, said her pong was stronger than the *coq au vin* he was cooking. He made the mistake of telling her when the weather warmed up and she got all huffy and left, just when I bloody needed the extra pair of hands. Never seen her since.'

'Could you give me a list of the employees at the time?'

'I had a nasty feeling you'd be asking me that. Come through to the office, no doubt I can find my copy of the pay slips somewhere.'

They added another four names to be run through the files and questioned personally.

They still hadn't struck lucky.

Driving back into the city centre, Pujol asked Morrison to pull over. Morrison blushed deeply and did so while Pujol scanned the street map he'd opened. 'I thought so. David Duval, the chap who does evening service at the restaurant, lives two streets away. Make a left, we'll see if we can catch him before he leaves for tonight's shift.'

Morrison knew he'd had it easy just ferrying Pujol about all day, listening to him interview dozens of suspects – hey, to him they were *all* suspects – and he knew now that instead of heading for the Hôtel de Police, Pujol was letting his enthusiasm run away with him and adding perhaps another hour to their day, and after that there'd be the *paperwork* to complete, and maybe more *research*. Morrison had worked hard to qualify as a member of the Police Judiciaire's Brigade Criminelle, and he was very enthusiastic about the work he'd undertaken; trouble was, he thought, as he flicked on the indicator and drew out into the increasingly thick five o'clock traffic, he hadn't been home for supper on time once, not once. And his Dad had promised him a thick ear if it went on much longer. Either that or worse. Much worse; he'd threatened to come and speak to Pel in person, tell him his son shouldn't be expected to miss his evening meal that Mum had cooked with tender loving care. His Dad was a Union man, knew all his rights, understood what a day's work meant, but he *didn't* understand – and Morrison almost trembled when he thought about it – what Pel was like. Union or no Union man, Pel would eat him alive. Not to mention putting a blight on Morrison's career thereafter. He'd probably be suspended, sacked or struck off, if policemen were, he wasn't sure.

'You missed the turning!'

Morrison blushed. 'Sorry.'

'Go round the block, we'll go into rue Freniot from the other side.'

When the car stopped outside number 103, both men climbed out into the gathering darkness. Pujol studied the buttons by the front door, then, satisfied he'd found what he wanted, he pressed the third from the bottom.

A voice came over the intercom. *'C'est qui?'*

'Police Judiciaire! Routine investigation about a girl you worked with in 1998.'

'D'accord. Entrez. Troisième étage.'

When they reached the third floor, a man about thirty was waiting for them; he was wearing trainers, jeans, and an orange sweat-shirt with 'FUN IN THE SPRING' written on the front. Pujol shook his hand, noting the clear blue eyes and firm handshake, showed him his identification, introduced Morrison, and they all went into the flat.

That's when Pujol got lucky.

On the oval table in the middle of the room stood two silver candlesticks. But he didn't say a word. Not yet.

Instead he conducted his interview exactly along the same lines as all the others.

'Yup, I remember smelly Renée. Sit down, do. What's she done?'

They sat at the oval table with the two silver candlesticks between them.

'She was murdered.'

'Et merde, is that right?'

'I'm afraid so.'

'Well, bugger me. Here, do you want a drink, bottle of beer or something? After what you just told me I think I'm going to.'

'Thank you, no. Has the news upset you?'

104

The answer came from inside a fridge in the adjoining kitchen. 'Well, yeah, it's not every day you get told someone you know got killed.'

'Do you still see her then?'

'Well, no. A figure of speech, what I mean is "know of", "have known", "did know once upon a time", if you get my drift.'

While the young man in the orange sweat-shirt swallowed the contents of his bottle of beer, Pujol continued with the questions, satisfying himself there was very little suspicious about David Duval, except perhaps the hideous orange sweat-shirt.

And the candlesticks.

As they were getting up to leave he picked one up and turned it over, noting the marks on its base. Just as he thought. 'A fine piece of workmanship,' he said easily. 'Where did you buy them?'

Duval laughed. 'Not worth much, I bought them off a bloke in the bar, only paid 100 francs.'

'Which bloke, which bar?'

'Hey, what is this! I thought we were talking about Renée?'

'We were, now we're talking about stolen candlesticks and a bloke in a bar. I repeat, which bloke, which bar?'

'Look, I didn't steal them if that's what you're thinking.'

'That's not what I'm thinking. I'm thinking maybe the bloke in the bar stole them.'

'Okay, okay. Jesus, it's my local, if I get the bloke done I reckon I can move. All that just to give a bit of atmosphere when the girlfriend comes to stay.'

'Which bloke? Which bar?'

'Texas Hole. I don't know the bloke's name.'

'What did he look like? What was he wearing?'

'*Putain, j'en sais rien moi! Si!* Pointed cowboy boots, well worn at the heel, it made the pointed toes stick up, that's why I noticed.'

'Anything else?'

'Leather jacket, a gold ear-ring and side-burns Elvis Presley would have been proud of.'

'Brilliant!'

'And I suppose you're going to requisition the candlesticks and I'll never see them again?'

'I'll give you a receipt.'

'Oh sure, and what bloody good will that do?'

Pujol handed him a 200 franc note. 'You can buy some more – from a shop this time.'

Going out into the street again, Pujol placed the candlesticks under the passenger seat of the car, but instead of climbing in and reaching for the safety belt as Morrison had hoped, he slammed the door closed and locked it, then set off towards a flashing neon light. Texas Hole! Texas Hole! Texas Hole! Sighing miserably, Morrison followed his partner along the pavement. He knew he was looking at that thick ear. Or worse.

Friday, 26th November

The sun was shining, bright and golden. Pel was surprised and feeling distinctly better. Slamming the brakes on suddenly, he came to a rocking halt at the traffic lights he hadn't noticed until it was almost too late. Looking across the park, where the lingering mist still covered the grass with a delicate film like a bridal veil, he could see small children already trudging along the paths towards the school on the other side. Mothers hurried them along, pushing buggies, or pulling outstretched, unwilling arms, their breath gusting like a car's exhaust as they shouted encouragement.

The driver behind leant on his horn aggressively and, glancing quickly up at the mirror, Pel noted a fat cigar then, waving an apologetic hand, he crashed his car into gear and accelerated away, with Fat Cigar hot on his heels. A kilometre further on, he put his right indicator on, slowed and turned carefully into the Hôtel de Police's forecourt between two saluting uniforms. He almost smiled to himself as the passing Fat Cigar tried to hide behind his steering wheel.

As the door crashed open, hitting the filing cabinets and making the chipped mugs on top tinkle, the members of the sergeants' room shuffled to attention. They were used to Pel's shock tactics and although Morrison's face turned a bright scarlet, no one else seemed impressed.

'Had your dad on the phone last night.'

'Sir . . . I –'

'Ticked me off for keeping you out late. Said your supper was going cold.'

'Sir . . . I –'

'If I were you, I'd buy myself a microwave to heat it up again. There's no way a member of my team is going to go bleating back to Mum because it's supper time, not if he's out on an enquiry.'

'Sir . . . I –'

'Talked him out of giving you a thick ear though, and congratulations on the arrest. Pujol said you handled yourself well for a beginner. Madame Darcy pleased to see her candlesticks again, was she? Not long a police widow, you know.'

'Yes, Pujol told me about Commandant Dar –'

'Shame you never met him, he could have taught you a thing or two. Right! Stop gawping, you lot, you were all beginners once and you haven't made much progress since. What's on the agenda?'

Pujol licked his lips. 'Maître Brisard's coming in to charge the thief this afternoon. I'd like to be there.'

'As arresting officer, you've got to be there, and make sure the statements, the charge sheet, your report and list of evidence are set out correctly and printed on to the right forms, with copies. If you're not sure how many, look it up. Brisard was always pedantic over procedure and since Chief Lambert has started encouraging him, he enjoys throwing his weight around. If there's the slightest error, he'll refuse the charge, which means we'll have to release the suspect, and Lambert'll be at our throats for losing a positive statistic. Twenty-four hours' observation maximum and he's just spent twelve of them in the cells, so you're going to have to be quick and thorough searching his flat. Have you got that sorted out?'

'Signed and stamped by Brisard, the *procureur* and Lambert, just the way it should be.'

'Good. Next?'

Pujol licked his lips again. 'I've still got twelve follow-ups for Renée Clavier – people she worked with.'

Septembre			Octobre			Novembre ♥ ♥		
M	1	S.Gilles	V	1	Se Thérèse E.-J.	L	1	TOUSSAINT FERIE ♥ ♥
J	2	Se Ingrid	S	2	S.Léger	M	2	Défunts
V	3	S.Grégoire	D	3	S.Gérard	M	3	S.Hubert _2_
S	4	Ste Rosalie	L	4	S.François	J	4	S.Charles
D	5	Ste Raissa	M	5	Se Fleur _2_	V	5	Se Sylvie _**_
L	6	S.Bertrand _2_	M	6	S.Bruno	S	6	Se Bertille _**** !!_
M	7	Ste Reine	J	7	S.Serge	D	7	Se Carine
M	8	Nativ.N.D.	V	8	Se Pélagie _**!_	L	8	S.Geoffroy
J	9	S.Alain*ChambreDeMétier*	S	9	S.Denis	M	9	S.Théodore
V	10	Ste Inès	D	10	S.Ghislain	M	10	S.Léon _3_
S	11	S.Adelphe	L	11	S.Firmin	J	11	ARMISTICE 1918 FERIE
D	12	S.Appolinaire	M	12	S.Wilfried _3_	V	12	S.Christian _**_
L	13	S.Aimé _3_	M	13	S.Géraud	S	13	S.Brice _****!!!_
M	14	La Ste Croix	J	14	S.Juste	D	14	S.Sidoine
M	15	S.Roland	V	15	Se Thérèse d'Av. _**!_	L	15	S.Albert
J	16	Se Edith	S	16	Se Edwige	M	16	Se Marguerite
V	17	S.Renaud	D	17	S.Baudouin	M	17	Se Elisabeth _4 ?????_
S	18	St Nadège	L	18	S.Luc	J	18	Se Aude
D	19	Se Emilie	M	19	S.Réné	V	19	S.Tanguy _**_
L	20	S.Davy _4_	M	20	Se Adeline _4_	S	20	S.Edmond _**** !!!!_
M	21	S.Matthieu	J	21	Se Céline	D	21	Christ Roi
M	22	S.Maurice	V	22	Se Elodie _**_	L	22	Se Cécile
J	23	AUTOMNE	S	23	S.Jean de C.	M	23	S.Clément
V	24	Se Thècle _**!_	D	24	S.Florentin	M	24	Se Flora **MOI 18!**
S	25	S.Hermann	L	25	Se Doria	J	25	Se Catherine
D	26	S.Damien	M	26	S.Dimitri	V	26	Se Delphine
L	27	S.Vinc.de Paul	M	27	Se Emeline _1_	S	27	S.Séverin
M	28	S.Venceslas _1_	J	28	SS.Sim., Jude	D	28	Avent
M	29	S.Michel	V	29	S.Narcisse _**_	L	29	S.Saturnin
J	30	S.Jérome	S	30	Se Bienvenue	M	30	S.André
			D	31	S.Wolfgang			

'Hand that over to . . .' Pel studied the duty roster. '. . . de Troq'
and Gilbert, they're waiting for information on articles removed
from her room. The rest of you – out questioning all carpenters,
joiners and cabinet makers within a 50 kilometre radius of
Larroque.' He held up the red pencil, letting the string dangle.
'This was found hanging from a curtain rail in the caravan where
the College Cadavre was killed. It was used regularly, I want its
owner. You got the lists, Nosjean?'

'What about the youngsters we've been chasing up?'

'From what Bardolle told us last night, they were joy-riding at
the campsite, using it as a summer bunk-hole to smoke in the
open air with an occasional bit of free love. You've covered a
good percentage of them, put it on hold, we'll come back to them
if the woodworkers give us no joy.'

While most of the team left the building, de Troq' crossed the
corridor as requested and went into Pel. Gilbert, as always, was
only a few steps behind.

'Shut the door and sit down.' Pel lit up. 'So, tell me about the
calendar in Renée's room.'

He had photocopies of the relevant months in front of him,
and passing one to de Troq', Pel exhaled noisily, pointing to the
misshapen hearts filling one corner. 'Did she have a boyfriend?'

'Her mother thinks not but that doesn't mean a thing. The
only man Renée ever mentioned was her teacher, Chouillou.'

Pel raised his eyebrows.

'He was kind to her, he and his wife invited her home for a
bath and a square meal. Madame Chouillou even supplied clean
clothes for her.'

'Does the Chambre de Métier's director know? What does he
think of that?'

'I'm seeing him this morning at ten thirty.'

'What about other male acquaintances, students, ex-working
colleagues?'

'Nothing so far.'

'Could the hearts mean something else? Perhaps she had a
secret crush on Chouillou?'

'It's possible. I asked Alex, she's sure the girl must have been
in love with someone. In view of her death, I'd like to follow up
the possibility of an amorous liaison.'

109

'Is that what they call it nowadays? I call it –'

'Gilbert! I know what you call it, thank you.'

'Okay, let's read it from the top.'

'9th September, she started her course. On the 24th Chouillou asked her home for the first time, he and his wife confirm this, that's the first group of asterisks and exclamation mark.'

'What about the numbers? You've skipped "3" and "4".'

'I'll come back to them in a minute. Two weeks after her first trip to the Chouillou house, she goes there again, on 8th October, also confirmed, and noted in the same way. From then on it's every Friday, as regular as clockwork.'

'Why didn't she just write in his name?'

'She'd suffered an incestuous incident with her father when she was fifteen and her mother made her promise never to talk about it. According to the psychiatrist I spoke to, the incident obviously marked her, but so did making the promise. She suggested that Renée grew up believing personal relationships, particularly with men, were to be kept secret, her mother had forbidden her to tell.'

'But she mentioned her teacher to her.'

'Yes, her teacher; teachers are allowed, she was at college. She didn't, however, mention she'd been to his house, that was personal and had to remain private.'

'Okay, passons. Why did the exclamation mark disappear for her Friday meetings?'

'It stopped being a surprise?'

'So what happened on Saturday, 6th November to deserve four asterisks and two exclamations? Where was she?'

'No one knows.'

'And why on the 13th are there three exclamation marks and on the 20th, four?

'Alex had a theory on that too.'

'Is she your bit of crumpet then?'

'Shut it, Gilbert!' Pel snapped. 'We're trying to discuss police business. If you can't participate intelligently, go and answer the phones. De Troq', *continue.*'

'She thinks these could be the dates when Renée had a meeting with her boyfriend. Which brings us back to the numbers

110

and Wednesday, 17th November. As you've already noticed, these numbers, one to four, appear once every seven or eight days. Alex thinks she was counting off the weeks of her menstrual cycle, and her period was due 17th November, hence the question marks – Renée was wondering if she was pregnant. By the 20th she knew either she was, or wasn't.'

'Her autopsy showed she wasn't.'

'So she went to her rendezvous with her boyfriend who was delighted, like her, that all was well.'

Hang on a minute, she didn't come back, she can't have done her doodling afterwards.'

'D'accord. So she did it before she left, anticipating his reaction.'

'Sounds like sense. But who's the bloody boyfriend? And why did he kill her?'

'Maybe she said she was pregnant, even though she wasn't.'

Both men looked at Gilbert.

'Go on.'

'Birds are like that, aren't they? Always want something from a bloke. The pathologist, did he mention she'd had an abortion?'

'No.'

'Was she a fucking virgin then?'

'Virgins don't, and no, she wasn't.'

'So, she'd been shafted by someone and hadn't got pregnant.'

'Congratulations, Gilbert, we decided that five minutes ago.'

'Maybe the bloke that was shafting her was bored and wanted to dump her, maybe he had already, and she thought by telling him she was pregnant he'd come back. Looking at those star things, I'd say he'd agreed to meet her, maybe to sort something out, but instead of shafting her and saying he was sorry for wanting to dump her, he fucked her with a bread knife.'

'Long-hinged blades.'

Pel pushed his glasses up on to his balding head. 'You have a curious way of expressing yourself, Gilbert, regrettable in a criminal detective, but I have to admit you may have something. However, we still come back to the original question: Who was the boyfriend? Until you find some trace of him, this investigation is, as you might put it, fucked. Or even shafted. So you'd better get going, questioning everyone who knew or came in

111

contact with her during the last eighteen months – the list is still a long one. And Gilbert, while language like that is accepted in the confines of our own offices, I hope you tone it down when talking to the general public.'

The general public were willing enough to answer questions when presented with police identification cards; unfortunately they were not particularly helpful.

De Troq' and Gilbert, who didn't tone down his language at all, slowly crossed the names off their list. No one could tell them anything about Renée, except that she smelt, poor kid. And no, they hadn't shafted her.

Pujol and Morrison entered the room in which the candlestick thief had been living and bagged up: Kate's kitchen radio, the two older boys' Walkmans plus a selection of cassettes, a dozen CDs – mostly classical music, but one of Dire Straits, another of Pierre Bachelet and a third of Joe Cocker, a string of imitation pearls, five gold rings – odd that, Kate hadn't had any stolen, she didn't wear jangling jewellery – four silver serving spoons, three diamond ear-clips' – three? Yes, three – two ticking watches and . . . that was about it. They also removed a collection of shoes, in the hope that their soles would prove the thief had been in the forest where Kate lived – and suddenly Pujol stopped. Why hadn't Rasputin, the monster dog, torn him to shreds? He looked capable of it. He'd have to ask Kate. Thinking about asking Kate, he allowed himself a private smile. It would be a good excuse to share another glass of wine, when he had the time.

Armed with the evidence, they raced over to Leguyder's laboratories, got a dressing down for giving him more work, he already had a pile of jumble for the Clavier case, then raced back to headquarters to start preparing all the paperwork so essential for a faultless charge to be brought. They finished just in time to see the examining magistrate, Maître Brisard, park his car in the courtyard behind the building and waddle towards the entrance, his large hips swaying like a washerwoman's.

Nosjean and Misset, his eyes glazed over as if he'd gone out, and Bardolle and Jourdain spent the whole day playing hunt the carpenter. It was a dead loss.

They came in tired, cold and discouraged, gave their verbals to Pel and went to write up their reports, or conclusions if you prefer, of the day's activities. A dead loss maybe but it all still had to be recorded, first into the virtual file, then printed out and added to the cardboard variety, lest the useless information be lost, misplaced or forgotten – *con*!

When they were at last shaking hands and wishing each other a good evening, when the computer screens had gone blank and the phones only rang occasionally, fielded fortunately by another team, when the door to the sergeants' room banged shut for the night, Pel stubbed out his cigarette and closed the file in front of him. For once he thought he might get away on time. It was 1955.

Buttoning up his overcoat, patting his pockets, just checking the emergency packet of Gauloises was still there, he stepped out into the corridor.

'Ah, Pel, a quick word if you don't mind. Rather important.'

Sighing, he followed Lambert into his office.

'Sit down, do.'

'I don't need to if it's only a quick word.'

'Commissaire, sit!'

Pel sat.

'Brisard and I . . .' Pel switched off his ears, he didn't want to listen to eulogies about a pompous *juge d'instruction* he'd never liked, and a snow-capped mountain, otherwise known as the Chief, that he knew he never could. The pair of them seemed very matey, which was bad for Pel. He'd been told, when asked, that Lambert and Brisard often lunched together, that, in fact, Lambert had been invited to Brisard's home on Sunday, and he wondered what they were up to. While it was perfectly normal for a magistrate and a policeman to be companionable, colleagues as they were, so to speak, in crime, this little combination had him worried. They could make life very difficult at the Hôtel de Police – had already got off to a good start – and although in the past he'd been able to outwit Brisard and keep him under control, Lambert was now established as his accomplice and the possibility of continuing to keep him under control had been well and truly cancelled.

'. . . therefore, as a result of this minor setback . . .'

What minor setback? Pel concentrated briefly. '. . . your team will have to remain as it is. The Minister of the Interior regretfully, but firmly, points out that while he understands fully the position of the police force, funding two more men in this county is not within the bounds . . .'

Now he understood. Since the summer, four officers had gone from the team; only two replacements had been appointed. It meant that everyone did weekend duty more often, that the hours were longer and the work more stressful, trying to cover the footwork and research normally done by the two missing men – or women. While Klein had his full quota of qualified detectives, and the other Commissaires in the building had theirs, Pel would have to make do with what he'd got. He looked up at the Chief's face – a good-looking man some might say, but a devious and jealous man. Lambert wanted his department to have the best statistics in France, he wanted to be congratulated and perhaps presented to the President, but he didn't want Pel to take any credit. He was sabotaging his team, giving him two frustratingly incompetent replacements; very soon he'd be suggesting Pel took early retirement, that he was past his prime.

'. . . I do wonder if, in fact, you are still at the peak of your career. Perhaps you need time to reconsider –'

Pel shot to his feet. 'I just have. Goodnight, sir!'

'Pel!'

The door slammed and Pel marched down the corridor visibly boiling with anger; Lambert and Brisard were campaigning to push him out and, ignoring the fact that he'd been thinking about retiring early, he wasn't prepared to go without a fight.

He shouted at all and any passing policeman – fortunately not many at that time of night – and stamped out into the street.

The Republic of France had 126,000 police personnel, of whom 15,846 were inspectors, 88,637 were peace agents, 3750 were investigators, and 2005 were superintendents. There were an additional 35,000 Parisian police – always a case apart – and 13,000 municipal police officers. State Police personnel totalled 91,263, of whom 2621 were officers, 79,936 were under-officers,

114

and 12,319 were other types of police personnel. Pel didn't know the exact numbers but he was definitely aware that of all the Chiefs of Police to choose from, and let's face it there had to be plenty, *he* had somehow got Lambert, and, he thought savagely, twisting the key in the ignition, my bloody brand new car's a week overdue.

8

Saturday, 27th November

The statistics of recorded convictions – convictions, not crimes – derived from the Directory of Justice statistics showed, for the previous year, 20,326 drug offences, 800 armed robberies, 735 rapes, and 625 intentional homicides. Of these 625 homicides, 373 were classed as murder, 212 as assassination, 15 as infanticide and the remaining 25 as other homicides. Of the 373 murders, a large percentage, something like 85%, were considered as domestic killings: wife killing husband, husband killing wife, wife killing husband's lover, husband killing wife's lover, lover killing lover's husband – you get the picture. The other 15% didn't fall into this category and had therefore been far more complicated, although a conviction was finally reached.

The College Cadavre case was complicated because the police didn't know the butchered trunk and arms had once belonged to a woman called Marianna Roquetas. Had they known, they'd have been able to trace her family and take it from there; however, they were still frustratingly working in the dark, so to speak.

The Renée Clavier case was equally complicated, because although they knew who she was, they couldn't find the mysterious boyfriend and everything seemed to point to him. Looking at the statistics it was logical, but not necessarily inevitable, that he was implicated, and they would, if nothing else, like to eliminate him from the enquiry.

Which made two complicated murders, or, as had been suggested, a double murder; whichever way you looked at it, it was still complicated. Consequently, the whole team – with the exception of Cheriff of course, who was at home with Annie and their newborn son – was in the office on Saturday morning, typing up the copious notes they'd made the day before. In all, fifty-seven people had been spoken to. Every interview had to be transcribed from their notebooks, put into the computer, printed out in quadruplicate – one for Pel, one for Lambert, one for the *procureur*, although he probably wouldn't read it, and one for the sergeants' room file – signed and distributed. It would probably take the best part of the day and no one was enjoying it, this was the dreariest part of police work but essential all the same. When the phone rang, it was snatched up with enthusiasm as a welcome interruption to the drudgery of spelling, punctuation and *point, à la ligne.*

The bright spot of the day was when Leguyder called Pujol with good news. A pair of trainers he'd brought in showed clearly that the wearer had been in an oak forest; the traces of loam, particles of leaves and staining from rainwater in the stitching proved it. Together with a previous record for pilfering, he now had enough to turn the charge into a conviction – another one to add to the Directory of Justice statistics – and, he thought happily, good news to give Kate when he dropped in that evening.

Leguyder shrieked down the phone, 'You still there, boy?'

'Just writing down what you told me.'

'Do that afterwards. Put me through to Pel, would you?'

The line clicked, buzzed and crackled mildly while Pujol did his stuff.

'*Pel à l'appareil, j'écoute.*'

'Leguyder here, I'm glad you're listening because I've got something for you to think about over the weekend.'

'What weekend? I've forgotten what a weekend is.'

'So have I! And all thanks to you, I've a mountain of rags here. De Troq' gave me the entire contents of Renée's room, including her filthy sheets. What exactly are you after?'

'Some hint as to where she went on the three Saturdays before she died. Everyone concerned admits knowing her, no one saw her. According to her diary –'

'Which de Troq' also left me, saying it was urgent. When isn't it urgent with your lot?'

'Not often. As I was saying, from the calendar, we think she met a boyfriend on the 6th, the 13th and the 20th, the day she died. As these meetings were kept a secret they probably took place in the same place, as yet unknown. Therefore –'

117

'*Entendu, j'ai compris.* So far, I've done her sheets and I can tell you this kid had a perspiration problem.'

'Tell me something I don't know.'

'She didn't wash before going to bed, there's mascara and lipstick traces on the bolster cover.'

'Mhmm.'

'And she had her period recently, the spots of blood are menstrual blood, not more than a fortnight old. If the bedclothes have remained unslept in, i.e. cold, since the night of the 19th, I would estimate these spots appeared around 16th, 17th or 18th November.'

'That fits.'

'That's the sheets, no sperm stains, no stray pubic hair, no alien traces at all.'

'Fine, we didn't expect any but needed to be sure.'

'Moving on to her clothes, I haven't finished yet but one of the woollen jumpers had a smear of paint in its fibres. Looks like her elbow brushed against a newly painted wall. You can hardly see it with the naked eye, the paint's almost the same colour as the wool, but that's what it is, E4-7 M, pale apricot to you, Satin 311, comes from Système Harmonip Color, manufactured by Omnium National Industriel des Peintures, known as ONIP to the professionals. It's not available in supermarkets or do-it-yourself stores. The main office is Kremlin-Bicêtre, Paris, their depot's in Hondouville, Eure.'

Pel was impressed. 'Do you have samples of all paints manufactured in France?'

'And the main Spanish, Italian, German, Swiss and Belgian marks. Recently we've even had to add the British ones, we're being invaded by them and the buggers bring their products with them instead of buying it here. What's wrong with French paint?'

'The instructions aren't written in English.'

'If they can't read the language of the country they've elected to live in, they shouldn't be here!'

'Do I hear a trace of racism?'

'No, certainly not, simply an objection to being colonised. Good day!'

118

Pel smiled, put the receiver down and thought about what he'd just been told. They certainly hadn't been redecorating at the Clavier house, from what he'd heard it'd been left to fester for the last hundred years or so. The Chambre de Métier? Or Renée's lover?

He pressed three numbers into the internal phone. 'De Troq', get in here, will you?'

A few seconds later, the aristocrat of the team was seated in front of him, looking clean and polished – even his hair looked polished, damn him. Pel's hand automatically stroked the remains of his, noting its rapid disappearance; every day there seemed to be less on his head. 'You went to see the director where Renée was doing her typing course?'

'Yesterday morning.'

'What did he say?'

'Not a lot, he hardly ever meets the students unless they misbehave badly or are continually absent. They've got nearly a thousand young men and women going in and out, he didn't even know what she looked like.'

'You've seen her classroom?'

'On a number of occasions.'

'Newly painted, was it?'

'It didn't look it.'

'What about the Chouillou house?'

'Rented.'

'Have they decorated it recently?'

'I doubt it, they're hoping to move soon.'

'Find out, and get back to the director, ask him if they've had the painters in recently.'

'They do courses in painting and decorating.'

'Ah, maybe we're on to something at long last. Add the students to your list of possible suspects. Pale apricot paint was found on one of Renée's jumpers, I've got a reference here. Does ONIP supply their paint? Leguyder said it's not on sale in retail outlets.'

'You'd better give me their full name and address. If we come up with nothing at the college, I'm going to have to do the rounds of all the local painters.'

119

'Don't forget to give all names to Debray and Rigal – they'll go through records, in case we've got a previous arrest for one of them. Do carpenters use paint?'

'Still think Renée's murderer might be responsible for both women's deaths?'

'I'm open to suggestions, de Troq'. Do they?'

'As far as I know they tend to use wood stains and varnishes, but I suppose some of them might, if a client demands it.'

'Check it out, would you?'

'Pel?'

'De Troq'.'

'We've got one hell of a lot of groundwork to cover, chasing our murderer or murderers, possibly hundreds of men and women to see. I'm perfectly happy to do that, as always, but please don't ask me to work with that slob Gilbert, he's nothing but an embarrassment.'

'Came up with a good idea though, didn't he?'

'Granted, but his vulgarity makes me cringe.'

'Discuss it with Nosjean, he does the duty roster, I just sign the thing.'

De Troq' left and turned right out of Pel's office, right again, straight into Nosjean's, who was busy making amorous arrangements with Anna for that evening.

Pel picked up the phone – it was ringing, he thought he ought to answer. Lunch-time or no lunch-time, duty calls, *n'est-ce pas*?

It was Leguyder again. 'I've just been looking something up and I think I should point out a detail you may have missed. When de Troq' brought me all this rubbish from the girl's room, he said in passing it was everything she owned.'

'That's what I was given to understand too.'

'I have in my laboratory one pair of worn, very worn, bedroom slippers, a filthy pair of cheap trainers, and that's it. No other shoes.'

'Except the pair she was wearing the day she died and which have since been disposed of.'

'*C'est exact*. Cast your mind back to the footprint we found on the banks of the Rin. It was made by a walking boot, size 39.'

'And Renée took that size.'

'Affirmative. One of my technicians has finally identified the boot. It was made by Salomon – they're well known for their *chaussures de randonnée*, basically leather with a rubber sole.'

'So what about it?'

'This particular pair, brand new by the look of it, would have cost 749 francs.'

'But that's ridiculous, my shoes only cost a matter of 400 and that's when I'm feeling extravagant.'

'Precisely, they are expensive.'

'What's the point you're trying to make?'

'Her trainers were mass produced, the manufacturers supply La Halle aux Chaussures, they'd have cost 150 francs, maximum. The slippers, it's difficult to tell, they were bought a long time ago but are hardly what one would class as a luxury item, say 80–100 francs. Her clothes are cast-offs and rags, her sheets and blankets were threadbare, so how come she was wearing a pair of boots worth 749 francs?'

'She couldn't have been.'

'Precisely,' Leguyder said again.

'Do many men have feet that small?'

'She was a girl.'

'I know she was, damn it! Answer the question!'

'Not many.'

'Male or female?'

'At the risk of repeating myself, she was an eighteen-year-old girl.'

'Not the deceased, you idiot, the killer.'

There was a sharp intake of breath. 'If you refer to me as an idiot, Pel, I shall refuse to reply to your questions.'

'I'm sorry, it just slipped out.'

'Then slip it back. I am not an idiot, I never have been and sincerely hope I never shall be.'

'Of course, I apologise, grovel and humbly beg your forgiveness. Will that do?'

'As I would imagine it's the best I shall get, I'm obliged to accept.'

'Alleluia. Now, was the killer a man or a woman?'

'I have nothing to suggest one or the other.'

'Except that the person we're talking about weighed 58 kilos.'

'The killer?'

'Yes! The sod . . .' Pel stopped and started again. '58 kilos, Leguyder, that's light for a man, isn't it?'

'Men come in all sizes, as do women.'

'An adolescent male?'

'Unlikely with a 39 boot. Youngsters, like dogs, give away their future proportions by the size of their feet at a very early age.'

'A pygmy? A dwarf?'

'Trust you to start being ridiculous.'

'Then tell me, for God's sake.'

'All I'm saying is that I doubt the boots belonged to the victim. It is more likely that they belonged to either a slim man with small feet, and they do exist, one of my technicians weighs no more than 60 kilos and he takes a 39 shoe, or a woman.'

'You always talk in ruddy riddles, Leguyder.'

'That's why I talk to you, Pel. You're a detective.'

'Where was your technician on the afternoon of 20th November?'

Leguyder disconnected.

'De Troq'!'

'*Patron?*'

'Chouillou's wife gave Renée clothes?'

'*Oui.*'

'Shoes as well?'

'No, the wife takes a size smaller.'

Shuffling the files round on his desk, he withdrew and opened the one marked RENÉE CLAVIER – MURDER' and started reading it once again, making notes as he read, '18, not a virgin, not pregnant, light for her height: thin/1m67. Sandy coloured hair. Bruising round the throat consistent with attempted strangulation. Woollen gloves, brown.' He stopped, reread what he'd written and underlined the word 'strangulation'. She'd been stabbed at least twice and her genitalia mutilated – they hadn't paid much attention to 'attempted strangulation'. 'Weapons: two long hinged blades and short sharp blade. Suggestions: decorators' scissors and Stanley knife'. Leguyder had found paint on the sleeve of one of her jumpers. They were getting closer. Surely Debray and Rigal would come up with a likely candidate soon. Patience, Pel, patience.

Patience is a virtue, virtue is a grace, Grace is a little girl who didn't wash her face. Renée didn't wash her face before going to bed. Renée was murdered by someone wearing size 39 walking boots. Who? Who!

Round and round the garden like a teddy-bear, one step, two steps . . . Pel sat up suddenly. It was possible, he'd didn't know why, although Gilbert of all people may have . . . No, it wasn't possible. On the other hand . . . it would be worth working it through.

As the city's church bells announced seven o'clock, Pel lit up, inhaled deeply, glanced at his watch, remarked it was a minute fast, blew out a stream of smoke, and stood up. Tomorrow, he told himself, tomorrow would be soon enough. It was already Saturday evening and he was going out.

Saturday evening: the moment everyone's been waiting for all week. Saturday evening, when there's nothing but crap and cabaret on the telly, when you're almost forced to go out, spend money – have a good time! Saturday evening, when you take your glad rags from the wardrobe and lay them on the bed, take a shower, have a shave, clip your fingernails and toenails, blow dry your hair so it flops seductively on to your forehead, add a splash of that aftershave the girls go wild about in the advert, and stand in front of the mirror to admire yourself, pulling in your stomach as you do so. Hmm, not so bad. Step into trousers, slip into shirt, pull on socks, do up shoes. Tie? Not tonight, Josephine. Add jacket, and hey presto! you're Prince Charming ready for action. No, hang on, don't forget your pay packet, keys, cigarettes and lighter. Maybe a handkerchief too.

Pel took two and, pushing them into his pockets, he smiled at his wife. She was dressed in elegant navy blue with matching shoes; her face was carefully and discreetly made up, her hair shining and healthy. Geneviève was a very attractive woman. What the hell she was doing with a bum like himself? He'd never been able to fathom it out; must be a masochist.

She smiled back happily. When he wanted to, Pel could look quite presentable – at least he was clean and neatly pressed tonight, even his shoes shone for once – but his dress sense, or rather lack of it, wasn't what fascinated her about her husband, it was his mind; more complicated than a computer, storing years of knowledge she could only hazard a guess at, and yet still always open to suggestions. A lot of her friends complained their husbands were predictable and boring after the long years of marriage. She had to admit, her Pel was very difficult to live with at times, often infuriating – 'a difficult little bugger' she remembered the old Chief called him – often absent, often absent-minded when concentrating on more important things, like terrorist bombs or murder, but he was always surprising, never boring. He'd do. She straightened his tie, which looked more like a hangman's noose than expensive silk, and kissed his cheek. She was looking forward to their evening with Kate.

Staring out through the window, Kate peered into the darkness. She'd been laying the table and had turned back to the sink for the salad servers when someone tapped on the glass, making her jump. A pale face appeared and she gasped. It disappeared.

The heavy oak door groaned open.

Pujol licked his lips. 'It's only me!'

'Come in, *imbécile*, you gave me the fright of my life. Glass of wine?'

'Mm, thanks. You really ought to shut the shutters, you know. You can be seen clearly from the track.'

'I do usually, except when I'm expecting someone, then I leave them open to check the arrival is who it should be, and not a marauding rapist. Where's your car?'

'I left it by the woodshed, where I turned round. Didn't Rasputin bark?'

Kate laughed. 'He probably didn't hear you above the television.' She looked over her shoulder and shouted, 'Turn it down a bit, boys!'

'We found most of your stuff. Obviously we'll have to hang on to it for the court case but you'll get it back eventually.'

'Thank you, Pujol. Darcy would have been proud of your efficiency.'

'Now you're not going to cry on me tonight, are you?'

'I promise if I do it won't be all over your shirt this time. Cheers!'

Pujol sipped and swallowed, studying the large dog watching him from just inside the sitting-room. 'He's finally realised there's someone here. You don't think he's a bit deaf, do you? How old is he?'

'Ten this year, and no, I haven't noticed any problem with his hearing. Do dogs go deaf?'

'I don't see why they shouldn't. Tell me, why didn't he tear the intruder to shreds? Even if he didn't hear him, surely he *saw* him?'

'No, he didn't, the silly ass had locked himself in the bathroom. He'd scratched half the paint off the door, and pulled up the carpet, trying to get out, so I reckon his hearing's okay after all. I found him up there when I got home. He's done it once before.'

'What was he doing in the bathroom – taking a shower?'

'Drinking out of the lavatory.'

'How charming.'

'I remember to close my bathroom, but the kids forget, theirs is smaller, the lavatory's behind the door, when Razz gets in there he must push it out of the way to quench his thirst. It slams shut and he's trapped.'

'So, your burglar got off lightly.'

'I doubt he'd have got a foot in the door if Razz had been around. Want to stay for supper? Cheriff and Annie are bringing baby Daniel over to meet the boys.'

Pujol's tongue darted out and did its work. 'Great. I'll help you lay the table.'

Jo-Jo the Butcher wanted to lay Miriam, at least that's what she said her name was. She was a bit young and rather immature, she'd giggled when he'd introduced himself at the bar. He didn't like gigglers. He didn't like young immature women much any more, not after the last one had come to such a sticky end. What he was looking for was a woman, perhaps thirty or thirty-five, someone with a bit of character and class. Not a go-go dancer like this one. That's all she seemed to want to do. He wanted more, he was doing his best to tell her. One hand was inside her tank-top, kneading a full and firm breast, the other was down

125

inside her leggings, kneading a full and firm buttock, and his erection was pressed into her groin, needing release.

When the slow came to a stop, she broke away and went to the bar for a drink before bopping back on to the floor.

By midnight, he was getting desperate and still the girl wanted to dance. It was nigh on impossible to have a persuasive conversation over the music belting out from the speakers. 'Come on, let's go back to your flat!'

She shook her head.

'I'm leaving! I've had enough!'

She nodded her head and blew a kiss.

He grabbed her and pulled her roughly to him. 'Come with me, you little bitch!'

She was struggling now, shrieking stupidly.

Half an hour later, he was out on the streets, alone. The bouncers had seen the argument and quickly put a stop to it; Miriam would never know how lucky she'd been.

Jo-Jo wandered about town, looking for a likely bar, but he knew it was too late now, all the tarts would be taken. He could go on to another disco, see what he could pick up there.

Pushing open the door of the Tropicana, he paid the entrance fee and went through the crowds to the bar. It was pretty full tonight, not much space for movement, all the better for preliminary groping. Smiling to himself, he ordered a whisky and drank it down with a gulp. 'Thirsty, were you?' The barmaid, thick with foundation and false eyelashes, her lips a livid scarlet slash, winked at him. Not his type.

Then he saw the two women come down the steps from the restaurant, well-dressed women, women with money, probably married and out for a bit of fun. Jo-Jo was ready to oblige.

It took a couple of drinks to loosen them up, put them both at ease, but it was worth it, eventually they agreed to dance with the good-looking stranger. They stepped out on to the dance floor and turned towards him, beckoning.

Jo-Jo shook off his jacket and followed.

Pel also shook off his jacket and, sitting on the edge of the bed, pulled off his shoes, thinking about their evening at Kate's. It had been very pleasant. She seemed almost back to normal, although he doubted she ever would be completely, but she was putting on a very brave face. Her voice had only stalled once, and that was understandable – they'd been talking about the Chinese picnic they'd had at the hospital, a tradition she and Darcy had started when the twins were born. So sad to be bringing them up without their father . . . He yawned and arched his aching back. Annie and Cheriff were still looking like cats that had been at the cream, and all the children had behaved themselves, as well as children can be expected to.

'Odd that, Pujol being there,' he said, parking his shoes neatly by the bedside table and starting on his socks.

His wife came into the bedroom already in her nightdress, brushing her hair. 'Not really, he'd got one or two minor details to clear up on the robbery. I'm glad you caught the chap.'

'But what was he doing upstairs?'

She kissed him on the forehead and climbed into bed. 'You really are a suspicious old rogue. He'd been trying to fix a bathroom door so Rasputin couldn't get locked in there.'

'How would he do that?'

'I honestly don't know, even he seemed a bit stumped, but no doubt he'll come up with something. He's bright, that one, reminds me of you.'

'Small, scruffy . . . I don't lick my lips before I speak!'

'I meant his mentality.'

'Oh.'

He finished undressing and wandered off to clean his teeth. 'You don't think –'

'Finish your ablutions, I can't understand a word!'

When Pel joined his wife in bed, he smelt of soap and toothpaste. 'Squeaky clean,' he said, smiling at her.

'What were you saying?'

'Forgotten.'

He kissed her goodnight and switched the light off, settling down under the covers with a contented sigh. Geneviève was just dozing off when he remembered.

'You don't think something's going on between those two?'

'Mm, sorry, which two?'

'Kate and Pujol.'

127

'No, I don't, although I do think Pujol's slightly besotted – after all, Kate is beautiful, though she's lost a lot of weight, poor love,'

'I sincerely hope he's not out of line.'

'One of these days she's going to have to rebuild her life with another man.'

'But it's too soon!' He counted silently. 'Five months!'

'And a half. As far as I can tell, she simply enjoys the company of an intelligent man. It must be very lonely without Darcy.'

'She's got four children.'

'The toddlers are hardly great conversationalists, and the older boys have homework, they're in bed by nine.'

'Even so!'

'Why do you think she invited us over, and Annie and Cheriff?'

'Because she likes us?'

'Obviously, but also because she misses being involved in police work. Darcy must have discussed what he was working on, the way you do with me. Not only is he dead but the contact she had with a whole crowd of familiar people has disappeared. Pujol is part of that crowd, I'm not in the least surprised she asked him to stay for supper.'

'But if it becomes a habit?'

'Pel?'

'Yes, dear?'

'Goodnight.'

'Yes, dear.'

Sunday, 28th November

Lambert arrived at Brisard's home at noon. He offered an expensive bunch of cut flowers to Madame Brisard, and a bottle of Bordeaux to the *juge d'instruction*. They ate a good roast lunch, with cèpes to complement the beef, and green beans turned in butter and garlic. Lambert wiped his mouth as he finished the cheese, feeling replete and relaxed, probably for the first time since he'd met Pel. As Madame Brisard cleared the table and prepared coffee, the two men retired to the sitting-room and sat down to wait.

'How's the double murder enquiry coming along? It's two weeks since the torso was found at the college, surely Pel should be making an arrest soon?'

Lambert sighed heavily. 'The only arrest his team's made since the story broke was a small-time thief who whipped a couple of candlesticks from Darcy's widow.'

'Should I move the case to Klein?' Brisard suggested. 'I could, you know.'

'That's who had it in the first place.'

'I mean the murders.'

'I don't think it would make much difference. Contumacious though he is, and he is insufferable at times, Pel is methodical – he'll get there in the end, if anyone can, even though he's got Gilbert and Morrison to handicap him. It's going to be a long one; the caravan was used by dozens of people, every one of them is being checked, both virtually and personally. So far there's no single person that stands out from the crowd as a possible suspect. And the Clavier case isn't any easier. She was in a class of seventeen, they all knew her, none well, no one had any idea what she did at the weekends. Her teacher is co-operative but can throw no light on her movements beyond the Chambre de Métier, the director didn't even know what she looked like, and her mother's worse than useless. It seems the girl was having a secret love affair, but for the life of me, I can't imagine who with. Apparently, she smelt.'

'Is Pel attacking the enquiry from the right angle? Perhaps a fresh mind would see more clearly.'

'You may be right. At the moment all he appears to be doing is amassing interviews and moaning about Gilbert.'

Brisard smiled with satisfaction. 'What's he done?'

'Been vulgar.'

'Is that all? For crying out loud! All policemen are vulgar at one time or another.'

'Pel's team don't like him.'

'Pel's team and Pel himself have had it their own way for too long. The old Chief let them get away with far too much, Lambert. I'm glad you're keeping a close eye on him.'

'Twenty-four hours a day; any deviation from regulations and he's in my office, swiftly being read the riot act.'

'He won't enjoy that!'

'He too can be very rude.'

'Partner him with Gilbert, it might calm the pair of them. That is, after all, why we chose him, to get under Pel's skin.'

Lambert ran a hand through his snowy white hair. 'Now there's an idea. I wonder why I hadn't thought of it myself.'

9

Pel was feeling much better. Boudet's shock treatment seemed to be working, the aches and agonies in his limbs had gone, his nose was no longer streaming, simply red and extremely delicate round the edges, and the cough was just a hacking cough, not the prelude to crippling bronchitis or pneumonia or some other equally debilitating disease. Yes, he really was feeling much better.

Until Lambert ordered him into his office.

'Come in, Pel, come in.'

The Chief was looking suspiciously pleased with himself; Pel expected the worst.

'Since I took up my post here in Dijon, we have, I'm sure you'll have noticed, had our little differences. Our relationship was certainly not an easy one, and still, if l may be so bold, is not completely comfortable. However, l have remarked a distinct effort on your part recently and wish to add my own.'

Pel stifled a yawn, Lambert was blathering again.

'My instructions, nay, my orders, were, right from the first day we met, that you were to spend more time in the office, delegating the footwork, and hence being present, and available, to receive and give instructions to your men out in the street, so to speak. I am pleased with the result; the efficiency of this Hôtel de Police – of *my* Hôtel de Police – has improved, the statistics remain stable and good. However . . .' He folded his hands and leaned on the desk in front of him in a confidential manner, emphasising the importance of what he was about to say. Pel stifled another yawn, Lambert was still blathering. 'However,' he said again, 'the murder of these two women is proving more difficult than anticipated, progress is slow, the tracks are going cold. With this in view, exceptionally you understand, I want you operating externally, personally following up the people involved. As an active member of the team,

131

instead of a passive member, you will obviously need a partner. I have studied, at length, the duty roster and rewritten Nosjean's feeble attempts at pairing off your officers with equilibrium.' He handed Pel a familiar sheet of paper. 'This is the order for the week. No changes are to be made, I want to see how the group works. Gilbert will be accompanying you.'

Uncharacteristically, Pel shuffled into the sergeants' room, where his squad was waiting for the morning meeting, and handed Nosjean the duty roster.

Nosjean sneezed, excused himself then snorted, 'What a bloody jumble! It won't work.'

'It's going to have to. Have you seen who wrote it?'

'But all the brains and dunces are together.'

'Have you seen who I've got?'

'You're on it? *Nom de Dieu*, hard luck.'

'Save your sympathy for the end of the week – by then we may all need it. Start the meeting, would you? I need to suck a Rennies.'

'Order!' Nosjean shouted, bringing the assembly to attention while he sneezed again and blew his nose. 'Partners for the week: Misset – Morrison; Bardolle – Jourdain; De Troq' – Cheriff; Pujol, you're with me; and Gilbert – you're with Pel.'

The startled faces began sniggering. No one wanted Gilbert; now Pel had got him. Poor old Pel. God help Gilbert.

'Who's manning the phones?'

'The same as last week, Sergeant Santonga, she's on her way up.'

'Nice tits.'

'Good legs too.'

'I like her smile, she's –'

'Murder!' Pel bellowed, his digestive system now back in acceptable working order. 'We've got two of them and not a single bloody suspect in sight. As we've all been remixed and ill matched, we might as well do the job properly and muddle matters furthers. Misset, keep stalking the carpenters. Bardolle, you too. De Troq', stick with the Clavier acquaintances. Nosjean, I suggest you and Pujol go back to the Chambre de Métier, it seems to pop up with odd regularity; the paint on Renée's jumper, her typing class, plus I now learn there is a carpentry course. Visit all the workshops, talk to as many students as possible, then bring a complete list of all the teachers and their students, all one thousand of them, back here for Debray and Rigal. Work with them to speed it up. Keep your eyes and ears open, all of you. For the moment all we know for sure is Renée's murderer was wearing size 39 hiking boots and weighs 58 kilos; it's not a lot but it's a start. Has her moped been found yet?'

'Negative.'

'It'll turn up, if not this week, next week, or the week after.'

'Next year?'

'And a fat lot of good it'll do us then.'

'Enough! That's Renée, we also have the College Cadavre. All we've turned up so far is that the killer marked the number of times he visited her in the caravan.'

'Where he shafted her.'

'Thank you, Gilbert, for your attention to detail, most enlightening. I, together with our eloquent colleague, am going to see Madame Chouillou. You never know, Renée may have confided something to her, as her only real friend, that she wouldn't have confided to her mother.'

Pel and Gilbert had to wait until play-time before being able to speak to Madame Chouillou. They sat in the warm sunshine, sheltered by the building, and stared, slightly frowning in Pel's case, at the clear forget-me-not sky, not a cloud in sight. It never ceased to amaze him how much weather they had; in five weeks they'd had it hot enough to eat outside at midday and cold enough to snow. They'd had storms, floods, fog and freeze; now the trees were still, their bare branches standing idle in the glorious autumn sun, and the nip in the air made him feel sharply alive. Until he glanced at Gilbert, who was picking his nose as if he'd lost his wallet up there, then he felt sharply repulsed. However, he told himself, give the man his due, he was the one who started a train of thought in my brain, even if he's not aware of it.

At ten thirty, doors banged open and children, all shapes, sizes and colours, streamed into the playground, shouting and yelling, and one or two fighting. Following in their wake were the masters and mistresses, shrugging themselves into overcoats, some lighting up surreptitiously and walking out of sight to smoke.

'*Je peux vous aider, messieurs?*'

Pel introduced himself, offering his identification to avoid confusion, and asked if it would be possible to speak to Madame Chouillou.

She was wearing flat sensible brown shoes, tan trousers and a fluffy pink jacket – 'old rose', Pel thought the colour was called – and pale pink lipstick. She came quickly towards them when called and shook hands efficiently before agreeing willingly to talk about Renée.

'Shall we sit over there on the bench? That way we won't be overheard.'

'Do you not want to be overheard?'

She looked at Pel as if he was an idiot, smiling slightly. 'It's not what I shall say, more what he may say,' she said, indicating Gilbert. 'I'm no prude but if any of these children go home having learnt a rude word at school, we, as their teachers, will be held responsible.'

'All kids swear,' Gilbert objected.

'Eventually, yes, but not at the tender age of three and we have twenty-five three-year-olds here. And, although the older ones do swear, they do not have your somewhat shocking eloquence yet.'

'Keep your mouth zipped,' Pel hissed and sat between them on the bench.

'Now, what can I tell you this time about poor Renée?'

'You saw her fairly frequently, you were kind enough to invite her to your home and let her have a bath, kind enough to give her clothes.'

'They were only cast-offs.'

'Even so, it was a great kindness. You were obviously the same size?'

'Not at all, she was longer and lacking in shape, as flat as a pancake.'

'But you must weigh approximately the same?'

'Possibly, I honestly don't know.'

'Renée weighed 55 kilos.'

'You surprise me, but then she was tall, wasn't she? I suppose that would account for it. I weigh a little less,' she chuckled, 'with the padding in different places.'

Gilbert leaned forward to look. Pel nudged him back into place, although he too would have guessed more.

'You told my man, de Troquereau, she was grateful. How did she express it?'

'I'm not sure what you mean. She said thank you, a lot, looked pleased, smiled at me, that sort of thing.'

'Did she tell you about her own home, her family?'

'Not really, except to say she didn't have a bathroom and her father was an invalid.'

'But you must have talked, say while you were preparing the meal, or while you ate it.'

'While the meal was being prepared, yes, I suppose we did chat, but not while we ate. Laurent was there then, you see. She was very shy, I suppose it was because he was her teacher, perhaps she was like that with all men. I really don't know.'

'Before your husband joined you, what did you chat about?'

'Oh, you know, this and that, nothing really, there wasn't much time, you see, once she'd finished washing, supper was practically ready.'

'Do you know if she talked to your husband on the way to your home, or when he drove her to hers?'

'You'd better ask him, but no, I don't think so, he never mentioned anything, except that she always said thank you as she got out of the car. Why?'

'We believe she had a boyfriend, one her mother knows nothing about. I was hoping she may have confided in you – you were the closest friend she had.'

'A boyfriend! Goodness, well, yes, why not? And you don't know who he was?'

'Not yet.'

'And you think it was this boyfriend that killed her?'

'It's possible.'

'What about the farm workers? Those sort of people can be pretty rough, can't they? And she did live out in the country, didn't she?'

'We've checked them with our records and done the rounds, we've talked to all the locals, both where she lived and where she died. We have no reason to suspect any of them.'

'Well, I'm sorry but I really don't know.'

'Prissy little piece,' Gilbert said as he manipulated the car out on to the road. 'What she needs is a jolly good rogering.'

'Keep your personal appraisals to yourself.'

'The other bit was all right.'

'What other bit?'

'The other bit of skirt, the brunette that spoke to us first. What's her name?'

'Joelle Dentreuil, *la directrice*.'

'That's right, that one.'

'You'd better behave, we'll be seeing her this afternoon.'

'Why's that then?'

'Work it out yourself, Gilbert.'

Gilbert hadn't worked it out by the time they arrived at rue Charrue, the address listed as Joelle Dentreuil's residence. It was 1645, Joelle had just arrived from the school quarter of an hour away. Pel gave her five minutes to get from the garage into the house and take off her coat, then he leaned on the doorbell. It was answered almost immediately by the brunette, who, though showing a certain amount of surprise, stepped back obligingly and invited them in.

They passed by the sitting-room where a ten-year-old boy was glued to the television and went into a modern kitchen. 'Coffee or drink?' she suggested.

Gilbert was about to agree to a quick snort, but Pel declined just in time, and started his questions.

'How long has Madame Chouillou been working with you at the school?'

'With me, five years, that's when I took over as principal. I think she was there another three before that.'

The back door opened, letting a blast of icy air race across the floor. Joelle's husband, Denis, shook hands, poured himself a pastis and stood in the background to listen. He was not much taller than his wife, quite small for a man, with fine bone structure, lightweight; around 58/59 kilos?

'What size shoes do you take, monsieur?'

Denis looked startled. '41. What the hell's it got to do with you?'

Pel sighed. 'Nothing.'

Embarrassed by the short exchange, Joelle Dentreuil brought two more glasses to the table. 'As the bottle's out, you might as well,' she encouraged, and to her husband, 'We were talking about Michelle Chouillou.'

'I can think of more exciting subjects.'

'You don't like her?'

'I don't *dis*like her, she's a fidget and a bore. Why're you interested in her?'

'She knew the girl that was found in the Rin a week ago.'

'Who was it in the end?'

'Renée Clavier. Laurent Chouillou taught her typing, both he and Michelle were very kind to her. They've told us what they can but information on the girl is very thin on the ground.'

'I'm surprised they had time to be kind to anyone, they don't have time to come round here any more.'

'Why's that, monsieur?'

'Their bloody house. Anyone would think they're converting a château.'

'Which house?'

'A house they bought, it's not much bigger than our garden shed, but the fuss they make about it – a whole evening to decide to paint the bedroom primrose yellow.'

'Have you ever visited it?'

'Michelle doesn't want anyone to see it until, and I quote, "it's all spick and span and looking lovely!" She must've told us a million times, after the first hundred, I stopped listening. It's somewhere out near Arney-le-Duc, I think.'

'Did you often spend evenings together?'

'Not any more.'

'But before they bought the house?'

'Yeah, we got on okay. When Joelle joined the staff at the primary school she gave a sort of party to get to know the rest of them. Laurent and I found we had something in common, our liking for jazz. Funnily enough, I met Michelle in town the other weekend and she invited us to a concert; trying to make up the lapsed friendship maybe.'

'But we paid for our own tickets!'

'What the hell, it'll be worth it – anyway, I like old Laurent. It's Michelle that gets on my tit.'

Gilbert was thankfully too busy scribbling to make any comment, obscene or otherwise, and Pel moved the questioning back to Joelle.

'What's she like to work with?'

'Easy, she's understanding with the youngest, firm with the oldest, and has the patience of a saint with self-opinionated parents. A valuable member of staff. In a way I quite miss them popping over, I found her fussing and fidgeting quite funny, sometimes she was just so absurd.'

'Well, I didn't,' Denis broke in again.

Pel waited for more, but instead Denis swallowed a mouthful of pastis and glared.

'Did either of them mention Renée?'

'If it was the waif and stray Laurent took home, then yes. Michelle rabbited on about her almost as much as the house, said it made her feel *so* warm inside to know she was doing something *good*.' Joelle chuckled. 'See what I mean? She always managed to make me laugh. Everything about her is exaggerated. She said it was the *least* she could do.'

'Between "it was the least she could do" and their ruddy paint charts she bored me rigid.'

Tuesday, 30th November

'Start with Arney-le-Duc and work your way out from there. Phone every Trésor Public listed in that area and find out where the Chouillous are paying rates for a house. De Troq' knew they were hoping to move soon, but we didn't know they'd already bought a place and were busy decorating it. And Gilbert, as we've been betrothed for the week, you'll do it right here in my office, where I can keep an eye on you.'

Nosjean pushed his way in, dragging his feet like a zombie. 'God, my head, it's worse than a bag of wet cement. I'm aching all over.'

'It gets worse,' Pel said cheerfully. 'Give Boudet a ring, he's got a shock treatment that did wonders for me. In the meantime, keep your microbes to yourself, I'm better. And just look at the sun! It's in its heaven and shining down on humanity, it's a glorious morning.'

'It's one hell of a morning. Look, we've just been comparing yesterday's notes. Bardolle and Jourdain were doing the carpenter rounds. They called at Entreprise Bois et Alu – made-to-measure wood and aluminium windows – 32 kilometres from the caravan at Larroque.'

'Is that as far as you've got?'

Nosjean sneezed twice, groaned and whipped out his handkerchief to mop up. 'They're thicker on the ground as we get closer to the city, and bigger. This place had more than forty employees. They spoke to every one.'

'Now you've finished making excuses, perhaps you'd get to the point.'

'The rapid question and answer routine brought nothing, most of the men were perfectly willing to help. One or two got huffy about talking to the police, and we now know why; they were the ones with records. One in particular, Bruno Estampe, wouldn't co-operate with Jourdain, tried to rub her up the wrong way.'

Gilbert raised his head, an obscenity wriggling on the tip of his tongue.

'Leave it, Gilbert! Go on, Nosjean.'

'She handed over to Bardolle and went on to the next name on the list. Bardolle got the questions satisfactorily answered. Last night, he checked all the names through our records and rang back this morning to find out if there'd ever been any trouble with the ex-cons. The answer was negative – until this morning. Bruno hasn't turned up for work. He's not off sick, he's not at home, and one of his sisters says he went out late last night and hasn't come back since.'

'What's he been done for?'

'Breaking a Moroccan's arm in 1991 – he claimed it was an accident and got off with a suspended sentence. Punching a woman in the face for pinching his parking place in 1993 – that time he went down for six months – and smashing tables and chairs in a gay bar, 1996, two years.'

'Sounds a charming fellow.'

'Not only that, but going through the Chambre de Métier's records, I discovered he did his training as a chippie last year, as part of a rehabilitation scheme.'

'Hold on, you've turned up a violent man working as a carpenter and who trained at the Chambre de Métier. Which murder are you working here?'

'It could be both.'

'Renée only started at the school in September.'

'And Bruno is still on day release, once a week, he could have known her.'

'And be mixed up with the College Cadavre?'

'It's possible.'

'Where does he live?'

'With his mother and three sisters in the council flats at Cantepau, a stone's throw from where Renée worked in the restaurant.'

'It is certainly one hell of a coincidence and I don't like coincidences, they tend to trip you up or send you off at an irrelevant tangent.'

'But the facts are too blatant to be ignored. One: he has access to, and uses regularly, a flat red carpenter's pencil. Two: his place of work is a short drive from the Larroque campsite where a woman was killed and cut up. Three: he has a record of violence, against anyone or everyone – an Arab, a woman, homosexuals. Four: he spends one day a week at the Chambre de Métier where Renée was at school. Five: he lives near where she worked for nearly a year. Oh, yes, I forgot, he's got a car, a second-hand Ford Escort, which makes getting from place to place, and away

140

again, simple. He was tricky with Jourdain yesterday and now he's disappeared.'

'Find him and haul him in quick for questioning. Get the details of his car from the Préfecture and put it out to the gendarmeries, the Police de Ville, as well as our lot. Go to Cantepau, talk to the mother and sisters, see if they've any idea where he's gone. And Nosjean, see if they can give you an up-to-date photo. If not, use what's in the files, have his picture printed and distributed – we must know what he looks like.'

'Press?'

'No. Keep the newspapers out of it for the moment. The odds are stacked against Estampe, but he's still innocent until proven otherwise. For the moment all we want to do is find him, okay?'

Gilbert slammed down the phone. 'Got it!'

'Got what, Gilbert?'

'La Garrigue, Arney-le-Haut, change of ownership in June 1999 to Monsieur and Madame Chouillou of 15 rue Renoir, Dijon.'

'Get your coat on, Gilbert, we're going out there.'

La Garrigue was definitely not a château. After the narrow streets – just two, crossing in the centre of Arney-le-Haut – twenty-three names in the telephone directory as opposed to Arney-le-Bas which had only seventeen, and Arney-le-Duc with an incredible fifty-one, and a tobacconist's where Pel bought a day's supply of Gauloises, handed the man behind the counter his *carte grise* and paid for the cigarettes and the tax disc for his car, patting himself on the back that he'd done it during the promotional period in November (10% more in December, and every month after that) but annoyed he'd had to, if his bloody new Peugeot had arrived on time it would have avoided this extra expense – they came out on to an equally narrow but very muddy country road that wound its way round the fields for another 3 kilometres before stopping at a T-junction: Le Bourg, Lincarque, Fougouzoo to the left, La Bouissonarié, La Garrigue to the right.

Gilbert swung the car to the right, down into a valley. They passed La Bouissonarié, shuttered and apparently empty, after three-quarters of a kilometre, then when they thought the lane, now only a stony track, was about to peter out to nothing, La Garrigue appeared round the corner. Set slightly higher than the lane, it looked pretty, highlighted in the sudden sunshine, and Pel could understand how a town-dweller could have romantic ideas about doing it up. It was definitely not unattractive: an oblong of pale stone, sitting with its back to a rising field of grass, a small fenced terrace in front, crying out for pots of geraniums and oleanders, wrought iron furniture and a large colourful parasol.

As he climbed out, an icy wind reminded Pel it was 30th November not 4th July in spite of the sun, and crossing to the terrace, he opened the squeaky gate and stepped up on to the concrete platform, going towards the front door. He put his ear to it, knocked and waited. No reply. He hadn't expected one. Putting his hand on the knob he twisted it; the door was locked, the shutters were firmly closed, he couldn't see in, but he'd certainly like to. Turning back to where Gilbert was standing in the yard scratching an ear, he could see the track they'd just come down ribboning its way up through the trees towards the T-junction at the top of the hill. If you didn't want visitors here, you'd have plenty of time to hide when you saw them approach. There wasn't another habitation in sight, even La Bouissonarié was hidden from view in the undulations of the bare autumn landscape. He glanced at his watch; not much more than half an hour from the centre of town.

'No, I will not authorise a search warrant.' Brisard sat down heavily, looking up from the paper in his hand to Pel's permanent frown. 'Lambert's been on to me about Chouillou. While he's perfectly willing to answer your questions, he thinks interrogating his wife at the primary school, in front of her colleagues and all the little children, is definitely going too far.'

'She didn't object.'

'She is polite. Unlike you. Being a policeman does not mean you can go barging into people's lives upsetting them.'

'I didn't upset her.'

'You've upset her husband. He asks for you to confine your questions to their own home.'

'Which one? They've got a house we didn't know about. It's out in the country, no neighbours, and excuse me for saying so, a perfect place to kill someone without being seen.'

'There is nothing to indicate Chouillou is the perpetrator. This,' he rattled the paper to make his point, 'is not justified. He's been as helpful as any man can be, his classes have been disrupted and now his personal life is being disturbed.'

'He knew Renée, better than we imagined.'

Brisard held up a pompous hand. 'I repeat, your suspicions are not justified.'

'And never will be at this rate.'

'You have no real reason to demand entry into their un-inhabited house.'

'What about hinged double blades, otherwise known as decorating scissors? And E4-7M, a pale apricot satin finish paint, for God's sake, they've been decorating the place for the last four months.'

'They are not the only ones with access to such things. For instance, the restaurant where she worked; they closed in September for the dining-room to be redone.'

'It was painted a cream colour.'

'What's to say one or two bedrooms weren't painted at the same time? Paid for in cash and not declared. And the shop where she worked, one of the girls got married, she and her husband have painted an entire apartment.'

'They did the whole thing white!'

'Am I to sign search warrants for every citizen who's ever bought a pot of paint?'

'Brisard –'

'Maître Brisard, if you don't mind.'

Pel sighed. '*D'accord*. Maître, the paint on her jumper is not available to the general public. It is however available at the Chambre de Métier where Chouillou works and although our enquiries have been extensive and time-consuming, he is the only person we've come up with who was, as far as we know, ever alone with Renée. He invited her to his home.'

'To meet his wife, Pel.'

'He was alone in the car with the girl before and after the evenings they spent with his wife. He could have taken her to see La Garrigue.'

'Why?'

'To meditate the complications arising from a typing course. How should I know? To ask her opinion on the colours they'd chosen.'

'To shaft her?'

'Gilbert, keep out of this!'

Brisard leaned forward. 'Let's recap, shall we? So far, all you've got is a print of a walking boot near where the body was found. Leguyder suggests . . .'

'Can prove.'

'. . . it was worn by a person weighing approximately 58 kilos with small feet. How much does Chouillou weigh? What size are his feet?'

'Look, the kid was murdered, stripped and dumped. The killer was clever, he's left us very little to go on, therefore it was carefully thought out, okay? If I start asking give-away questions and I happen to be asking them of our killer, he's going to know why and destroy any evidence that may be left – like for instance his ruddy walking boots, or blood-splattered clothes.'

'It will be interesting to hear what Bruno Estampe has to say, *when* you find him. He is, as far as I'm concerned, a far more likely candidate for conviction than a happily married man who happened to teach one of the victims. I signed the *avis de recherche* for him, it was a logical request. This isn't. You will not search the Chouillous' country cottage.'

'And as far as I'm concerned,' Pel muttered as he walked back to the car, '*Maître* bloody Brisard can go shaft himself.'

'I knew a bloke once that could actually –'

'Shut up, Gilbert!'

At seven that evening, with Gilbert grumbling by his side, Pel sat outside 15 rue Renoir waiting for Chouillou to come home.

'Good evening, monsieur. I beg your pardon for disturbing your evening but, as I'm sure you'll understand, we are engaged in a murder enquiry. You have been very helpful in the past and I wonder if you could indulge me a little longer.'

Laurent Chouillou squinted at the two detectives and stepped back. 'Sure, come in. You want to ask more questions, is that it?'

Pel sighed apologetically. 'That's it exactly. You and your wife are the only ones we can find who had a relationship with Renée resembling anything close to a friendship. The examining magistrate responsible for the case has asked me to ask you, together with a number of others of course, a few simple questions to clarify things.'

Chouillou looked at Pel with one eye; the other seemed to be fixed on Gilbert, sitting beside him. 'Anything I can do to help.'

'How much do you weigh?'

Laurent laughed. '73 kilos.'

'What size shoes do you take?'

'42.'

'Where is your wife, by the way? Surely she should be home by now?'

'Aerobic classes, she wants to lose a bit of weight before Christmas.'

'Very wise. Next question: where were you on the afternoon and early evening of Saturday, 20th November?'

'1 haven't got a clue. Is it important?'

Pel fixed on his right eye, the one that seemed to be doing the work. 'Very.'

'Over a week ago, oh God, honestly I haven't got a . . . yes I have! That was the Saturday Michelle bullied me into going to Beaune. Conforama were having a pre-Christmas sale and she wanted a dishwasher. It was peeing with rain but no, she wanted her dishwasher.'

'You went to Beaune, almost 40 kilometres away, to buy a dishwasher?'

'I know it sounds slightly ridiculous but yes, I did.'

'Can you prove it?'

'Well, I've got the till receipt and the stamped guarantee.'

'What time did you leave the house?'

145

'Two, straight after lunch.'

'What time did you get back?'

'Ooh, around five, I think.'

'Can you be more specific? Did someone see you? A neighbour, for instance?'

'Yes, I asked Bashir next door to give me a hand unloading the thing. He did, we got it into the kitchen and then we had a drink. It was nearly six by then.' Now it was his left eye dodging about.

'Muslims don't drink alcohol.'

'I know, I tend to forget he's an Arab. He always laughs when I offer. He had a glass of grenadine, I had a beer.'

'What did you do after that?'

'Plumbed the damn thing in.'

'When you're moving so soon?'

'Not till the spring. When it gets a bit warmer.'

'Did anyone see you while you were working?'

'I shouldn't think so, I was on my hands and knees behind the kitchen units.'

'What time did you finish?'

'Just before my wife walked in around seven.'

'Tell me about the house you're moving to.'

'What about it?'

'How often do you go there?'

'Every weekend.'

'What do you do there?'

'At the moment, paint the walls.'

'Does your wife go with you?'

'No, I go alone. She's allergic to the paint, it makes her sneeze and her eyes run, gives her a migraine, that's why I've got to do it before we move. She'll make up for it later, making curtains, covering the sofas and things, generally prettying it up, she's good at that.'

'So normally on a Saturday, you are decorating at La Garrigue?'

'That's right.'

'But the Saturday Renée was murdered you were at Conforama in Beaune?'

'Yes, I was.'

146

'Will you be decorating next Saturday?'

'I should think so. Michelle's very anxious to get it finished.'

'Which room are you painting at the moment?'

'The sitting-room.'

'What colour?'

'We had difficulty with that one. I wanted something dark and sultry, you know, a bit sexy, but Michelle said it would be gloomy in winter and we could create the same effect with subtle lighting. In the end we settled on a creamy sort of orange.'

Both eyes were wandering now. Pel fixed on a point between his eyebrows. 'Pale apricot?'

'That's exactly it!'

'Traces of pale apricot emulsion were found on one of Renée's sweaters.'

'Oh . . .?'

'How often did you take her there?'

'I didn't, I wouldn't . . .'

'Just to show her the house your wife talked about so often?'

'Well, I suppose there's no harm in admitting that.'

'And to shaft her?'

This time Pel didn't shout Gilbert down, he watched in fascination as Laurent Chouillou almost cringed before the question.

'Well, did you?'

'I was her teacher!' His eyes weren't dancing independently any more.

'We know that.'

'It would have been terribly wrong if . . .'

'But did you?'

'Sure he did, he's been shafting her rigid for weeks.'

'I have not!'

Pel stood up and crossed to the window, leaving Chouillou under Gilbert's gaze. 'My lieutenant doesn't think you're telling the truth.'

'I would have lost my job, my wife would leave me –'

'*Did* you?'

'It's not allowed –'

147

'I'm beginning to believe Gilbert is right, and I'm also pretty certain we can prove it. You'd better tell us everything, monsieur. If you prefer, we can do it in the presence of a stenographer to take down your exact words and Maître Brisard, our *juge d'instruction*, as witness, plus a lawyer if you wish to appoint one. You can reread the statement, changing your story as often as you like, before signing it, after which you will be charged with the murder of Renée Clavier.'

Pel knew he was exaggerating, but he knew he'd shocked Chouillou. He'd not been totally fair either; he could not prove the man with his head in his hands, sobbing on the sofa, had had intercourse with Renée. If he could have, he'd have done it long ago and avoided wasting so much time looking for the elusive boyfriend. And the last thing he wanted to do was involve Brisard, he'd only be a disruptive element at this stage. But Pel was well aware that the idea of accompanying two plain-clothes detectives back to the Hôtel de Police, to sit guarded by a uniformed officer in a stark interview room while the necessary officials were contacted and assembled, then to answer questions in front of those officials while a stenographer tapped out every spoken syllable, put the fear of God into most people, particularly those with something to hide, and Pel was sure now Chouillou did have something to hide.

And he'd had enough time to think about it. Pel came back to stand in front of the suspect. He laid a hand firmly on his shoulder, making the man jump. 'Well, did you?'

Chouillou twisted round, tears in his eyes. 'Only twice. Look, I know what you're thinking, oh God . . .'

'*Je vous écoute.*'

'Oh Jesus, what will become of me? Yes, yes, I picked her up and we went to La Garrigue on Saturday afternoons.'

'Did you on the 20th?'

'No! I was in Beaune, I can prove it! Check with Conforama!' The voice was full of panic. 'Look, I'll tell you everything if you promise to keep it to yourself.'

'I can make no guarantee.'

'She was young and vulnerable, she needed loving, she'd never been loved or cared for in her life, I couldn't help it, she wanted to do something for me to show how grateful she was, she'd have done anything for me. When I told her she mustn't breathe a word of our . . . our liaison, she simply nodded, she understood. In class she behaved just the way she always had, sitting at the back, ignored by everyone. Poor Renée, in a way I was glad to give her a bit of pleasure, a little happiness. And she *was* happy with me, the afternoons we spent together were tender and sweet. We were going to spend the night of the 20th together, the whole night, wake up in each other's arms the next morning, but Michelle wanted her ruddy dishwasher. I nearly told her to fetch the thing herself! You see, there was no way of letting Renée know I couldn't meet her, I could hardly ring and apologise with my wife in the room, and by the time I got to Beaune Renée'd already left for our rendezvous. I felt awful about standing her up, and not just for the afternoon; as I was leaving I heard Michelle on the phone, inviting guests for a meal at seven thirty, I wouldn't be able to get away even after fetching the dishwasher. But I couldn't make a fuss, Michelle would have wanted to know why, and I couldn't tell her. Now of course, I'm terribly grateful to her for keeping me busy. I saw the newspapers on Monday morning and thought, my God, and Renée not in class. Then I thought she was probably just upset that I'd let her down. Well, when I found out the 'teenage girl slain' *was* her, I breathed a huge sigh of relief. I thought, thank God I was miles away, there's no connection to me. No one'll know. I'm safe.' He looked up at Pel, beseeching him to understand. 'And the evening was spent with my wife, her brother and his wife. So you see, you're wrong, it *wasn't* me.'

Pel gave Chouillou a receipt for the dishwasher's stamped guarantee and till ticket confirming payment by cheque, thinking what a pathetic little man he was; a teacher who'd allowed himself a huge sigh of relief when he'd discovered one of his students had been brutally murdered. He walked down the path to the car, sadly satisfied. It was late and he was feeling very tired and very old, not in the mood for talking to a dippy teacher with a fluffy pink jacket, but that's where they were going next, to the sports centre where Michelle was attending aerobic classes.

Two suspects; one down, one to go. And Gilbert farting about, patting ruddy Chouillou on the back. 'Come on, Gilbert, get a move on!'

As Gilbert moved the car away from the kerb, he turned to Pel and grinned. 'Just having a word. See, I told you he was shafting her.'

10

Michelle Chouillou was perspiring heavily. In a pink leotard and tights she looked rather like a shiny marshmallow. Pel could see why she wanted to lose a bit of weight before Christmas. He waited patiently, leaning against the wall by the exit while she showered and changed, and would have missed her if it hadn't been for the pink fluff. She came out of the changing rooms in a huddle of red-faced women, all slightly overweight, and it was only when she was level with him, about to step out into the chilling night air, that Gilbert nudged him and he came to life.

'Oh dear, not again,' Michelle replied to his request. 'Yes, of course I'll answer your questions. Follow me home, we can talk there.'

'We've just come from rue Jean Renoir. Isn't there a bar or something here?'

'They only serve fruit juices.'

'That'll do.'

'Through there.'

Sipping disconsolately at a lukewarm apple juice, Pel went cautiously into action.

'I apologise for the questions I'm about to ask. They are being asked of all those who knew Renée Clavier. I hope you'll bear with me.'

'It's the least I can do.'

'Thank you. What size shoes do you take?'

'I've already told you that. Well, I told someone. 38.'

'How much do you weigh?'

'55 kilos but going down.'

'The last time we met you said you weighed a little less than Renée. She weighed 55.'

'Which is exactly why I enrolled for these classes! After I told you that I got on the scales. I didn't weigh a little less, I weighed a little more.'

'How much exactly?'

'I really can't see what that's got to do with you.'

Pel sighed. 'Just answer the question.'

'A little more, 56, I've never weighed that much in my life before.'

Pel noted it down, wondering why women always lied about their weight.

'Where were you on the afternoon of 20th November?'

'The 20th, when was that?'

'Ten days ago. Your husband claims to have gone to Beaune for a dishwasher.'

'Ah, yes, I remember. I went into town to do the shopping and buy a present for my niece. My brother was coming for supper with his wife, she's expecting a baby and I wanted to buy something nice for her, it's a girl. I thought I'd save the postage after the birth.'

'What time did you leave the house?'

'Two, just after Laurent.'

'What time did you arrive in town?'

'About half an hour later. I went right into the centre and parked in one of the underground car parks, it was pouring with rain.'

'What time did you leave?'

'About six thirty as the shops were shutting.

'What did you do during these four hours?'

'Shopped, of course.'

'Did you see anyone you know?'

'I don't think so.'

'So no one can confirm you were in the centre of town all afternoon?'

'Oh, I see what you're getting at. Well, no – except of course my MasterCard receipts – Laurent had taken the cheque book, so I used the banker's card. They should have the time on them, shouldn't they?'

'Would you be kind enough to let me have copies?'

'I might just have them still on me, I haven't sorted out my bag since then. Hang on.'

She opened a large brown tasselled shoulder bag and disappeared momentarily inside, coming out triumphantly with a handful of tickets. 'There! That one's for the pink rabbit I bought Vikki – that's what they're going to call the baby. This one's for, oh, well, it's for a bra and panties I bought myself, rather frivolous but there you are. This one must be the butcher's – steak, pâté and *rillettes*, my brother loves *rillettes*. Bricorama, Maison Moderne, and this one's for the bank – I needed groceries after that and hardly thought I could pay for 10 francs' worth of potatoes, a salad and half a dozen apples with a piece of plastic.'

Pel shuffled the receipts, putting them in chronological order.

'This last one is for ten past four, only an hour and a half after you arrived.'

'I've just explained, I paid for the rest in cash.'

'So you have no proof you stayed in town until six thirty?'

'I don't like your tone of voice. Are you accusing me of . . . What are you accusing me of?'

'I'm not accusing you of anything. I'm just trying to establish your whereabouts on Saturday, 20th November.'

'I was in town! I've told you, 1 was shopping. When I'd finished, I left my bags in the boot of the car and went window shopping, trying to get ideas for Christmas, and unfortunately for me they don't give receipts for that!'

'Did you go into any other big stores, where security cameras film the public?'

'No. For heaven's sake, don't you listen, I was *window* shopping.'

'I thought you said it was pouring with rain?'

'I had an umbrella! A modern invention but very useful.'

'So two and a half hours on Saturday the 20th remain unaccounted for?'

'You horrible little man!'

Pel raised his eyebrows; being called 'horrible' was fair enough, but 'little' he objected to.

'Yes,' she went on, unaware of his feelings, 'if that's the way you want to put it . . . there are two and a half hours . . . no there aren't . . . the concert tickets!' Her head disappeared once more inside the voluminous brown bag and came out a moment later with a leather ring-file organiser. 'I put them in here for safe-keeping, in the pocket at the back. There!'

Pel held in his hand two blue tickets for SOIREE JAZZ to be held at the old Cornmarket, on 11th December. Stapled to them was a receipt:

```
              CARTE
             BANCAIRE

          MARCHE DE GRAIN
             21 DIJON
        Le 20/11/99   17:16:11
           Marché de Grain
          4681191 5651 10
         5131891020153204
            02/01      101
        3C3C6F1063E9D77B A
               08D0
        001 001 (1) 000009 C
             640,00FRF
           Pour information:
           Mont: 97,57 EUR
        Taux: 1EUR = 6,55957FRF
               DEBIT
          TICKET A CONSERVER
          MERCI AU REVOIR
```

Pel compared the card number, the one starting 513 and ending 204, with the other receipts and they tallied. She'd bought the tickets at 17 hours 16 minutes 11 seconds. There was no disputing it, she'd been in town all afternoon. 'Is this the concert you're going to with the Dentreuils?'

'As it happens, yes. How did you know?'

'Monsieur Dentreuil mentioned it. He also mentioned he

bumped into you in town – it would have been the afternoon in question?'

'That's right! I'd forgotten. There you are, you see, I'm not telling you fibs. And I think,' she went on triumphantly, 'I can persuade you I stayed there until six-thirty. Go and see the nasty little Arab chappie who works in the Beauparc car park. He'll remember me! He made me pay 250 francs for an afternoon's parking.'

'What did he do? Wrap your car up in cotton wool and rock it to sleep?'

Gilbert!

'Don't be facetious! I lost my ticket. I got to the exit barrier and couldn't find it, and this Arab said if I couldn't find the ticket I'd have to pay the forfeit! I was furious and I told him so. He didn't budge an inch, just pointed to a sign where the prices were displayed and I had to agree it was quite clearly marked: in the event of loss or destruction of ticket, a forfeit of 250 francs will be charged. I still protested. He said, if I didn't like it, he'd call the gendarmes and they could sort it out. Well, by then there was a queue of cars behind me, honking and hooting, all wanting to go home, so what could I do? I handed him my MasterCard. It was *so* embarrassing, in front of all those glaring motorists, I had to go into his smelly little office and wait for him to put everything on to the computer and for *it* to print the receipt.'

'Why didn't you pay in cash?'

'I didn't have enough left, I only drew 300 francs out of the bank, *un retrait rapide*, just enough for the groceries and a few bits and bobs.'

'Do you still have the receipt from the car park?'

'It might be in the car. I was so angry I just screwed it up and threw it on the floor.'

'But you say the incident is registered on their computer?'

'After all the arguing and trouble, I damn well hope so!'

'And it was the same banker's card as this one, the same number?'

'Yes it was. We're not called de Rochefoucauld, you know!'

'When you left the city centre . . .'

'At *six thirty*!'

155

'. . . where did you go?'

'Home, of course – my brother was coming for supper.'

While Pel and Gilbert were entertaining and annoying Michelle Chouillou, Nosjean, heavily dosed but now running a temperature, and Pujol were being entertained by Estelle Estampe, Bruno's younger sister. They'd gone to the block of flats at Cantepau and taken the stairs – the lifts weren't working, did they ever in council flats? – up to the sixth floor and knocked – no bell – on the door marked 604.

Estelle was nineteen and fat, and the ugly bulges of her body were accentuated by the tight clothes she was wearing; they looked ready to burst. She studied the police identification Nosjean offered her, shrugged and said, 'Yeah, whadja want?'

It took a few moments of explanation but she appeared to get the drift of what they were after and finally stepped back, inviting them in. 'Wanna beer or something?'

'Perhaps a cup of coffee, thank you. It's been a long day.'

'Only got instant, what about tea?'

'That's fine.'

While she wedged herself between the kitchen units to boil water and drop tea-bags into mugs, Nosjean and Pujol glanced round the room. Slovenly was too kind a word to describe it and Nosjean realised that if he didn't watch out, his own flat could rapidly deteriorate into the mess he was sitting in. There were dirty clothes strewn across the floor in piles, as if the wearer had simply stepped out of them and left them there. On the table, an assortment of beer bottles, mugs, glasses and bowls, together with opened letters, magazines and newspapers, waited to be dealt with. The windows were clouded with condensation and the large television set's screen was grimy with fingermarks. And by his side was a child's pot that smelt. At least he didn't have that in his flat. Not any more. He allowed himself a few brief moments to wonder how his four-year-old daughter was, whether she missed him the way he missed her. Anna was good fun, and good in bed, but the cuddles Erika had given him . . .

156

''Ere you are then.' Estelle placed two stained mugs in front of the detectives and banged down a carton of sugar cubes; in it was a sticky teaspoon. 'So you want to know about our Bruno? Mum works night shift at the factory, she won't be back till six tomorrow morning, and my sisters are out at the cinema. I've been left to sit my nephew, Tyron, that's Natacha's kid. What's Bruno done now?'

'Your brother hasn't been into work, and we were wondering if you know where he is.'

'Haven't seen him for a coupla days. Pissed off the other evening after supper.'

'Did he say where he was going?'

'Nah.'

'Or why he was going out?'

'Nah'.

'Did he seem upset or moody, anxious, angry?'

'Nah, none of them.'

'He just got up and walked out?'

'Took his hold-all, the one he uses for his work overalls and his lunchbox, 'cept he didn't have his lunchbox, he'd left that for Mum to wash.'

'But the hold-all appeared full?'

'I reckon so, didn't really notice.'

'Did he say anything between coming home and leaving?'

'Nah. Never does say much, our Bruno. Shouted at me last week that I was a lazy cow and should get a job. 'Snot easy, you know, unemployment being what it is, and anyway, who'd look after Tyron if I was at work? Go on, tell us, what's Bruno done? Been thumping someone again?'

'Does he do that often?'

'Yeah. Trouble is he doesn't know his own strength, when he gets his fists out, he always manages to break something. Broke my wrist once.'

'Why did he do that?'

'I said I'd tell Mum what he'd done. I did too, even after he'd bust my wrist!'

'What had he done?'

'Killed the bleeding cat. I don't think he meant to though, it was asleep on one of the tyres. When he reversed, it just flopped

157

off and fell under the wheel. It jerked a bit afterwards but its belly was squished flat. Mum loved that cat. We got another but that was a disaster, it had kittens in his bed. The whole blooming lot disappeared the next day, don't know what he did with them, poor little bleeders.'

'The car he reversed, was it his?'

'Yeah.'

'A Ford Escort?'

'Something like that, it's white.'

'Doesn't he like animals?'

'I don't think it's that. He says they're a nuisance, that's all.'

'Does he like women?'

'Oh yeah, he likes them all right. Had a girlfriend once, spent Sat'days and Sundays with her, I think, he certainly wasn't here. Maybe he's gone off to live with her – no, that can't be right, the last two weekends he's spent in front of the telly, farting and belching. He went out last Sat'day evening, or was it the Sat'day before, anyway, whatever, he was tucked up in bed on Sunday morning.'

'Could we have a look at his room?'

'Rather you than me, but help yourself.'

She led them from the living-room into a narrow corridor where there were four doors. Behind the first were Bruno's belongings. Nosjean didn't touch a thing – not allowed without a warrant – he simply studied the chaos. An explicit sex magazine lay open on the unmade bed, pictures of nude women were pinned up on the walls, some in Sadistic harnesses, brandishing whips. Two empty beer bottles lay on the floor together with a large muddy pair of boots. 'Note the boots, Pujol,' he croaked, 'we'll come back for them later.'

'If the *juge d'instruction* co-operates,' Pujol pointed out.

They turned back into the scruffy sitting-room. 'Thank you for your help, Estelle. Tell me, I don't suppose you'd have a recent photograph of your brother?'

As the two policemen left the block of flats, the swing doors banging back into their frames, Nosjean stopped dead, pointing speechlessly at the unmarked grey Citroën they'd left locked on the forecourt.

158

The wheels were missing.

'Half an hour! Half an hour and they've whipped our bloody wheels!'

'And probably sold them too,' Pujol added gloomily. 'Still, look on the bright side, at least they left the rest.'

Wednesday, 1st December

Persuaded that, while they waited for Bruno Estampe to appear and be brought in for questioning, it would be a good idea to have a few of his belongings examined by Forensics, in order to establish whether or not he had been near the caravan at Larroque, or near the small river Rin – which would be a step in the right direction – or perhaps to discover traces of blood on or in the fibres of a piece of his clothing or footwear – a hypothesis they hoped would be the case, particularly if it was proved to be the College Cadavre's blood, or Renée Clavier's – or, of course, they might just find the murder weapon itself, which would mean they could actually book the bugger – Brisard signed the necessary papers after only twenty minutes' argument.

Armed with the necessary requisition note 'for the confiscation of personal property belonging to, or in the possession of, Monsieur Bruno Théodore Estampe at Flat 604, Bâtiment E, Cantepau, relating to, directly or indirectly, the police enquiry here above specified . . .', Nosjean – dosed up to the eyeballs with every cold and flu treatment he could find in the local chemist's – together with Pujol, went back to Cantepau and, politely refusing another cup of vile tea and a cuddle with Tyron whose nose was emitting unsavoury pale green and yellow bubbles as he breathed, they collected Bruno's muddy boots, had a quick whip round his room for anything else that may or may not implicate his involvement in one or more murders, and, with a car that still had its wheels when they came out – thanks to an official-looking notice on the dashboard, 'POLICE VEHICLE', made hastily the night before – delivered them to Leguyder at the Forensics lab. Particular emphasis was put on the importance of the muddy boots.

Question: 'Do you want to know what they're made of? Or where they've been?'

Answer: 'Both.'

Reaction: 'You lot, you're worse than any other team in town. It's Pel's fault.'

Pel's fault or not, Leguyder's work was invaluable and conclusive. They weren't asking for much, just enough for a rapid arrest, followed by a few pertinent questions, and the prosecution of the answers, all done during the twenty-four hours they could detain their suspect, before, they hoped, charging him and taking the case to court – maybe in six months' time.

If they found him.

But at last they seemed to be closing in on the Butcher.

And possibly Renée's killer too.

No such luck, tell me another fairy story.

The connection with Renée was vague though. Pel wasn't convinced. A secret friendship springing from an occasional meeting at the Chambre de Métier – no one had ever seen them together. The possibility that they'd met when she worked in a restaurant not far from Cantepau was still *only* a possibility. These two suggestions had not been substantiated, therefore remained doubtful, and, in the absence of any other suspect, he and Gilbert continued checking the Chouillous' movements on 20th November.

December had announced itself with a thick frost and, as they set off out of the city, the countryside was frozen white. The peaceful Charolais cows had gone from the petrified fields, passing the winter inside the massive modern barns built behind the ramshackle farms that punctuated the plains. The hillsides were lost in an icy mist, making the landscape desolate, cold and somehow strange. It seemed even the birds had disappeared.

They arrived on the outskirts of Beaune at 0935, and at Conforama – famous for its dishwashers, and other household machinery – seven minutes later, conveniently placed as it was on the northern part of the city's bypass. Buttoning their heavy overcoats across their chests, they walked smartly across the enormous car park to the shop's entrance.

'Yes, sir, may I help you?'

Pel leaned over the long counter and let the smart assistant study his identification, while he studied the badge on the young man's jacket: 'Jean-Pierre Marco CONFORAMA SALES CONSULTANT here to help YOU.'

'We're trying to trace the movements of a Monsieur Laurent Chouillou. This is a receipt for an electrical appliance he bought. Can you confirm its authenticity?'

'Er . . .'

'You'll have a bleeding record of it on your computer, won't you?'

Thank you, Gilbert.

'Oh, yes, I see. Certainly. Date of purchase, please?'

'20th November.'

'Sorry, what was the name again?'

'Chouillou, C-H-O-U-I-L-L-O-U, Laurent.'

Marco tapped the information on to his keyboard and pressed Enter. 'Ah yes, here we are, a Candy dishwasher, one year guarantee, paid by cheque, registered at 1526, *carte nationale d'identité numéro* 97071100123.'

'Who made the sale?'

Marco looked puzzled. 'As a matter of fact I did.'

'Do you remember him?'

'Well, no, I deal with so many members of the public, I –'

'He came all the way from Dijon, does that help?'

'Ah yes, I do remember him. Odd that, we have a branch there. I wondered at the time why he'd driven so far. He told me he should have been decorating or something but his wife had set her heart on our special promotion and they were out of stock in his home town.'

'Were they?'

'I don't know, I didn't bother to check, just made the sale, that's what I'm here for, not to question customers' actions. I'm not a policeman, you know.'

Gilbert sniffed loudly. 'We'd noticed that, mate. As a bleeding salesman did you happen to look at him?'

'Yes, of course!'

'So describe him.'

'Well,' he was ordinary really.'

Pel hadn't anticipated much more. 'Nothing particular about him?'

'Like his eyes, nose, mouth,' Gilbert suggested, 'accent, big ears, his cock hanging out?'

Pel winced. Fortunately, Jean-Pierre Marco didn't, he was thinking hard. 'Now you mention it, yes, he had a slight squint. I wasn't sure which eye to concentrate on when talking to him. We're trained to give constant eye-to-eye contact, it makes the consultation personal, thereby boosting sales.'

'Anything else?'

'I don't think so.'

'It's enough, thank you.'

'He really was there then?'

'It seems so, Gilbert. Did you time our journey here?'

'Fifty-seven minutes, but this is Wednesday, the traffic would've been much denser on a Saturday afternoon.'

'How long were we in the shop?'

'No more than fifteen.'

'He'd've had to choose the dishwasher, find an assistant . . .'

'Saturday afternoon again, *patron*.'

'. . . go to the till and so on.'

'Say half an hour minimum?'

'He left at approximately two, arrived here at three, left at three-thirty . . .'

'Went round the back to load the machine, Saturday afternoon, he'd've waited a bit for his turn.'

'. . . left at three forty-five then, plus another good hour to get home, brings us to nearly five o'clock, at least. Let's go and see Bashir.'

'He'll be at work.'

'This evening then.'

'Why not at work?'

'We don't know where.'

'I do.'

'How . . .?'

'As we were leaving Laurent Chouillou's yesterday, I asked him how come he had a dirty Arab for a neighbour. He took offence.'

'I'm not surprised.'

'Told me, all righteous like, that Bashir was very respectable, and "I'll have you know," he said, "is an investments manager at la Caisse d'Epargne." '

'Good God, Gilbert, you surprise me.'

'Yeah, me too, a dirty Arab earning more than me.'

'That's not quite what I meant.'

'Please come in, gentlemen, take a seat.'

'Monsieur Bashir Azedj?'

'Correct. How can I help you?'

'You live next door to Laurent and Michelle Chouillou?'

'I do.'

'This is a routine enquiry to clear up one or two confusing events on Saturday, 20th November. I believe you helped him unload a dishwasher.'

'Yes.'

'What time was it?'

'Before dark. We unloaded, carried it into the kitchen, stripped off the carton casing, then we had a drink. By then it *was* dark, nearly six, so say, about five thirty.'

Thanking Azedj, a *very* respectable investments manager, Pel stepped thoughtfully into the street. 'I don't suppose you know where Michelle's brother works?'

'Sorry, guv. Maybe his wife'll be at home – they live on an estate in St Juery.'

'You have been a busy boy.'

'Easy, looked up Michelle's national identity card, had her maiden name on it, Lafon, and her place of birth, Vézelay. Rang the mayor's office. Yeah, they said, we've got a Lafon born in Vézelay, Christian Lafon, lives in Talant. What's his address, I said, police business, I said.'

'Good work!'

'Mm, well, I want to get home to the missus on time, haven't shafted her once since this all started.'

Why did Gilbert always have to spoil it?

'Madame Lafon?'

She was a small mousy woman, and was, as Michelle had told them, expecting a baby very soon. When she moved, her hands held her pregnancy as if she was frightened it might drop off and roll under the table.

'Yes, we went to Laurent and Michelle's that evening. We arrived around seven thirty and left just after eleven. I was tired.'

'Did either of them, at any time, leave the house?'

Her face crumpled in anxious concentration. 'I don't think so. I helped Michelle in the kitchen while the men talked in the sitting-room. I'm afraid I didn't help her with the washing-up afterwards, she said not to, her new appliance would do it. How I'd love a dishwasher, she is lucky. No, no, neither of them went anywhere. Why do you ask?'

'Routine questions, madame, nothing to worry about.'

After a few more minutes, they all stood up and walked towards the door. Pel politely shook her hand and thanked her.

Gilbert also shook her hand and grinned evilly. 'Keep your legs crossed, love, you look ready to split.'

'Gilbert!'

He went on grinning and followed Pel down the concrete pathway. 'No luck, huh? The Chouillous didn't do it.'

'Back to the drawing board. Maybe one of the others has come up with a new suspect.'

They hadn't.

Nosjean, in desperation, had been to see Boudet but the shock treatment made no difference. His head still thumped as if someone was trying to demolish it with a sledge-hammer, from the inside, his legs felt like eels in runny aspic, and his nose screamed 'Mercy!' every time he blew it, which was with monotonous regularity. Remembering the suicide victim laid out on one of the lab's metal tables, he decided that's how he felt. He would have been glad to curl up and die by six o'clock.

No such luck.

There was one small stroke of luck however.

As the students streamed out of their various classrooms and workshops, he did come up with a lad of nineteen who, while he wore size 43 boots, admitted selling his sister's new Salomons for 150 francs. 'I needed the dough! She never wore them! She'd had them six months and I'd only ever seen them on her feet once! Works, doesn't she? On the tills at Intermarché. I put an advert on the students' noticeboard, funny that, it was old Chouillou that bought them, couldn't work it out, weird. Anyway, I worked it out the next week, that smelly Renée was wearing them. Maybe it was her birthday, maybe Chouillou's wife didn't like them, how'm I supposed to know? My sister? She hasn't even noticed I snitched them yet.'

So now they knew where the size 39 boots had come from, he thought dismally, dabbing at his skinned nostrils. Contrary to what Leguyder had surmised, apparently it was Renée who'd been wearing them, and subsequently made the print near the stream – where she'd been dumped – carrying something weighing 3 kilos – or riding a kid's trike. Somehow it just didn't add up, and they still had no idea who'd killed her.

Except maybe Estampe, and he was still on the loose.

Génial.

Everyone was fed up. It had been a long drab day, producing very few results. They were no nearer to finding their elusive suspect for two horrific murders, and no nearer solving any of the other five million cases that had landed on their desks during the past four weeks. Muffled against the chilled mists, they'd walked their legs down to stumps; on farmers' endless muddy tracks, along smooth but never-ending pavements, over gravel drives, across neat lawns, and up and down flights of steps – ask a policeman how high they build the blocks of flats in the city, but step back before doing so. They'd asked questions until they were hoarse. They'd scribbled, calculated, puzzled and argued, and, in the end, what did it change? *Quedale. Nada. Niente. Niet. Walou. Rien.* Sod all. It changed nothing; they still had five million cases on the books, plus of course the two horrific murders. Their reaction to almost ten hours' useless exhaustive work was unanimous: *putain de merde*, shit a bleeding brick, or as the Arabic speaking members of the force would say, *rlla*.

One couldn't really blame them.

As the team were heaving on overcoats, looking forward to an evening at home instead of out on the streets tramping from one address to another, the phone pierced the contented rumble of another bloody day over. Pujol held up his hand and the sergeants' room fell silent, every one of them hoping it wasn't an emergency.

It was.

11

When he crashed the phone back into its cradle, Pujol licked his lips urgently. 'Bruno Estampe! Misset's giving chase! Tell Pel! I'm on my way!'

Seconds later, the whole squad was mobilised and tearing across town, blue lights flashing and sirens wailing through the darkened streets.

Gilbert was driving like a lunatic and Pel had difficulty shouting coherently, bouncing about unavoidably under the safety belt. 'Holy mother of . . .! Mind the Mercedes! Misset! Where are you?'

'Going south-east down avenue de la Première Armée! Stopped at traffic lights and there he was, sitting right beside me! Morrison's having trouble keeping up, I think he's spotted us. *Watch that* . . . bike. Jesus, a near miss. Coming into the square now. White Ford Escort, going like the clappers.'

'Registration number, Misset?'

'8644 . . . PR 21.'

'Pujol's approaching from rue Cazotte. He'll try and pick you up in rue de la Liberté to take over. Keep the line open.'

The two pairs of headlamps were weaving dangerously through the dawdling home-goers; a fist was raised by a lorry driver and his mouth worked its way round a long stream of swear words. Morrison didn't wait to find out what they were. Twisting the wheel roughly in his hands, he swung out round the stopped lorry and accelerated hard. Hundreds of red tail-lights ahead. Which ones was he supposed to follow?

Suddenly, the white car broke free, nearly knocked a pedestrian flying, and roared across the crossroads, bringing the traffic in all directions to a screeching halt. Morrison's feet were working fast, standing on the brakes, hitting the clutch, then recklessly, stamping on the gas. He was perspiring nicely now, terrified but exhilarated, the adrenaline pumping into his bloodstream, his heart pounding; all the same, he still wanted to close his eyes as they hurtled across the congested junction, waiting for the resounding crunch, the shuddering ricochet as another motorist hit them.

It never came.

The Escort was still on the wrong side, forcing its way through the oncoming cars, leaving a stream of hurriedly stopped vehicles parked at odd angles along the edge of the road. As they flashed past the two lanes waiting for the lights to change, Misset noticed startled faces caught briefly in the headlights, ghostly and white, eyes wide. Like faces from a grave; they reminded him of his mother-in-law and he nearly smiled.

Another roundabout. Wheels screaming, ignoring the speed limit of 50, they attacked it at 90 kilometres an hour, narrowly avoided a Renault Espace that braked violently to miss the Escort just coming off the hard shoulder, and swerved across the edge of the roundabout's carefully planted garden. The tyres spun momentarily before they finally caught, throwing up mud, and gravel, and a couple of dozen mangled pansies, purple and yellow petals flying in all directions. A traffic cop on the other side lifted his whistle to his lips and got no further: the two racing cars were gone, shrieking into the night.

'We've lost him!'

'*Merde!*'

'No, got him again! Turning right into rue du Chapeau. Slow down, Morrison! He thinks he's shaken us off.'

'Pujol, move into rue Bossue, then rue Michelet, be ready for him to emerge.'

Silence.

'Pujol!'

'Already on him. Accelerating, going fast towards Place St Philibert. Misset's behind me now.'

'De Troq', where are you?'

'Place St Bernard.'

'Too far. Keep closing. Nosjean?'

'Railway bridge, rue Monge.'

'Get into rue Condorret. Cheriff, close in from rue Mariotte.'

'He's turned left! Now in rue Condorret!'

'I'm there! It's narrow enough for . . . Road block operative . . . now!'

'*Putain*! Turned into rue du Mouton! He's stopped! Road works, we've got him!'

As the Ford Escort slowed to a halt, the council workmen, busy packing up for the night, turned and shouted. The car door was flung open and Bruno leapt out, running full tilt for the red and white barriers.

"'Ere! You can't go through there, mate!'

'Take cover! He may be armed!'

Cheriff, Misset, Morrison and Pujol were sprinting through crouched figures, jumping over fallen shovels and piles of sand then leaping the barriers like Olympic hurdlers. Except Misset, he ran round.

'*Stop! Police!*'

Bruno didn't stop, he didn't even hesitate, his feet kept pounding towards the end of the road. Cheriff had his pistol in his hand, Pujol was pulling his. They chased Bruno at full speed into Rampart Miséricorde, arms pumping, legs pumping, hearts pumping, praying Nosjean would be there to cut him off.

Nosjean was, out of his car, waiting, nose shining like a beacon, behind an open door, gun raised and balanced on the roof, taking careful aim.

'*Stop! Police! Or I'll open fire!*'

Bruno stopped. He stopped dead, twitched his head from side to side and leapt on to the wall in front of him. In a second he was gone.

Nosjean scrambled up just in time to see him land badly, bellow with pain and crumple in a heap. On the well-lit railway lines below, Bruno went on bellowing. Cheriff joined Nosjean on the wall, looking urgently to his left.

'*Merde*! There's a passenger train arriving on that track, we've got to get down there, haul him off.'

'Only access is over there! He's had it!'

A long shadow caught their attention, flickering to their right; it left the wall swiftly, like a bird, and flew inelegantly down to land beside Bruno. It stumbled, fell, cried out, then on hands and knees, put long lanky arms under Bruno's shoulders and dragged him clear. The passenger train hurtled past, its horn blaring as it went.

'Bloody hell,' Nosjean said and sneezed twice.

* * *

Two men were in hospital.

Two men had broken ankles.

One of them, under guard, was a suspected murderer: Bruno Estampe.

The other, blushing uncontrollably, was a policeman: young Morrison.

Pel was staring at Morrison. He looked about sixteen years old, pink in the face, his ankle suspended from a pulley in the ceiling, the rest of him wrapped in pristine clean white sheets. 'Did you notice how your seniors didn't attempt to commit suicide?'

Morrison went a deeper shade of puce. 'Yes, sir.'

'Pel.'

Morrison turned red. 'Yes, sir Pel.'

'No, drop the sir, just Pel.'

Morrison, now beetroot. 'Yes, Pel.'

'One reason was the fast train approaching. The lights were green, it wasn't going to stop. Another was they'd already seen the result of a man jumping; he broke his ankle. And policemen with broken ankles aren't much good to me.'

Morrison looked as if his head was about to explode. 'Yes, Pel.'

'You are lacking experience, you didn't think, you reacted hysterically and broke *your* ankle. Now you're no good to anyone.'

'I also got the bloody bugger though!' Pel blinked, it was the first time he'd ever heard Morrison speak, his voice was surprisingly deep and manly, for a bloke who blushed as soon as you looked at him. 'If I bloody hadn't he'd've been bloody mincemeat.'

' "Bloody" being the operative word, and I was coming to that!'

Morrison was back to glowing red. 'Yes, sir, er, Pel.'

'Congratulations.'

Morrison was doing impersonations of a beetroot again.

Thursday, 2nd December

Surprisingly it was sunny and warm, it made a nice change after the chilly winds and sudden frost, and Pel was whistling with cautious satisfaction as he knocked on the door of the forensic laboratory. It swung open and a technician allowed him entry. 'Finished the workman's boots?'

'I'm not sure, Leguyder's working on it personally.'

'What about the clothes and prints?'

'You'll have to ask him. He's in there. Monsieur! Commissaire Pel.'

Leguyder didn't look up from the microscope. 'Tell him to wait!'

'Too late, I'm already here.'

'Then sit down and don't interrupt. You spoiled an evening I was looking forward to, it's the last time I leave a private number with the police.'

'You were warned.'

'I missed the whole of *La Bohème*.'

'Like opera, do you?'

'Don't try and butter me up by saying you do too, I shan't believe you.'

'Well, actually, it's a bit above me, but my wife loves it.'

'I don't know how she puts up with you.'

Pel frowned, he didn't either. In fact, thinking about it, he wouldn't have given himself house room. 'She's an exceptional woman.'

'She must be. Did my technician frisk you?'

'What on earth for?'

'Cigarettes! They have strict instructions to refuse admittance to anyone carrying tobacco on their person.'

'I know the rules.'

'And you forget them every time you come here.'

'Give it a rest, will you?'

'The rest of what?'

Pel sighed, some days he hated scientists. 'Did you find anything on the workman's boots Nosjean brought in?'

'I found plenty. Do you want the complete list or simply the conclusion?'

'The conclusion.'

'The boots had not been to the campsite at Larroque, the mud didn't match.'

'What about the banks of the Rin?'

171

'No.'

'What!'

'The mud on the boots had a high limestone content, chalk to you, and diesel oil plus a lot of sawdust – they were the main ingredients, you understand. My guess is the wearer works as a chippie to the north-east of the city.'

'What about the laces, the stitching?'

'The same. No blood, no human tissue, we took them apart. All we found was sweat, rain and the mud I described.'

'Could he have washed them?'

'No soap, no detergent.'

'What about the clothes?' Pel asked desperately. 'There's got to be something!'

'Most of the stains are beer, gravy and coffee. On the trousers I found mud splashes again and diesel fuel. However, on the cuff of the shirt . . .' Now he looked up. '. . . there was blood.'

'Yes?'

'I compared it with the DNA profile of the College Cadavre . . .'

'Yes?'

'It didn't match.'

'Renée Clavier?'

'Not her either.'

'Another body we haven't discovered yet?'

'Incredibly, it's the blood of a cat.'

'It can't be!'

'Come and see for yourself!'

'What about the fingerprints and footprints we sent over last night?'

'They don't match with any found in the caravan.'

'They've got to!'

'They don't!'

'You've found nothing!'

'I would like to point out I can only find something if *you* provide me with the wherewithal. You have not.'

'Nosjean!'

'*Patron?*'

'Feeling better?'

172

'No, although my temperature was normal this morning.'

'About time. Leguyder can offer us no proof whatsoever. Who's at the hospital with Bruno?'

'Pujol plus two gendarmes.'

'Has Bruno said any more?'

'Only that he doesn't know what the hell we're talking about.'

'Has he asked for a lawyer?'

'Not yet.'

'Get a search warrant for the whole of his mother's flat, I want every single article of clothing from his room, search the lock-up cellar if they've got one, take his car over to Forensics.'

'*Patron?*'

'What!'

'I checked his story, that he was with a girlfriend every evening from six, when he knocked off work, to nine when he left to eat his supper, and that until the 13th he spent every weekend with her, all weekend. Our torso was murdered between the 3rd and the 10th.'

'The girlfriend could be lying.'

'She could be, but she works in a bar cum restaurant and has rooms over it. Her employer, who also lives on the premises, confirms her story. He encouraged Bruno to hang around, he spent money.'

'He could be lying.'

'We have half a dozen regulars to the bar who say the same thing, they all knew Bruno well.'

'Ever any trouble?'

'While he was going out with the girl, he was calm and well behaved. She chucked him on the 13th and they had a blazing row in front of all the customers. He started busting the place up but the owner and a couple of other brickies managed to get him out into the street.'

'Other brickies?'

'From the building site down the road, Entreprise Ubaldi. Bruno's firm are supplying the windows for the office block. He has a heavy-goods licence and had made a couple of deliveries, that's how he met the girl; they all went for a beer one evening after work. By the way, his employer says for an ex-con he was remarkably trustworthy. Most of his men lose tools, a euphemism

173

for swiping them for their own use. Bruno didn't. He was thinking of employing him permanently after his apprenticeship is finished.'

'For crying out loud! You're making him sound like a sodding saint, and we know he's not! Three acts of violence already registered and convicted.'

'He could be going straight.'

Pel snorted. 'So why did he take flight when Misset tried to pick him up?'

'He says he panicked, he's got a record and thought the ex-girlfriend had reported him for starting a fight.'

'So where's he been hiding?'

'In a boarding house in rue Chaudronnerie. He said he was fed up with interference, his sisters and mother always on at him, they never gave him a moment's peace, then we were there asking questions and stirring up trouble; he moved out. I went out there first thing, the landlady corroborated his story and let me into his room. There was precious little but it's on its way to the labs now.'

'I don't believe it!'

'I've sent Bardolle and Jourdain out to Larroque with his pictured. They're asking questions of the locals there and in the surrounding villages, someone may have noticed the white Escort near the caravan site, or Bruno himself, he's a big bloke, not easily missed. De Troq' and Cheriff have gone to Entreprise Bois et Alu to search his locker and talk to the men he worked with, and we'll do all the petrol stations between his home, his place of work, the bar and where the murder took place but unless we come up with something positive we've got no case against him.'

'What about Renée Clavier?'

'He says he doesn't know her.'

'Where was he on the 20th?'

'Having a tooth filled.' Nosjean dug into his pocket and pulled out his notebook. 'He woke up in the night with toothache and rang the dentist the next morning. They told him he could come in that afternoon but would have to wait while the appointments were seen. He waited from three thirty to four forty-five. He left quarter of an hour later and went into a bar for a glass of whisky.

174

The barman remembered him, there were very few customers because of the heavy rain. Bruno played on the electronic game Bazouka Balls, drank another whisky plus two beers, leaving at seven, it had stopped raining for a bit, when he went home. I've checked every detail, that's what he was doing.'

'Damn, blast and buggeration!'

'And another thing . . .'

'What? What now!'

'Boudet's shock treatment – it doesn't work. I'm aching all over. I feel a hundred years old.'

'That's nothing, I felt at least a thousand.'

'1000 francs?' Kate stood back, stroking Rasputin's head, to study the small desk again. 'Is it worth it, Monsieur Pancart?'

'To restore it to its former glory? Only you can make that decision, madame. It's an attractive piece, a fine example of Louis-Philippe, but in a very poor condition. It'll need quite a lot of work on it, one or two of the panels will have to be completely replaced.'

'Oh well, okay. How long will it take?'

'I could drop by tomorrow to collect it with the trailer, then, say, a week to ten days to do what's required.'

'Fine, it's a deal, I think I can just about afford it. Would you like a cup of coffee, or perhaps a glass of beer? You've been so kind coming all this way to advise me.'

'That would be most pleasant.' Pancart followed her through to the kitchen. 'Did you pay a lot for it?'

'That I couldn't tell you. My husband found it and brought it home, he said he thought it was a bargain, it was a sort of birthday present.'

'He must be a very generous man.'

Kate put the beer bottle on the table in front of him, next to the glass, and smiled. 'Yes, he was.'

Pancart noted the past tense. 'Are you divorced now?'

'No, no, he died last June.'

'I'm so sorry, I shouldn't have asked.'

'Don't apologise, how were you to know? Anyway, I've got to get used to talking about it.'

'What was he?'

The eyes watching her were dark and slanting, slightly foreign, they were inquisitive, searching eyes, wanting to know, attempting to make up for the unintentional faux pas, she thought; they were sympathetic and friendly.

'He was . . . an artist in a way. But also a scientist. He fitted small things together, rather like pieces in a puzzle.'

'A sculptor?'

'No, not really. Nothing so tangible. His puzzles were always built on fact, from a sound basis of knowledge, bit by bit, and the result was nearly always a surprise.'

'Beautiful? Like you?'

She laughed at the compliment. 'No, the end product of his work was satisfactory but definitely not beautiful. It could be very ugly.' Why was she playing games with this man? Because talking about Darcy in this way hurt less, she found it didn't make her want to cry, and she didn't enjoy crying, particularly in front of strangers.

'But you were able to appreciate its worth?'

'Definitely. Sometimes it would take months to reach its conclusion, in fact it was a relief when one of his cases came to an end.'

'Cases?'

'That's what he called them.'

'I think you're hiding something from me'. He smiled broadly, showing regular white teeth. 'I think your husband was, mm, perhaps a psychiatrist.'

It was a reasonable deduction, showing an astuteness she hadn't expected. 'How long have you been restoring antiques?'

'A little more than ten years now. I started in Paris in 1989, that's where I learnt the tricks of the trade, but it was a rat-race in the capital – not my business, that's always been calm, almost soothing, no, I mean just living. I moved here two years ago.'

'To get away from it all?'

'In a way. Paris is a suffocating place, here I have a larger workshop and pay less rent. The flat over it is adequate for a single man and my clients are, *comment dirai-je?*, more interesting and more interested, they take the time to discuss. Like you this evening.' He stood up and offered his hand for shaking. 'It's been a pleasure, thank you, Madame Darcy. I'll be back tomorrow, about seven, would that be convenient?'

Friday, 3rd December
Between short explosions into his handkerchief, subsequently blowing his nose and flinching, and the occasional hair-raising coughing fit, Nosjean took the morning meeting. Pel had gone to raise a rumpus *chez* Peugeot; his new car was now three weeks overdue. He was told 'first thing Monday' and went off muttering into the fog, back in force that morning. Now he was pestering Leguyder again and was sent away with a flea in his ear for the trouble. 'I've transmitted my findings. If you bothered to look at your e-mails occasionally you'd stop wasting my time and yours.'

'I came directly here.'

'You should have gone directly there!'

'I need information.'

'You're not the only one! I work for many people, not just your team, you know, and every article, every sample we receive demands my laboratory's concentration and time. Forensic science has become more and more precise, hence extremely complicated and thus time-consuming in the analysis, since its rudimentary application in the mid-1700s. It is undeniably essential in criminal detection, providing proof where the police would otherwise be left guessing. Sherlock Holmes would be flabbergasted by the progress we've made, although, it is interesting to note, the principle has always remained the same: observation. He only had his magnifying glass –'

'Stop prevaricating and tell me.'

'I am not prevaricating – and tell you what? That you make my life a misery, sending me piles of filthy overalls, muddy boots and smelly underpants?'

'I don't arrange it that way.'

'I wouldn't put it past you.'

'What did you find?'

'Read the e-mail!'

'Leguyder!'

177

'Plenty, I found hundreds of interesting particles and stains, but as far as you're concerned I think the word 'nothing' about sums it up.'

'Nothing, not a bloody thing,' he reported to Nosjean. 'Have one last talk to Bruno, and hurry it up. Last night Brisard was belly-aching about removing the police guard, our twenty-four hours are well and truly up.'

'He was released this morning.'

'What!'

'The *juge d'instruction* insisted, he was at the hospital himself. He also insisted we drove him home.'

'Jesus.'

'It wasn't him, *patron*, his belongings were clean – well, certainly contained no evidence against him. Leguyder's good at his job, he'd have found something had it been there. Everyone we spoke to yesterday didn't necessarily like Bruno but he was where he said he was, doing what he said he was doing. We even managed to find the petrol station he used. He was as regular as clockwork, every Saturday morning he put 100 francs' worth of petrol in the Escort. We've worked it out, he couldn't have gone further than to work, to his girlfriend's place of work and home. The stations on the way out to Larroque couldn't identify him and they're small country stations with a small local clientele, they notice strangers.'

'He could've filled up in an automatic machine at a supermarket.'

'He doesn't have a banker's card.'

'He could've paid by cheque or in cash.'

Nosjean sneezed loudly. '*Patron?*'

'*Oui, oui, je sais*, back to the drawing board.'

'*Mais non*, I just wanted to ask you, how long before Boudet's shock treatment started working properly?'

Brigitte Cluzel should have started work at nine o'clock. She was one of the secretaries employed by AXA Assurances, in their avenue Bouloc agency. This morning, however, after a great deal of thought, she'd made a decision and, ringing the office at half-past eight, left a message on the answerphone, apologising and saying she'd be coming in late, she'd explain when she arrived.

Parking her car carefully, adjusting the cardboard disc to show her arrival time in case an anti-social member of the Police de Ville strolled by, parking tickets at the ready, she zipped her jacket up and, shivering, made her way back up the street to the Hôtel de Police. As her heels clicked across the entrance hall, she was feeling just a little nervous but, sure she was doing the right thing, her duty, continued walking steadily towards the sergeant on duty.

'Madame?'

'I, um, I'd like to speak to someone about, well, about a man I met on Saturday evening.'

'Last Saturday evening?'

'Yes.'

'What about this man?'

'Well, he was weird. Not at first,' she said hastily, trying to justify her stupidity, 'it was afterwards.'

'After what, Madame?'

'After we went out into the street. He forced me into his car, he said I'd regret it if I didn't do what he wanted. It was horrible, very frightening, I think he was going to rape me.'

'You prevented it?'

'No, well, yes. As he was driving off, I jumped out and ran like hell back to the club.'

'Did he follow?'

'I don't know, I didn't have time to look. But, well, what with that . . . that thing that was found at the college, and the other girl murdered in the stream, I thought I ought to report it.'

'Just a moment, please, I'll call a detective for you. What name is it?'

Nosjean sneezed four times, blew his bright red nose, and staggered down the stairs. 'Madame Cluzel?'

They shook hands and went through the electronically operated security doors – operated by the desk sergeant, allowing detectives out whenever they wished but preventing the public from entering without first announcing themselves and being

179

accompanied by a member of the Hôtel de Police – back up to Nosjean's office.

When she was comfortably settled into the chair opposite him, he asked her to repeat what she'd told the officer downstairs. While she did so, he sucked a Strepsil and went on feeling lousy.

'He behaved perfectly normally inside the club?' he asked as she came to a stop.

'Well, yes. We danced, had a drink and danced a bit more. Then my friend, the friend I went with, Jeanne, started looking at her watch and said she ought to be making tracks, which left me with Jo-Jo.'

'Jo-Jo?'

'He introduced himself as Jo-Jo.'

'What was his surname?'

'I don't know, he never said.'

'Did you give him your full names?'

'No, only our Christian names.'

'Your addresses?'

'Certainly not!'

'Places of work?'

'No, we didn't talk about work, in fact we didn't really talk at all. He chatted us up, then we danced.'

'What about when you had a drink?'

'We talked about the club, the music, what people were wearing. Mind you, it wasn't easy, it was terribly noisy.'

'Fine, so Jeanne left, go on from there.'

'Well, we danced a couple of slows, it was that time of night, and he said he was getting tired and would like to go to bed. I was so stupid! I just didn't think, I said something like, yes, me too. We got our coats and went out into the street.'

'What happened then?'

'He said his car was parked round the back of the club. I said that was fine, mine was parked across the street. That's when he got nasty and I realised I'd made a terrible mistake, he thought I wanted to go to bed with him! I apologised, laughing, you know, and said I was very flattered but I really should be going home. He grabbed me and dragged me into the car park. He was really rough, I've still got the bruises on my arm. Then he

180

opened the car door and shoved me inside. I was so shocked I didn't know what to do. Anyway, when he stopped at the exit to see if anything was coming, I leapt out and legged it back to the club. Stayed there until they closed at six the next morning and asked a bouncer to see me across the road to my car. Thierry and I had a hell of a row when I got home.'

'Thierry?'

'My husband. I'd promised to be back by two.'

'Can you remember what Jo-Jo's car was like?'

Brigitte closed her eyes, in an effort to recall. 'It was a dark colour, that's all I can tell you.'

'Hatchback, break, saloon?'

'Not a break – I'm sorry; I can't remember, it happened so quickly and I was scared.'

'Can you remember him?'

'I'll never bloody forget him!'

12

It was worth a shot. Picking up the phone he tapped in the number for Debray and Rigal's room. 'Bringing Madame Cluzel down to look through the files. Slip the car-chase chap in among them, would you?'

He escorted her back down the stairs and introduced her to the two computer whizzes, then, offering her a seat, asked her for a basic description.

'Tall, dark, and handsome.' She was clearly embarrassed by this statement, smiling apologetically. 'But he was!'

They went through the file of appropriate and less appropriate mug shots. She shook her head at every one, even Bruno Estampe.

'Are you sure?'

'Certain. That's not him.'

'Okay, we'll try and build something up.'

Rigal put an empty face on the screen.

'No, his chin was more pointed.'

Rigal changed it.

'His eyes slanted slightly upwards. He was clean shaven, very clean looking – otherwise I wouldn't have danced with him. No, the hair was just a bit longer – but not over his ears. The lobes were smaller.'

'You remember his earlobes?'

'We danced a couple of slows, they were right by my nose.'

It took nearly an hour for her to be satisfied with the results. 'Yes,' she said at last, 'I suppose that's about right. It's not perfect but I honestly can't tell you how to make it so.'

Between Strepsils, Nosjean saw her out and thanked her. As she left, she smiled kindly at him. 'I was stupid, wasn't I?'

'Perhaps a little lacking in caution,' he replied and sneezed.

'Well, thank you for your help. I hope you catch your killer, and you know . . . it's none of my business, but you really ought to take something for that cold.'

Nosjean was feeling gloomy as he went back to Rigal. 'Print me a dozen, would you?'

'Sure thing. You sound awful, why don't you take something?'

'Just print the bloody things, will you!'

Armed with the bloody things, Nosjean wearily climbed the stairs and distributed the portraits to the remaining members of the team, or left a copy on each uninhabited desk with a note: 'Do any of your carpenters look like this? Renee's friends or neighbours?'

Pel picked one up and looked at it. 'Who is it?'

'A man who tried to abduct a woman from a night-club car park.'

'And?'

'She was intelligent enough to run for it.'

'You think it's the Butcher?'

'I think I'm about to expire.'

'If you do, I'll have you suspended.'

'Thank you for your few kind words.'

'It's only a cold, man.'

'Yes, your sodding cold!'

Gilbert was sitting with his feet up on Pel's desk as he walked in and slammed the door. 'What do you think you're doing!'

'Reading, guv.'

'*Playboy*? *Lui*? *Tits and Bums*?'

'Renée Clavier.'

'Good God! You don't mean you're actually working?'

'Can't think how it happened.'

'You must be slipping, Gilbert. And what has your short burst of erudition told you?'

'Not a lot.'

'So why did you bother?'

'I don't know . . . except . . . well, it's not what's written here, it's what's missing that's worrying me. Can't put my finger on it, there's something written between the lines and I just can't make it out.'

'Give it to Pujol, he's got special glasses for that sort of thing.'

Gilbert frowned, totally confused.

'Oh, for God's sake, Gilbert, stop looking so thick, you're worse than Misset.'

'Not quite, guv, I plug my brain in every morning and right now it feels as if it's about to blow a fuse.'

'Well, don't do it here, the cleaners'll complain. What's bothering you?'

'That's just the trouble, I don't know. I think it's the timing. The Chouillous both have cast iron alibis and yet . . .'

'And yet they are the only ones who had any real contact with Renée, except her mother.'

'Right, and she wasn't shafting her.'

'Does your mind ever deviate from its one track?'

'Not often. On the other hand Chouillou was, regularly.'

'But he was in Beaune, we've done the trip and it's impossible for him to have got back, picked the kid up, killed her, disposed of her and been back at his house when he was.'

'Yeah but . . .'

'You want to check again?'

'Sort of.'

Pel sighed, signed the letters on his desk, read his e-mails, replied to three, and went out with god-awful Gilbert to 'sort of' check.

The bank manager was very helpful, after having Pel's credentials verified, of course. As he explained, he couldn't give out confidential information about his customer's account to anyone who just walked in off the street. Having got that cleared up, he tapped in the number of the card, marked clearly on the receipts Michelle had found at the bottom of her bag.

'Here we are, Monsieur Laurent et Madame Michelle Chouillou. What did you want to know?'

'The times of purchases paid for by her card on 20th November.'

'The 20th . . . here we are. 14.15.11: New Baby – *Vêtements et accessoires pour les tous petits*. 14.41.23: Lingerie de Luxe.'

'Forget the seconds, they're of little importance.'

'Very well. 1505: Dubois Viande. 1535: Bricorama Do-it-Yourself. 1559: Maison Moderne. 1610: Crédit Bourgogne, *un retrait rapide*. 1640: Stop Presse. 1721: Marché aux Grains Theatre and Auditorium. 1800: Vins du Terroir. 1833: Beauparc Parking.'

'Stop Presse?'

'Mhm, 1640, for the sum of 83 francs.'

'And Vins du Terroir?'

'1800, for 246 francs.'

'We haven't got either of those.'

'Well, it's here on the computer, there's no mistake.'

The two men sat in the car and studied the confirmed times. 'The longest pause between the purchases is only forty-one minutes; it's not enough, not nearly. It would still take nigh on an hour and a half to make the return journey to the stream, plus the time it took to kill and dump the girl. The discrepancy should be more like two hours.'

'We're flogging a dead horse.'

'It certainly looks like it.'

'Speaking of horses, I'm hungry enough to eat one. What about lunch, guv?'

Denis Dentreuil was less helpful. 'Look, I'm just leaving. Can't you come back later? It's Joelle that works with Michelle, not me.'

'Perhaps we could accompany you to your place of work and explain to your employer. I'm sure he'll allow you a few minutes to help the police with a murder enquiry.'

'I'm not going to work, I'm self-employed.'

'What do you do?'

'I'm a househusband, actually I was just off to the cinema.'

'This won't take long.'

Dentreuil sighed impatiently, obviously annoyed at the intrusion. '*Putain, d'accord.* You'd better come in.'

'The last time we spoke to you, on the 29th, you said you'd bumped into Michelle Chouillou and she invited you to a jazz concert. That would've been on the 20th.'

'The concert's on the 11th.'

'I would like to establish the day you saw her in town.'

'Oh, yeah, I don't know, it was a Saturday – not last Saturday, the Saturday before. It was pissing down.'

'20th November.'

'If you say so.'

'I do say so because I have a copy of the box office's receipt with that date for four tickets for a concert on 11th December.'

'Then it must've been.'

'But I remember your wife saying you paid for your two tickets. How do you explain that?'

'I paid her back afterwards.'

'So she invited you to the concert and went to buy the tickets alone?'

'No, I bought them.'

'But you just implied she was the one that paid for them.'

'She did. She gave me her card and I did the queuing.'

'Do you know her code?'

'She wrote it on my hand, said to pay for all four and I could reimburse her later.'

'When was that?'

'Well, actually it was a couple of days later.'

'Hang on a minute there, guv, she had her card on her when she left the car park at 1830.'

'I gave *that* back to her immediately.'

'Let's get this straight. What time did you bump into her?'

'I don't know, I don't wear a watch.'

'She gave you her banker's card and you queued for four concert tickets and paid with that card.'

'Right so far.'

'Then you returned the card to her immediately but paid her back a couple of days later.'

'Well, when I say I gave it back immediately, what I mean is the same day, when I met her at the car park.'

'And between her giving you the card and the car park, you had it on your person?'

'I couldn't give it back if she wasn't there, could I?'

A gleam came into Pel's eye, he was beginning to understand.

'Are you responsible for 83 francs being paid to Stop Presse and 246 francs to Vins du Terroir?'

'So what if I am?'

'Answer my question, are you?'

'Yes. She said I could. She said, "Buy yourself a mag to read while you queue and a bottle of wine for supper." So I did.'

'More than one magazine, n'est-ce pas? And more than one bottle of wine, I think.'

'So I bought a couple of magazines, it was a long wait.'

Gilbert grinned evilly. 'And the wine, you greedy bugger.'

'Don't you call me a bugger!'

'How many bottles did you buy, monsieur?'

'A case.'

'Six?'

'Yes, so what! I told her. She didn't seem to give a shit, said not to worry about it. So I didn't.'

'Go on.'

'What?'

'What happened after you met her at the car park and you returned her card to her?'

'She drove me home.'

'Why was that?'

'Christ! There's no law against it!'

'Of course there isn't, just explain why, would you?'

'I went into town by bus, okay? I don't drive. She said if I did the queuing she'd run me home afterwards. Told me to meet her by the south entrance of Beauparc car park at six thirty. So that's what I did. We went down to the car and she couldn't find her ticket. There was a fuss about that, specially when she didn't have enough cash to pay. I didn't either, then I remembered I had her card.'

'And that's when you gave it back?'

'Sure.'

'Shame, you could've gone on using it for days.'

'You rude bastard!'

'Take no notice of him, monsieur. Tell me about the concert tickets?'

'Oh hell, all this fuss about a couple of concert tickets. No, I kept them.'

'All of them?'

'It wasn't deliberate! She was in a hurry, her brother or some-thing was coming for supper, so I just left it, she dropped me off and drove away. I gave two of the tickets plus the receipt for payment, plus a cheque for our two, to Joelle. She sorted it all out Monday morning at school.'

'What about the mags, mate, and the wine?'

'She said not to worry!'

'She drove you home?'

'I just said so, didn't I?'

'Did you notice anything in particular about the car?'

'Like what?'

'Anything out of the ordinary. Were the wheels muddy, for instance?'

Dentreuil thought for a moment. 'No, I don't think so,' he said, 'but I'll tell you what, it was bloody hot inside and full of condensation.'

'It was raining, her coat must have been wet.'

'She wasn't even wearing a mackintosh, just that repulsive pink thing.'

'But it was hot inside the car?'

'Bloody stifling. When she went off to pay, I turned the heater off. She didn't seem to notice when she came back, but then she was a bit flustered. Normal enough after being forced to pay 250 francs for a few hours' parking.'

The man in Beauparc car park's small office was, as Michelle had indicated, of Arab origins. He was sitting behind a large glass observation window, watching the cars come and go, mostly young women in a hurry to collect children from school. It was 1615, the primary schools were due to finish lessons in quarter of an hour. Pel waited until the eight queuing drivers had paid, then walked across the echoing concrete vault. By now the attendant was holding a cup in his left hand and a green tartan thermos in the right; he was pouring coffee, while a cigarette smouldered in the ashtray. Pel knocked at the door and opened it.

'Afternoon, missieurs. You boys loss your ticket?'

'Does it happen often?'

'Less an' less. Too esspensive, missieur.'

Gilbert closed the door behind him and flashed the police identification necessary before engaging on official business.

'I've din nothing – nothing I can think of.'

'Non, mon frère, t'inquiète, we'll citch you later.' Gilbert being obnoxious.

'You are not my brother, and I'm not worried. Assou Aanaoui at your service.'

'Bonjour, Assou'. Pel offered his hand and, putting down his coffee, Assou shook it. 'I'm Commissaire Pel, we're checking a woman who claims to have been parked here all afternoon on 20th November. She paid 250 francs by banker's card.'

'Be on my computer.' Assou tapped and fiddled until the relevant date came up on the screen. 'Jist one that day.' He rolled his eyes. 'I remember her too, wearing a pink fluffy jacket. Made a fuss because I charged her the fourfeet. That's the rule, written up there on the wall, in big bold letters. No ticket, pay 250 francs. And everyone honkin' and hootin' behind her.'

'What time was it?'

''Scuse me, Missieur.' A square white ticket appeared through the slot in the window. Assou took it, fed it into a square box and smiled at the driver. '20 francs, please.'

Two ten franc coins dropped into the dish. 'Thank you, madame, bon après-midi.'

The barrier rose and the car disappeared.

Another ticket.

'20 francs, please. Merci, bonsoir.'

The barrier rose again.

'What was the question?'

'What time did the 250 franc woman leave here?'

Assou turned back to his screen. 'Six thirty-three and thirty-two seconds.'

'Was she alone in her car?'

'No, sir, she was with her hubby.'

'Can you describe him?'

'No, sir, he stayed in the car.'

'What makes you think it was her husband?'

'Because he gave her the banker's card. "Here,", he says, "pay with this." '

'You heard what he said?'

'Yes sir, he leaned over and stuck his hand out, but I didn't see his face. Sorry 'bout that.'

'Don't worry about it, *mon frère.*'

Assou flashed a look of irritation in Gilbert's direction.

'You ought to try working with the creep,' Pel said to Assou, who grinned, showing perfect clean white teeth. 'Tell me, was the woman argumentative?'

'Oh yes, sir, says she's only here since after lunch-time. I says, sorry, if you got no ticket, you pay the fourfeet.'

'Thanks for your help.'

'Don't be surprised when you leave,' he said, grinning again. 'Minimum charge 10 francs, it's written up there, see, in big bold letters.'

ALL TICKETS MUST BE SHOWN AT THE BARRIER

IN THE EVENT OF LOSS A FORFEIT OF 250 F

WILL BE CHARGED

FOR HOURLY TARIFFS SEE BELOW

Minimum charge of 10 F

Gilbert turned back from the notice. 'Just a minute, mate.'

'It's the rule! Even for policemen.'

Gilbert was still pointing at the red-lettered words. 'Explain that.'

'It's legal, sir, it's all written up there −'

'Yeah, we know, you Arab twit, in big bold −'

'Shut up, Gilbert. Assou, I think he'd like you to explain exactly how the system works.'

'Well, sir. You come down the ramp and take a ticket from the machine at the entrance. When you leave, you hand the ticket to me, I put it in the machine. It tells me how much and the price lights up outside so the driver can read it.'

'In case they're bleedin' Arabs and don't understand French.'

'Gilbert! Go on, Assou.'

'Well, that's it really, except if you lose your ticket, then –'

'You pay a fucking fourfeet, you said that ten times already'.

'Gilbert! So,' Pel continued, 'if I wanted to, I could come in at eight, stay two hours and leave, having paid 10 francs. Then I could come back later stay another two hours and leave, having paid another 10 francs.'

'If you wanted to.'

'Or I could have come in five minutes ago, lose my ticket and have to pay 250 francs.'

Assou shrugged. 'That's the way it works.'

'Thank you, Assou, it's been a pleasure talking to you.'

'The pleasure was mine, sir.'

'Drive out of the city centre on the D996, heading for Arney-le-Duc. When you get to Arney-le-Haut, drive on to La Garrigue. From there you're to take the D32 to Auberive, I want to have another look at the Rin. Then bring me back here as fast as you can, into this car park and stop. If I'm right in what I'm thinking, we will then be paying a call on the wine merchant and Stop Presse.'

Gilbert sighed wearily. 'Anything you say, missieur. Have you got 10 francs on you, guv? Your new best friend, Pain-in-the-Assou's waiting by the barrier and if his grin gets any wider the top of his head'll fall off.'

'Now will you give me the search warrant?'

Brisard leaned back in his chair and folded his hands over a rich man's stomach, bulging under his loud striped tie. 'There is still is no proof.'

'The search warrant will give us that.'

'I'm not satisfied.'

'You never are. How am I supposed to arrest Renée's murderer if you won't let me look in this damn house?'

'What are you looking for?'

'The size 39 boots, her clothes, anything that can place her and the murderer in the same place at the same time on the afternoon of 20th November.'

'It's not specific enough, Pel. You're working from supposition not hard evidence.'

'But my supposition is not impossible.'

'Slightly far fetched but –'

'Premeditated murder often is. You'd be amazed at the ingenuity criminals can come up with when they want to get away with something.'

'Even so –'

'Oh, sign the fucking thing, Brisard. You might like twiddling your fingers but I want to get home to my missus this evening, I haven't shafted her ever since –'

'Lieutenant! How dare you speak to me like that! I'm an appointed examining magistrate – a little respect, please!'

But he signed it.

'Pompous old windbag,' Gilbert muttered as they made their way out to the car.

'Congratulations, you've at last managed to make a pertinent observation, and without swearing.'

Kate was swearing silently, she'd just shut a finger in the drawer after looking for a biro. She hadn't found one.

'I had dozens of them a week ago, bought a whole new pack, I can't think where they've got to.'

Monsieur Pancart smiled understandingly. 'Don't worry, I've got something to write with. If you could just find a piece of paper, I'm sure we'll manage.'

'Pour yourself another glass of wine, I'll go and search.'

She came back a moment later empty-handed and apologising. 'I think my twins must have had a prolific drawing session, there isn't a sheet of paper in the house.' Picking up the diary she kept by the phone, turning to the section marked 'Notes', she tore out a page. 'Sorry, it's the only thing available.'

Pancart smoothed the page on the table top then, taking a pencil stub from his pocket, asked her to repeat her telephone number.

Kate watched while he wrote, checking he got it down correctly, then sat down to finish her drink. 'About a week?'

'It should take at least that. I'll give you a ring when it's finished and you can come and inspect.'

'Oh. Won't you just deliver the desk back here?'

'I'd rather have your approval first.'

'I suppose you'll want paying then?'

'As you wish, either then or when I do deliver, for the moment that's not what's worrying me. I must confess I'm a little concerned about one of the legs, I didn't notice yesterday but it's rotten. I'll have to find a wood-turner for that and I don't know one offhand. It may take a little longer than anticipated. I'll keep in touch, let you know if there's going to be a delay.'

They shook hands, wished each other good evening and Pancart drove off along the remote track, his headlights, flashing across the tree trunks, making eerie moving shadows, gaunt and black in the night. She patted Rasputin's solid body, glad to have such a faithful companion to guard her and the boys. 'Come on, Razz, let's stock up for the evening.'

It was only when she went back inside with an armful of logs for the fire that she noticed he'd forgotten his pencil: a small flat red stump, attached to a piece of string. She picked it up, turning it over in her hand, then, deciding it couldn't be very important, put it on her diary by the phone, thinking she'd return it the next time they met. Calling the children through for supper, she began laying the table, unaware of the eyes watching her through the window.

Saturday, 4th December

'Very nice,' Pel said as the tour of inspection finished. Laurent Chouillou hadn't been pleased to have another afternoon's decorating interrupted but was looking happier now. 'I see you have central heating too, very efficient.'

'I keep it on at a low temperature so the pipes don't freeze.'

'And so it's warm enough,' Gilbert added, 'to walk around starkers in between –'

Pel interrupted. 'But from the look of it, I see you also use the fireplace.'

193

'To burn rubbish and old pallets. Once I've got it going I bring in the fallen branches from the yard, it makes it nice and cosy, and brings the temperature up quickly while I get started.'

'. . . shafting?'

'Gilbert, I'd appreciate it if you'd shut your mouth and open a sample box, we need the contents of the grate.'

'What on earth for?'

'Just checking, Chouillou, just checking.'

'Another evening ruined! I'm sure you do it deliberately, Pel.'

Leguyder was standing with his hands on his hips just inside the lab door.

'I promise I don't. But the results are very important, you could confirm the identity of a murderer.'

'Or not, as the case may be.'

'Please don't keep me in suspense. What did you find in the ashes?'

'For convenience and rapidity, I'm prepared to indicate a number of substances we have been able to distinguish quite quickly but you understand our work isn't yet finished, there may be other things we've not yet uncovered. These tests take time.'

'Just tell me!'

'Let me frisk you first.'

'Oh, for God's sake,' but Pel lifted his arms and allowed two packets – two packets? Ah yes, current and emergency – to be removed from his person and placed in a tray by the door.

'Follow me into my office. With all the rubbish and rags you've been giving me, I'll have to refer to my notes.'

For once it wasn't a computer screen that divulged the information; instead, Leguyder leafed through an ordinary paper notepad. 'I haven't had time to collate it all properly,' he explained, frowning at his own writing. 'Ah, here we are: a large amount of melted plastic, small amount of melted rubber, we think rubber gloves, paper, rags, some woollen and synthetic fibres all incinerated, and five metal buttons from a pair of jeans.'

'But the boots, what about the boots?'

194

'No boots.'

Pel's face fell.

'But we did find something that may help, although it must be identified as originating from the Salomon sportswear factory.'

'What? What!'

'Sixteen hinged metal eyelets and twelve riveted hooks, the sort used for lacing walking boots above the ankle.'

'Bingo! I love you, Leguyder.'

'Good grief.'

'Gilbert! Ring your missus, tell her not to wait up for a shafting! Ring my missus, tell her you're invited for supper! Ring Brisard, ruin his evening, ring Lambert, ring the bells of Notre Dame, I think we've cracked it!'

Sunday, 5th December

The appointed lawyer was not best pleased to be called out so early on a Sunday morning. He'd been on his way back from his girlfriend's favourite disco and now he was tired, shifting from foot to foot in his highly polished dancing shoes, loosely fitting black trousers and very snazzy shirt, as he stood with the group of men round the wooden table and chair on which was sitting the only woman in the room. Maître Brisard was standing next to him, also looking angry; he'd already threatened Pel with a stiff reprimand if this was a false alert. Gilbert was picking his teeth with a broken match. He'd just completed the necessary caution – 'You are not obliged to say anything, but if you do it may be used in evidence against you . . .' – for the second time, so that it was on record in front of irrefutably acceptable witnesses, and asked if she understood what he'd said. She'd shrugged, the expression on her face bored, as if she considered Pel and his partner as a very much lower form of life. 'Yes, I understand.'

Pel lit a cigarette and studied the small face poking out of the pink fluffy jacket. He inhaled and exhaled, savouring the moment, knowing he'd got it right. All the way over and back in the car, he and Gilbert had been going through the details; they'd got the timetable right, they'd got motive, they'd got evidence. It had occurred to them, as they brought the suspect up from the cells, that the only thing they hadn't got was the murder weapon, but in these days of advanced science it wasn't much of a handicap. They knew what it was and the likelihood of Michelle having it in her possession or access to it was great enough for it to be accepted in court.

'You are Michelle Lafon, wife of Laurent Chouillou?'

'Of course I am.'

'Where were you on the afternoon of Saturday, 20th November?'

'In the city centre, my banker's card receipts prove it.'

'We have a witness willing to testify that you left that card with him between approximately 4 p.m. and six thirty, and that with it he purchased two magazines, four concert tickets and six bottles of wine.'

'Six!'

'Yes, madame.'

'I'll kill him!'

The lawyer opened his mouth, yawned and closed it again.

'I've spoken to at least one shopkeeper who remembers the man with the code written on his hand. I would therefore like you to account for your movements while he was using your card.'

'I was window shopping.'

'Why didn't you wait to buy the concert tickets yourself?'

'I hate queuing.'

'So you went window shopping?'

'Yes.'

'For two and a half hours?'

'Yes.'

'You didn't go to your car?'

'I don't need a car to go window shopping.'

'When you did go to your car, at half-past six, didn't you find it strange that it was so warm inside?'

'I can't remember.'

'Monsieur Dentreuil says he had to switch the heater off – he described it as stifling.'

'Then yes, I suppose it was.'

'Why was it stifling if it had stood empty all afternoon in a cold underground car park?'

'I don't know, it works well. There's a booster fan.'

'Or perhaps you'd been cold driving into town and switched it on then? It was a very chilly day.'

The young lawyer frowned and began cautioning her but was interrupted by her reply.

'*N'importe quoi.*'

'He also said you were flustered?'

'He's got a big mouth!'

'Why did you give the impression of being flustered?'

'I was in a hurry, my brother and his wife were coming for supper.'

'Of course, you had to get the meal ready.'

'That's right.'

'Green salad, ready washed, dressing from a bottle, rillettes and pâté bought that afternoon, and grilled steak, followed by fruit. For four people. Is that correct?'

There was a pause.

'For the sake of the recording, please note Michelle Chouillou nodded her head. Madame, the meal I have just described takes approximately ten minutes to prepare, with a few extra minutes to grill the steak, a total of about 15 minutes. For your information, I bought the ingredients yesterday evening and took them home. Present for the experiment was my housekeeper who did the cooking, my wife, an impartial participant who timed the operation, Lieutenant Gilbert, standing on my left, and, of course, myself. We arrived at my home at just before nine, the entire meal was on the table by twenty past.'

'I like things to be just right.'

'Neat and tidy, everything in its place.'

'Yes.'

'Did you know that when you burn walking boots the eyelets and hooks needed to fasten the laces don't disintegrate?'

Michelle's eyes lifted abruptly. 'I beg your pardon?'

'Buttons from jeans don't either.'

She looked from Pel to Gilbert and back. 'What's that . . .?'

'We found both in the fireplace at your house in La Garrigue.'

She was frowning. 'It's not poss . . . when did . . .? Laurent!'

'It's also interesting to observe that the journey from Beauparc car park to La Garrigue takes approximately an hour there and back. You could easily have gone there after meeting Monsieur Dentreuil and been back in time to meet him at six thirty and then drive home. This could explain the car's warmth and your being flustered. It had perhaps taken longer than you'd anticipated?'

Now she was on her feet, the chair tipping over and clattering to the floor, pointing an accusing finger at Pel. 'No it didn't, you bastard! I'd timed it perfectly . . .'

13

It took a while to calm her down, then sitting once more at the table she gave her story to the police.

'It was quite by mistake I found out, actually. Laurent had gone, as he always does, over to the house after lunch to paint, leaving me to do the housework, the shopping and prepare our evening meal.' Her voice was nonchalant, she was sure of what she was saying and apparently proud of her achievement. 'Well, during the afternoon, once I'd finished the housework, I had a shower, put on clean clothes, a new pair of designer jeans and a dear little pink jumper that showed my tummy button, and thought, well, what a waste. There I was all prettied up and Laurent was at La Garrigue. We weren't receiving guests that evening, all I had to do was heat up a *blanquette de veau* that I'd bought, and I thought, well, what if I pop over and see how Laurent's getting on. It was 6th November, I remember it clearly, there was hardly a soul on the streets, the whole country, it seemed, were stuck in front of their tellies watching the Australians beat the Blues in the rugby final in London.'

'Cardiff,' Pel corrected, he also remembered the French defeat clearly. Such a disappointment.

'I beg your pardon?'

'The final was in Cardiff, Wales, not London.'

'What's the difference? They're both in England! Where was I?'

'Remembering clearly that there was hardly a soul on the streets.'

'Yes, because of the rugby final and my poor Laurent painting the walls of our sitting-room pale apricot. It's such a warm, soothing colour, so complimentary to my complexion. I felt sorry for him, you see, working away like that, and decided to pop over and tell him to come home early, perhaps rent a video for after dinner, something romantic, like *Titanic*, you know, to set the mood. Well, off I went, full of the joys of spring, well, autumn really, thinking it would be a lovely surprise for my husband. I parked the car in the drive and walked up. It was a frisky sort of day, bright sunshine but cold. I didn't call out, because, well, I wanted to surprise him, creep up behind him and give him a cuddle, and say, come home sweetie, let's celebrate. Well, something like that, if you know what I mean. But I couldn't find him. Not in the *still* undecorated kitchen, not in the sitting-room he was supposed to be finishing that day, so I went upstairs, thinking the poor thing had perhaps been tired and dropped off on the mattress. I should explain, sometimes he stayed the night if he wanted to finish something vital, he'd camp there, and carry on working the following morning then come home for Sunday lunch, sleeping most of Sunday afternoon. Poor Laurent, I thought. My God! When I got to the landing, I could hear the most revolting animal noises, it sounded as if he was in pain. I crept closer, and well, there they were. There in our newly decorated bedroom, the primrose yellow all glowing and pretty, and those two on the mattress. It was disgusting! They were sucking and licking each other, I've never seen anything so degrading in my life, and all the time this moaning from Laurent's throat, while she dribbled all over his . . . his thing. I turned and fled! I didn't want to be witness to such debauchery. I ran down the drive and drove off. On my way home, I was thinking more and more clearly, and it occurred to me that this dirty little girl, who we'd shown nothing but generosity and kindness, wanted my husband. *My* husband! We were married in church, in the sight of God, until death us do part. And that's when I decided to get rid of her. Until death us do part you see, it was the only solution. It took a while for me to work it out though, another weekend passed, another weekend when Laurent was at La Garrigue. I went there again, just to make sure, you understand, and it only reinforced my desire to defend my property. Laurent was mine! After that, I did a couple of test runs in and out of town, to and from the house, and from there into the country to a very remote stream. I was sure she wouldn't be found for weeks. My timing was right, it was just possible to get to La Garrigue, do what I had to do, undress her and burn all her belongings then drive her to the stream, and make it look as if she'd been raped, I hoped you'd think it was the same man that butchered that other poor creature at the college. How disgusting that was! Well, all went well until I met her. She was sitting on the terrace in the rain waiting for Laurent. I beckoned to her and she crossed the yard and I told her to get into the car, I had a message for her. In all honesty, I lost my courage, with her sitting beside me, I knew I just couldn't go through with it, I'm not a murderer, you see, and she seemed pleased to talk to me. She told me she'd promised to help with the painting, to pay us back for everything we'd done for her. I told her to keep her hands off my husband. At first she acted the innocent until she realised I'd actually seen them in their depraved activity. I told her exactly what I'd seen. Well, she couldn't argue with that, could she? I could feel my heart pounding, I told her she was a dirty little bitch, after our kindness and generosity, I told her she could go back to her hovel and rot! And do you know? She told me that Laurent was going to leave me for *her*. She told me she was pregnant. She said she knew I didn't want children, but Laurent did, she would have announced it that afternoon. She told me, they'd planned it, hoped for it, prayed for it. Prayed for it! I don't suppose she even knew what prayer was, and even if she did, I'm sure the good Lord wouldn't listen to *her*. Well, I saw red, who wouldn't under the circumstances? I don't really know what happened next but I do know all of a sudden she was limp and floppy, her mouth open, her head back, her eyes staring out through the windscreen. I'd done it! I'd throttled the cheap little bitch. Then of course I had to act quickly, cover it up, the way I'd planned. But you know, even at a time of extreme stress, my brain was functioning perfectly. I was brilliant. I stripped her and took her clothes into the house, put on Laurent's painting overalls, and a pair of rubber gloves and, adding her thick peasant socks, put on her boots. Ugly clumping things. Laurent had bought them off a student at the Chambre de Métier for a pittance. The boy was only asking 100 francs, Laurent gave him 200, it was the least he could do, fair's fair after all. He brought them home all proud and pleased, said, look what I've got for Renée, these'll keep her warm this winter. Well, she was thrilled to bits, apparently they're in fashion for young girls as well as young men, personally I can't understand it, but that's kids for you.'

They waited in silence for her to continue, the tape recorder clicking quietly as it wound its plastic tape from one spool to another, but Michelle had lost impetus.

'You'd had a brilliant idea and were putting on her boots,' Pel prompted quietly.

She jumped as if prodded with the sharp end of a needle. 'Yes, that's right, so clever! I laced them up, thinking *if* I left any footprints, they'd be hers, not mine. Then just to make sure she really was dead, and to confuse the police when and if she was found, I went out to change her appearance. It was incredibly difficult puncturing her skin but I managed the essential cuts and sat back. That was when I discovered the Stanley knife in Laurent's overalls and set to work on her thighs and things. Once I was satisfied with the effect, I put her back in the car, wrapped and taped into plastic sheeting, I was careful to fold over the corners, so no blood would escape – there was a lot of blood when I'd finished her erroneous rape. Luckily it was raining hard and washed the yard clean.'

Gilbert interrupted. 'What did you use, love?'

'The big scissors Laurent used for cutting the wallpaper. It livens a room up, doesn't it, having one wall covered in pretty paper.'

'What did you do with them afterwards?'

'Threw them in the brambles of course! That place has been so neglected, brambles and nettles everywhere, just below the yard there's an enormous tangle of them, you could hide a horse in there, if, of course you could persuade it to co-operate!' She laughed, a tinkling girlish laugh.

Gilbert didn't. 'Is that where you hid her moped then, love?'

Michelle smiled at him. 'You're not so stupid after all, are you? Yes, just pushed it to the edge of the yard and in it fell. The brambles closed over it like a puddle of mud. Perfect, you see, I'd thought of everything.'

Once again she dried up, confused by the diversion.

'You'd just wrapped the body in plastic.'

'Ah yes, body wrapped, in the car. Then what? Oh golly, I nearly forgot, I put the little folding trolley we use for moving heavy things in the boot and drove down the drive. All the time, I was thinking, working it out, making sure I hadn't made a mistake.'

'Could you describe the trolley, please?'

'I don't see why I should, but if you insist. It was Laurent's invention. When we bought the house there was a dreadful amount of scrap metal lying about. I dropped a lot of it into the brambles, that's how I knew they were good at hiding things. I suppose one day we'll get round to clearing them away. I thought we could replace them with a nice flight of steps down into the field, with statuettes either side – yes, that would look rather smart.'

'The trolley.'

'The trolley. Sorry, I digress, yes, in amongst the scrap metal, Laurent found a rusty old three-wheeler. He converted it into a trolley with a folding handle. Not particularly difficult at all. What's so interesting about a stupid trolley?'

'You'd just put it in the boot.'

'And was driving down the drive, making sure I'd done everything in the right order. I had. When I got to the stream, I got the trolley out, put her on it, pulled it over to the water and tipped her in. All I had to do then was slip the plastic sheeting out from under her, put it in another plastic bag I already had in the car, and arrange her legs so the current washed her . . . her cavity clean, and go back to the house to tidy up. You know, burn the plastic, the rubber gloves, and her wretched boots, they'd been so uncomfortable! Make sure her clothes were no more than ashes and drive swiftly back into town. I was a few minutes late meeting Joelle's husband, but that wasn't my fault, a lorry had shed its load in the middle of St Seine-l'Abbaye and we were sent all over the place before returning to the right road. It didn't matter though, he'd done as I asked and paid for the concert tickets with my card, and his wine, six bottles, how could he do that to a friend who trusted him? Some people are awful, aren't they?'

No one replied.

'Yes, so I had receipts at various times during the afternoon, proving that I'd been in town all afternoon. I disposed of the parking ticket I'd taken half a minute earlier and created a fuss when that nasty little Arab wanted 250 francs. There must have been dozens of people witness to my departure at six thirty. Home by seven, had a shower, I felt I needed it even though hadn't touched the filth with my bare hands. My brother and his wife arrived at seven thirty sharp and stayed until shortly after eleven, when we went to bed. My husband and I, no more smelly Renée. I took the car to a car-wash the following morning, just in case, hoovered out the boot, made it spick and span, just as new, and boiled Laurent's overalls. Perfect, don't you think?'

'Not bad for an amateur.'

'All because your old man was giving her the occasional poke.'

'Michelle, do you feel any remorse about what you've done?'

'Remorse? She was only a peasant, plotting to take what wasn't hers. Dirty little peasant girl, it was a fitting end to such a useless squalid life.'

Brisard was obviously stunned, he was blinking a lot. 'Tell me,' he said, 'did you ever visit a caravan at Larroque, near Pontailler?'

Now everyone in the room was looking stunned, Michelle included. 'I wish to see my lawyer. I shan't say another word without him being present.'

The snazzy shirt made a move. 'Madame, I was appointed to represent you.'

'Oh, well that's all right then.'

When Lambert arrived at nine thirty, he offered Maître Brisard a cup of freshly made coffee from his own personal *cafetière*, while Pel shuffled round his office waiting to be called. Michelle had been charged with deliberate, premeditated murder and taken to 70 rue Auxonne – as the local prison was lovingly known.

Gilbert was bored, and Pel was bored watching him pick his teeth, his nose and any other extremity available. He sent him home at ten. He was silently reaching boiling point when he heard the door down the corridor open, pompous voices congratulating themselves and, finally, after a last bit of back-slapping, 'Commissaire Pel!'

The meeting was short and snappy.

'I don't care what Brisard says, she had nothing to do with the College Cadavre!'

'How do you know?'

'Lambert, this was a crime of passion – well-planned, I grant you. Chouillou was shafting the girl!'

'Pel!'

'Sorry. The accused's husband was involved in a sexual relationship with the victim.'

'Perhaps he had other lovers?'

'Oh, grow up, Chief, this was the first time he'd ever been disloyal to fluffy Michelle. It was a mistake, he was frustrated in his marriage, bossed by his wife, she didn't want kids, he did, et cetera, et cetera, a nubile kid comes along and wants to thank him for his kindness, she was ready to do anything for him. You can see it happening.'

'You may be able to –'

'If you can't, mate, you shouldn't be Chief of Police.'

'Commissaire!'

'Yes, I know – dismissed.'

Pel spent the afternoon in front of the television pretending to watch thirty fully grown, highly trained, well-paid and mostly intelligent men trying to pound each other into the quagmire at Toulouse. It had been introduced as a 'friendly' game of rugby – the World Cup was well and truly behind them – but watching the players pile one on top of the other, fighting for the ball, sweat and mud flying in all directions, he wondered what an 'unfriendly' game would look like; probably like a battlefield out of *Braveheart*, a film he'd surprisingly thoroughly enjoyed until he'd been called out to . . . what was it that evening? He couldn't remember. Not that it worried him for long. Gradually his eyes grew heavy, his head nodded forward and, although he jerked it up several times, his chin finally slipped on to his chest. He was fast asleep.

'Your wife says do you want a whisky!'

Pel leapt a metre out of his chair. 'You stupid woman! It's a good thing I'm not armed, I could have shot you!'

'Your wife says –'

'I heard you the first time! Where is she?'

'Flambé-ing a rabbit in Calvados.'

'Good God, poor little bugger. What's she doing that for?'

'So you can have a change from toadstool stew.'

'I think we may be going out this evening.'

'Not blooming likely! She's been working her fingers to the bone doing a gourmet meal, while you've been snoring like a hog in here.'

'I do not snore like a hog.'

'You ever heard one?'

'Have you?'

'Do you want a whisky, or what!'

'Yes, yes, woman, bring me a whisky, not a what, and make it snappy, I'm gasping with thirst'.

'*Jawohl, mein Kommandant!*' She goose-marched away, her hob-nail boots crashing across the *carrelage* floor.

'A man has to be a saint living in this household,' he said a few minutes later as his wife handed him a tumbler half-filled with golden liquid and two large ice cubes chinking against the sides. 'A saint with cast iron armour. *Merci, chérie.*'

'You have good training at the Hôtel de Police, some of your men must be worse than Madame Routy.' She sat down and sipped at her own less full glass.

'Like the witch in the kitchen, they're an ugly bunch.'

'Alex isn't!'

'I'm sure she sticks her fingers in a faulty plug every morning to get her hair to stand on end.'

'Nonsense, all you need is styling gel, my girls use it all the time at the salon.'

'Oh, how disappointing.'

'And de Troq' isn't ugly either, he's always perfectly groomed.'

'Yes, damn him, standing beside him makes me feel like a tramp.'

'And Nosjean, and Cheriff . . .'

'All right, you win. They're not an ugly bunch. They're fine, handsome and beautifully brought up.'

Geneviève chuckled. 'How are the two new men?'

'Morrison broke his ankle and can only answer the phones.'

'Surely he shouldn't even be in the office?'

'Apparently he's insisted on participating, even if it's only in the paperwork, from tomorrow morning.'

'A brave youngster.'

'A foolish one. When he gets to my age, he'll realise that breaking an ankle is a blessing in disguise. I'd stay at home.'

'You know jolly well you wouldn't, and anyway, you and Madame Routy would have declared full-scale war by the end of the first day.'

'It wouldn't take that long, I assure you.'

'What about the other new man, Gilbert, the one you brought round last night?'

'He's foul-mouthed, racist and rude. Most of the team refuse to work with him.'

'But?'

'But what?'

'I thought you were going to say 'but'.'

'No.'

'Oh.'

'Would you like to go out for dinner?'

'Not tonight, I've prepared something special after our odd picnic last night. What was that all about? Madame Routy had to give the soufflé she'd cooked to the dog next door.'

'In the end it didn't have a great deal of relevance, but I had to justify every minute in a woman's day.'

'Women in general, or a particular one?'

'A very particular one. She carved up a seventeen-year-old girl with a pair of decorating scissors and a Stanley knife.'

'*Mon dieu*! Why on earth did she do that?'

'Because her husband was sha . . . having an affair with her.'

'I see. Who made the arrest?'

'Well, actually it was Gilbert, I thought he almost deserved it.'

'Another whisky?'

'Mm.'

'I'll get it.'

'Thank you.'

Geneviève left Pel puzzling over Gilbert. He was a repulsive man, the sort of bloke he'd have great pleasure slinging into a cell for twenty-four hours to cool off, but . . . His wife had been right: there was a 'but'.

She handed him his refill. 'How's the College Cadavre going?'

'Off, and rather rapidly, I would imagine. It's weeks since the poor woman was murdered, and we keep drawing blanks. We still don't know who she is – I mean, was. The investigation is going round in circles, the men are worn out and don't know where to turn next. We've covered almost every possibility.'

'Almost?'

'A figure of speech.'

'Ah.'

'Dinner's ready when you are. Take your time, there's no urgency.'

'For once in my life,' Pel muttered as she wandered off.

But he was wrong.

There was a very definite urgency, although he couldn't possibly have known it.

Jo-Jo, the Butcher, was feeling bad. He'd tried, God how he'd tried, to forget what he'd done, but the sticky slippery feel of blood under his bare feet, the warm flesh as he sliced through it, the wrench of the joints as they separated in his hands, and the glassy eyes, still open in the severed head, watching him as he worked . . . He couldn't forget those eyes, they haunted him. Every time a woman looked at him, he could see those eyes. He longed to close them, be at peace. Stop them following him everywhere, criticising, chastising, disapproving. And yet . . .

He opened the magazine again, studying the nude, putting his thumb over the model's face, and remembered weighing Marianna's small breasts in his crimson-covered hands. The smell of a woman passing in the street excited and disgusted him, they smelt so sweet and were so sour. And yet . . .

There was one woman . . .

The psychiatrist's widow; now there was a woman with class and intelligence. She'd smelt of . . . of what? Oranges? Cinnamon? Bitter-sweet, not sour. Two days since he'd been in her house. She'd been brave when she'd caught her finger in the drawer, didn't want to show she was hurt. And the game she played about her dead husband; didn't want to show her grief, or perhaps she hadn't cared a toss for him and it amused her to play games with men? She was a strong woman though. Very

208

desirable. Beautiful. Fulfilled – how many children did she have? Four. If she hadn't cared for her husband, why had she given him four nippers? He smiled, perhaps she liked fucking. A real woman.

That evening, he'd watched them all from the enveloping shadows of the forest while they ate supper and talked, and laughed together. She seemed happy, or was she faking it? When they'd cleared the table, the kids had gone through to the other room, leaving her alone, stacking plates in the dishwasher. She'd stopped and gazed out through the window, it seemed straight at him. His heart had thumped in his chest even though he knew he was hidden. Then she'd looked sad, terribly, tragically sad, as if beseeching him to appear and comfort her. The following evening, she'd shut the kitchen shutters and he'd had to work his way through the undergrowth to the back of the house. He'd heard the dog bark inside, noisily, aggressively and had fled through the trees to a safer distance. Later, cold and angry, he'd dared to return only to find the sitting-room had thick curtains and they were closed. One by one the lights had extinguished as the children went to bed and he'd waited longingly for her to do the same, to catch sight of her undressing.

It was nearly midnight when she'd finally gone upstairs and he'd had to hurry round to the front again, scratching his ankles on thorns and thistles. The dog had barked, but only briefly, and he'd stood well back, staring up at the rectangle of light. Kate's silhouette was framed in it, not for long, quickly stripping off her clothes and stepping economically into a man's pair of pyjamas. It had been enough, he'd glimpsed the curve of her breasts, a pointed pink nipple, he'd caressed her taut belly with his eyes, and roamed hungrily over her buttocks. It had taken no more than seconds but she was imprinted on his mind.

He wanted her.

He carefully closed the magazine, closing his eyes at the same time, unzipping his trousers and holding himself carefully, preparing for the pleasure. It had been a month since he'd had a woman, his aching need was growing stronger, and the stronger it grew the more desperate he became. Those two middle-class tarts at the disco had been disappointing, although he'd thought for a moment that Brigitte was keen – stupid bitch, jumping out of the car like that and running off. She could've been hurt. He chuckled at his humour, working rhythmically on his member, coaxing himself to ejaculation. Then the blonde yesterday, nothing more than a common whore, openly leading him on, flirting, rubbing herself up against him, then the moment he made his move, introducing her bloody husband. Thinking about husbands – out of sight but still present to protect when necessary; or temporarily absent, silly men who let their wives go out alone; or, in one case, permanently absent – his deranged mind once more wandered back to the psychiatrist's widow. And the more he thought about Kate, the more he knew he would have to possess her, completely, if only momentarily. He would have to have her, even if it meant killing again.

He half opened his eyes and watched with satisfaction as the semen ran on to his hand, spurting gently like a small, warm, milky fountain.

14

Monday, 6th December
Pel had a headache, which didn't help his mood. But he did have his beautiful new car which cheered him up slightly. Peugeot had exceptionally opened their doors that Monday morning – usually a day off – and allowed him into their well-equipped garages to take possession of the shining Burgundy red – what other colour could Pel have chosen? – Peugeot 406. He'd signed all the necessary papers, was pleased to see the tax disc was already on the windscreen, less pleased to see it had been added to the invoice, had a quick but unsatisfactory argument with the sales manager and left, grumpily agreeing he'd made a fine choice. As he made his way back through town, he paid particular attention to his driving, knowing that sometimes he was apt to think about other things while at the wheel and had in the past had one or two near misses – plus one or two scrapes, the car he'd left behind him in exchange looked as if he'd been at it with a length of lead piping. He was determined to get his brand new, very smart and extremely expensive Peugeot home that evening without a single scratch. This car, he told himself, would see out his career as a *commissaire de police*.

Proud of his slow but uneventful journey, he recklessly leapt up the stairs to his office two at a time, missed his footing, and bent his wrist saving himself on the banisters then stubbed his toe on the last step. This, plus the headache, now pounding between his temples, was not conducive to improving his level of tolerance of idiots, nor patience with the rest of the human race. However, he managed to phone his wife in peace to give her the good news about the car – 'Take care of it, it cost a lot of money.' 'I know, I ruddy paid for it!' 'See you tonight, *mon cher*, you can take me for a spin, have a drink somewhere perhaps?' 'If you insist.' – before Lambert ordered him in for a conference.

Lambert the drone.
Lambert the bore.

Lambert the Chief.

How come he'd got Lambert?

How come he'd got Gilbert, and Morrison for that matter?

How could you take a chap seriously with a name like Morrison? It wasn't even French. He'd claimed when asked, and Pel had made a point of asking, that his grandfather had come from Scotland, thus explaining the peculiar name and his shockingly orange hair. One would have expected him to be dubbed Carrot Top or something similar; in fact he seemed to have acquired the nickname Haricot Vert, either out of perversity or because he was very tall, painfully thin and professionally extremely green. And he was, Pel had noticed, sitting in the sergeants' room, his plastered ankle poking out under his desk, a hazard to all passing traffic, waiting to apologise when someone tripped over it, or for the phone to ring. And how come his cold had come back? Have to have a word with Boudet about that. Nosjean was looking better, he no longer had the flushed face of a fever-ridden policeman. Pel's face felt as if it was building up to bursting into flames any minute.

He glanced up at Lambert's: puffed up and pink, mouth opening and shutting, like a goldfish coming up for breakfast, a goldfish with a white wig. The thought amused him even though he was exhausted.

Kate was feeling exhausted. Her parents had been for the weekend and although she loved them dearly, it had been very tiring; she'd been pleased to see them leave that morning. While she was ready to sell the house in the forest and move back to the Tarn, allowing them to share some responsibility for her children, fetching them from school while she was still at work, for instance – and she knew she was going to have to work for a living – she certainly didn't want to be organised into it. They were only trying to help, she knew that, but sometimes she wished they wouldn't. They'd been round the estate agencies finding out about houses; they'd been round the schools, finding out about them – 'The children's education is obviously an important factor when deciding where to live'; and, damn it, they'd been prospecting for jobs – 'Now he's a highly intelligent man, I'm sure you'll get along very well. All he needs is two days a week, Wednesdays and Saturdays, when his wife is with their children.' So where does that leave mine? Being entertained, and very probably spoilt rotten, by Mum and Dad two of the three days they don't have school. That's not what I want! The situation was hopeless. She had a thirteen-year-old at college, a ten-year-old doing his last year at the village school, and two almost-two-year-olds who weren't anywhere, except with themselves and her. And what about the holidays? What she needed was something she could do at home. Earn a little money to tide them over, until they were in full-time education.

Another two years. Two years was a long time. And doing what?

The monthly bank statement she'd received that morning made it clear she'd soon be in trouble. The few savings she had didn't amount to much, and her regular income was minimal, just enough to cover the cost of the older boys; thank goodness their father was never late with his cheque. If only she'd agreed to become Darcy's wife sooner – a police officer's widow was entitled to a reasonable pension. As it was, she'd buried him the day they'd planned to be married, and was therefore entitled to nothing. And if only the lawyers would hurry up and complete probate, at least then she'd know exactly where she was, though she didn't expect it to make much difference. Whatever Darcy had left would go to his two baby sons; under French law they were his next of kin, not her.

The phone cut through her thoughts, and leaving the kitchen table where she'd been pondering, she unhooked it from the wall.

'Madame Darcy?'

'Monsieur Pancart, how are you?'

'Very well, but concerned. I've found a wood-turner but he's unable to make the legs for your desk exactly as they were. He's given me drawings of what he can do, and I was wondering if you'd help me choose the style that goes best. Would you mind coming to my workshop to discuss it?'

'Yes, of course, when?'

'This evening?'

'I'm not sure I can, my children, you see . . .'

'I do see. What about tomorrow?'

'Same problem.'

'I understand. Perhaps while they're at school? When you come into town to do the shopping? It is quite urgent – if you want to have your desk back quickly, that is. It's coming along nicely, soon be finished, except for the legs of course.'

'I'll try and find someone to look after the children for a couple of hours, it shouldn't be that difficult. I'll give you a ring as soon as I'm organised.'

'Yes, that would be kind.'

She disconnected and wandered through into the sitting-room where the twins were playing with an assortment of cars and lorries and cushions, untidying the tidiness her mother had left – if only her parents had stayed another twenty-four hours . . . She chuckled at her own absurdity. In the old days, she'd asked Annie and Cheriff to come over if she and Darcy wanted an evening out alone. Before that there'd been the girl at the end of the track, but she'd moved away and the cottage was empty now. She sat down to watch the little boys for a minute, unwelcome tears welling up in her eyes.

Moving to Burgundy had been an adventure, buying the forest house with Daniel exciting, decorating it, moving the furniture into the finished rooms and living there together so happily – it all seemed like a dream now. She wasn't lonely, the children filled in the days and part of the evenings, but how she missed Darcy's arms round her when he came home at night, always late but always loving, and his warmth in the bed when they woke in the morning, the comfortable hours they spent in front of the crackling log fire with a glass of brandy discussing this and that. She missed him terribly. Perhaps her parents were right after all, perhaps moving away would help heal the wound, a new start would force her to stop reminiscing, shroud the memories that lived with her here. But she wasn't ready to forget, not yet. She still slept with the shirts she'd taken from the linen basket that smelt of Daniel, although less and less – he was fading rapidly, disappearing, though not completely. Just occasionally, even now, she'd find something he'd hidden, like a bar of chocolate behind the books, knowing she could have a sudden craving for it, too late to buy some, and she'd sit down with a bump and weep at his thoughtfulness.

And she missed him sharing his cases with her, explaining why he was anxious, or angry, or disgusted. It had been fun when the Pels and the Kamels came for supper, almost like old times. And Pujol too. He was sweet.

An idea struck her and, blinking back her tears, she returned to the phone.

Coincidentally, it was Pujol who answered, and without hesitation, before she changed her mind, she put her question.

'Certainly,' he replied immediately, 'I'd be delighted to babysit for a couple of hours. I've got a bit of a cold, though – does that worry you with the babies?'

'Not a bit. I'll give you a remedy if you like, one that works.'

'Okay then, I should be able to be there just after six thirty, if nothing goes wrong. I'll ring you if we have an emergency.'

Kate was pleased. She was also quite surprised she'd dared, but she did want to see the desk Darcy had bought restored to – what had Pancart called it? – its former glory. It was going to be the Daniel Darcy Memorial Desk. She tossed her hair over her shoulder, smiling again, and dialled Pancart's number.

He couldn't work that afternoon. He sat in his silent workshop and stared at Madame Darcy's desk. He hadn't touched it since he'd brought it in, he didn't want to, what he wanted was to touch her. This evening at seven o'clock she was coming to see it, to discuss the turned legs. He hadn't seen a wood-turner, he had no intention of doing so. No need. When Madame arrived, he'd invite her into the flat on the pretext of searching for the drawings the wood-turner had given him. While they were up there, he'd offer her a drink – 'After all,' he would say, 'you were kind enough to offer me one when I came to your house, at least let me return the hospitality.' Of course the drawings would be impossible to find, they didn't exist, and after a while she would become suspicious. That's when he'd say, 'They must be in the workshop, let's go down, it would be better anyway to talk with your desk in front of us.' And once she was in the workshop,

215

he'd lock the door and turn on the huge circular saw to cover any sound, so if someone walked past the property, with his dog or something, he'd say, 'Hmm,' to himself, 'that chap's keen, working at this hour,' and walk on, leaving Jo-Jo to do what he had to do. He must remember to keep the wood-burning boiler alight and hot. That's where he'd put the stray city cats when they wandered in looking for warmth; the next morning there'd been nothing left but a few carbonised bones.

When Pujol arrived in the forest, Kate was ready and waiting. 'They've all had supper, I fed them early. The older boys will help you get the twins to bed at seven thirty, or if you can't face it, let them stay up, it won't hurt for once. I should be back well before nine to sort things out and tuck everyone up for the night. We'll have supper together afterwards if you like, I've prepared a *salade niçoise*, all we'll need to do is grill the steaks in the fireplace.'

It sounded wonderful to Pujol.

'There's white wine in the fridge, red wine on the table, or whisky in the cupboard. Help yourself. If you need anything else ask Patrick or Jack, they know where everything's kept. Oh, and don't let Rasputin out, he'll try and follow the car.'

'Don't worry, we'll be fine, it's only for a few hours. But take care on the roads, it's below zero, minus three already.'

Satisfied by the arrangements and Pujol's confident smile, Kate pulled on her coat, gathered up her handbag and car keys, and drove off down the forest track to meet Monsieur Georges Pancart, *Restaurateur de Meubles*, or so it said on the wall above his workshop – also known as Jo-Jo in the bars and night-clubs he frequented at weekends; the man the police had nicknamed the Butcher.

An hour later, Pujol was helping Jack with his mathematics at the kitchen table, showing him an easier way round a problem, when one of the twins pottered into the kitchen asking for paper. Jack slipped a file out of his satchel and handed him a sheet, and the contented toddler lay full length on the floor beside them to

216

scribble. It was a full five minutes before Pujol glanced down at him and noticed what he was scribbling with. Abruptly, he jerked the pencil from the chubby hand. The child looked up and started complaining loudly.

'Where did you get this!'

Jack glanced up from his maths. 'Hey, what's the matter? He found it!'

'Where?'

The small boy was sitting up and crying now, upset by the aggression and confused by the sudden change in mood.

Jack stared at Pujol, his young eyes bright with hostility. 'He doesn't know what you're on about. Give it back!'

Pujol whipped his head round. 'Do you know where he got it?'

'No! It's been lying around for days, Mum must've given it to him.'

Pujol held the string between two fingers and let the flat red stub dangle. He was breathing heavily, trying to stay calm. 'Sorry, I didn't mean to shout, but this is important. Very important. Do you know how it got into the house?'

'No idea, so what's the big deal?'

'Nothing. Where's Patrick?'

'In his room, doing his homework.'

Pujol galloped up the stairs, banging into the bedrooms until he found the thirteen-year-old bent studiously over his books. His head lifted abruptly as Pujol burst in. '*Qu'est-ce qu'il y a?*'

'Patrick, do you know where this came from?'

'No, why?'

Pujol had to do a bit of quick thinking. 'Police business. We've been looking for a man using a carpenter's pencil just like it, to, er . . . help us with our enquiries.'

'Maybe it was the antique restorer's.'

'Which antique restorer?'

'The one Mum's gone to see tonight.'

'*Merde!*'

'What's wrong?' The startled adolescent ran after Pujol as he flew done the stairs again and all four children watched wide-eyed as he hurried to the phone, snatching it from its cradle and tapping in numbers as if he expected to win the jackpot.

217

'Commissaire Pel, it's urgent!'

'Who's calling?'

'Pujol!'

'Ne quittez pas.'

The forty seconds it took Pel to answer seemed like an eternity, forty dangerous seconds that could save Kate's life.

'Oui, j'écoute, and this had better be important. I was just about to sit down for supper.'

Pujol licked his lips and swallowed, collecting his thoughts together. 'The red carpenter's pencil attached to a piece of string in the caravan.'

'Yes, what about it?'

'I've just found another, one of the Darcy twins was drawing with it.'

'Then ask Kate where he got it.'

'That's just the point, she's not here. I think she's gone to see the man who left it.'

'Oh my God. Who?'

'Hang on. Patrick, do you know the man's name?'

The teenager shook his head.

'They don't know but he's an antiques restorer'.

'Jesus, it could take hours to find him. Stay on the line, I'm looking in Yellow Pages.'

'Jack, find me the telephone directory quick!'

'Pujol, there are hundreds. Where was she going, into the city centre or somewhere else?'

'She expected to be back well before nine, so the round trip, plus the meeting, would have taken less than two hours.'

'So he's probably within a 30 kilometre radius of her house. Try some names on the boys, starting with those listed under Dijon.'

Pujol started reading them of: 'Alibert, Daniel; Antiquités Farenc; Blanc, Jean-Pierre; Bel –'

'Put the forenames first!'

'Marc Bel; Nicolas Bleuze; Vivian Bonaffet; Marie-Claude Cintas; Patrice Cintas . . . *Patron,* they're shaking their heads, this could take all night!'

'Keep going. Geneviève, not now! I've an emergency on my hands.'

'Pierre Crozet; Michel Daux . . .'

Pujol heard insistent mutterings on the line while Pel's wife interrupted. 'Damn it, go away, you silly woman.' He only whispered it, but Pel heard.

'Hold your horses, Pujol, the silly woman is very interesting. Kate asked her to recommend a restorer, we had a grandfather clock done a few years ago and she sent her to the same man. His name was Bernard . . . and bugger it, we can't find him listed anywhere.'

'Maybe he's moved?'

'He did, he experimented with a workshop in the city for a while, but went back to the country. The building's been rerented to another restorer, that's the one dealing with Kate, so my wife says. Hang on, she's found the address! 10 avenue St Pourçain, that's near the canal. Name: Pancart, Georges. Jo-Jo! Have you still got the picture of him?'

'Who?'

'The bloke that got rough with Brigitte Cluzel outside a disco. I know Nosjean gave you a copy!'

'Probably still in my jacket pocket. Yes, I've got it.'

'Show it to the kids then!'

Pujol unfolded the crumpled photocopy of the 'tall, dark and handsome' man with slightly slanting eyes and passed it to Patrick. He and Jack studied it for a moment then, looking up with a frightened expression, shrugged. 'I'm not sure, it could be him, but . . .'

'Not sure,' Pujol repeated, 'could be, but.'

'Does the name mean anything to them?'

'Pancart! Georges, or Jo-Jo, Pancart?'

Patrick frowned. 'Pancart? *Oui, peut-être.*'

'I've got a maybe here.'

'It's enough. Let's go, pick me up on your way through!'

'I can't, I'm babysitting!'

'What's the time?'

'Seven forty-five.'

'Get off the bloody phone then!'

Pel didn't wait. Dropping the receiver into his wife's hands, he was already hammering a well-known number into his mobile.

'Hôtel de Police, Dijon, Commandant Nosj –'

'Nosjean, thank God you're still in the office.'

'Just leaving, Anna's train arrives at –'

'Shut up!'

'*Patron?*'

'Who else is still there?'

'Misset, he doesn't seem to want to go home.'

'He'll have to do. 10 avenue St Pourçain, I'll meet you both there, as fast as you can make it!'

'But Pel, Anna's –'

'Fifteen minutes and alert the gendarmerie to give us back-up, a dozen men, I want the place surrounded!'

'*Patron?*'

'*Move!*'

Jo-Jo moved papers haphazardly across the table, looking for the non-existent drawings. 'This is embarrassing, I appear to have mislaid them. Ah, just a minute, perhaps I left them in the work-shop downstairs. I'll nip down and have a look. Or better still, if you wouldn't mind accompanying me, we could continue our discussion there, in front of your desk it'll be easier comparing the different models of legs that way.'

Kate swallowed a mouthful of the kir Pancart had served her; it was rather flattering, she had the feeling he'd bought the wine and blackcurrant liqueur with her in mind. '*D'accord*,' she said, picking up her coat. 'Then I really must be going, I promised to be back well before nine.'

'What a shame, I've enjoyed talking to you. I'd rather hoped you might stay for supper.'

Good grief! I do believe he's flirting with me! 'That's very kind, but no, I've left an inexperienced babysitter with the children and I don't think he'd be very pleased if I'm late.'

'He?'

'A friend of my late husband's.'

'Isn't his wife with him?' Jo-Jo opened the door and led the way down the steps into the walled yard. 'Be careful, they're icy.'

'He's not married.'

'*Votre copin?*'

Kate laughed. 'Oh no, we're not going out together, he's just a gentleman willing to help out.'

'*Et votre copin?*'

Kate frowned. 'I don't have one. Daniel only died in June, it's too soon, I don't think I could bear anyone else touching me.'

'One day though?'

The conversation was becoming more personal than she liked. 'I can't imagine it, not yet.'

'I wonder what your babysitter would have to say? Don't you think his kindness has ulterior motives?'

'What do you mean?'

'You are an attractive woman, very attractive. Now you're a widow you must be careful of the way men look at you, question why they wish to help.'

'No, not Pujol, he's a sweetie.'

'It's only a warning, take it or leave it. I'm a man, I know the way they think.'

'You may be right, but don't worry – I'm perfectly safe with Pujol.'

'Perhaps, but there will be others who are not so polite.' Would she understand what he was trying to tell her? He had to try and make her – that way, if she remained, it would be an invitation for him to go one stage further.

Kate stood patiently by his side, waiting to be let into the workshop. She folded her arms across her breasts; it was freezing outside and he was beginning to give her the creeps.

Jo-Jo pulled the keys from his pocket. Now he was nervous, already perspiring in spite of the cold. She was so close, he could smell her perfume. Why didn't she run away? The gates to the street weren't locked, he'd left them that way deliberately, giving her a chance. The keys dropped from his trembling fingers, and stopped on the end of a slim chain. 'I . . . I have to attach everything,' he explained, his laughter brittle, 'otherwise I can never find a thing.'

'Like the drawings.'

'Yes, like the drawings.'

He fumbled the keys into the lock and turned, opening one of the heavy wooden doors to the workshop, then, switching on an overhead light, invited her in. She stepped over the mounds of wood-shavings surrounding the machinery and cautiously crossed the floor towards her desk, sitting in the far corner.

Jo-Jo closed the door, watching her all the time.

For a moment Kate was puzzled, running her hand over the old wood. 'But you haven't started it. You said it was almost finished . . .' Her voice stalled as she heard the keys in the lock again. She turned and stared at Pancart. He had a strange expression on his face, not helped by odd highlighting from the single electric bulb; he looked weird, excited, almost sinister. His skin shone with perspiration as he came slowly towards her. Blinking, she told herself not to be silly, that there was nothing to worry about, but the hairs on the back of her neck began prickling, warning her she had made a terrible mistake.

He bent down and pressed a large red knob on one of the enormous machines. It growled and sprang into life, the circular saw turning rapidly in the cast iron platform, slicing the air and sending sawdust shooting towards the high ceiling. The noise was deafening, rasping and shrieking into the shattered silence, cutting off all sound from the city outside, effectively shutting them off from other human ears.

And making conversation impossible.

Now she knew they hadn't come here to talk.

She backed away, bumped into her untouched desk and stopped, cornered and very frightened.

15

The gendarmerie vans screamed through the streets, scattering pedestrians and cars as they approached, passed and disappeared, leaving a shrill echo of ringing in their ears, blue flashing lights imprinted momentarily on their sight.

Pel drove like a maniac, his hand on the horn when he could, climbing on to the central reserve when a halted vehicle blocked his way, jumping the queues at traffic lights, causing near pileups at every junction. Thank God there weren't many people about on Monday evening.

Nosjean slammed the *girofar* on to the roof of the large grey Citroën, reached under the dashboard and set the siren wailing, then, reversing out of the parking place, forced his way into the dawdling traffic and accelerated fast up the avenue. He had no idea what the panic was about, but he knew that's what it was; Anna would just have to wait. Again. 'Give me the directions, Misset! Hurry up!'

'Get out of the fucking way!' Pel hissed to himself, willing every other driver to understand the urgency. He hurtled dangerously past a van, then cut it off dead as he swung back to the right again, crossing its path suddenly, and shot down a side street.

'First right, second left, no, that's one-way! First right, third left!'

Misset was swinging under his seat-belt, the torch beam playing on a street map. 'Cross the canal on boulevard Gorgets, mind the hump-backed . . . bloody hell . . . bridge. Okay, sharp right and you're there! Slow down so I can see the numbers!'

Skidding on to the Quai Galliott, Pel held on to the car with difficulty then, as its bonnet straightened, he stamped on the pedal under his right foot. 100 metres further on, he turned into avenue St Pourçain and slowed down.

The wrong end – 110, 109, 108 – but going the right way. He

accelerated again, cruising now at a more reasonable speed, his eyes flicking, counting off the numbers.

There were headlights coming towards him, glaring and bright. They extinguished, the car had stopped, could be Nosjean and Misset, or the gendarmes. Must be sure. 64, 63, 62.

Another pair of headlights.

Extinguished.

It had to be Nosjean. 19, 18, 17.

It was Nosjean and a vanload of uniformed police, parked outside the gates of number 10, behind Kate's Espace. Nosjean and Misset were already out of the car, flashlights in their hands, breath like smoke in front of their faces.

Pel cut the engine, joined them at a run. 'Switch those things off!'

'What's the fuss about, *patron*?'

He didn't answer, but twisted round as a high-pitched roar pierced the peaceful night. 'What's that noise?'

'Sounds like a saw mill.'

'Jesus Christ!' He turned towards the uniformed officer who was waiting for instructions. 'Is this all the men you could muster?'

'Another van parked round the back, sir.'

'Tell them to be out and ready, guns drawn.' Then to Nosjean, 'Have you got ours?'

'*Patron*, you didn't –'

'Never mind! Take them off the uniforms.'

'With all due respect, sir, gendarmerie regulations say –'

'Bugger gendarmerie regulations, there's a woman in there about to be murdered. Hand them over! Then position your men, don't waste time! We've only got seconds.'

'*Patron*,' Nosjean whispered, 'what's this all about?'

'All you need to know is Kate Darcy is in there with the Butcher.'

'What!'

'Exactly, and I don't like the sound of that saw.'

'It's turning in thin air at the moment,' Misset offered.

'If he starts cutting something up, we're too late.'

'All ready, sir!'

224

'Try the gates. If they're locked, bring the van up, we'll go over from its roof.'

They were all surprised when one of the gates swung open. They stopped, listened, guns swaying from side to side as they watched for any tell-tale shadow of movement.

Nothing but inanimate planks and piles of wood, a wheelbarrow and a stack of neatly cut logs.

One by one they stepped through into the cobbled yard, alert and anxious. In front of them were the double doors to the workshop; lights glowed dully from the flat above, throwing rectangles of pale, colourless light on to the ground, shining on small frozen puddles, turning them into odd-shaped silver mirrors. 'Get a couple of your men up there, hanging out of the windows, front and back.'

As two gendarmes mounted the steps, Pel put his ear to the solid oak door. All he could hear was the shrieking drone of the circular saw. Then, as he listened, another noise joined it. Misset grabbed his arm. 'That's either a drill, or a hand-held jigsaw.'

Pel closed his fingers gently round the icy metal handle, pressed down and pulled.

It was locked.

'We'll have to break it down.'

'*Patron*, both doors are hinged to open outwards, we'll never do it, we need a battering ram of some sort.'

Pel's eyes narrowed: Misset had plugged his brain in.

'It'll take too long, even if we could find something suitable. What about the police van?'

'Too wide, sir, its wings would hit the cement block wall and fold without making any impression at all on the doors.'

'It would also warn the Butcher that we're here.'

'I don't care about that, but we mustn't let him escape, and we must get in there before he kills Kate.'

'If he hasn't already.'

Pujol was fidgeting, unable to stay still, fretting from room to room. Patrick and Jack were being as grown-up as they could but they weren't stupid, they knew that the sudden change in him from tolerant babysitter/friend-of-the-family to active policeman, bellowing questions and shouting into the phone, concerned their mother. They'd asked, over and over again. He'd said there was nothing to report and to be patient. They too were frightened now.

Sitting in front of the television, pretending to watch *Toy Story* with the toddlers, they kept glancing at each other and turning to look at Pujol who was pacing in the background.

'Can't you ring and find out?'

'I just have.'

'It's nearly nine o'clock.'

'I know!'

'Why isn't Mum back yet?'

'Been delayed.'

'We ought to be going to bed.'

'Do you want to?'

'Not really.'

'Then stay where you are.'

'What about the babies?'

'What about them?'

'They're yawning.'

'Shall we put them to bed then?'

'They'll cry, the film hasn't finished.'

'Look,' he said kindly, forcing his voice to stay level, 'I'm no good at this sort of thing. What do you do when there's no school tomorrow?'

'Sometimes Mum lets us bring our duvets down from the beds and we all curl up on the sofas. Often the littles fall asleep.'

'Fine, let's do that then.'

'Coo, can we?'

Kate pressed herself into the dimly lit corner, her eyes darting from left to right, searching for a weapon with which she could defend herself. Incredibly, there was nothing.

Where she would have expected to find screwdrivers, hammers, discarded table legs or simply a short length of wood, there was nothing. Pancart hadn't touched his tools for nearly a week, they were neatly arranged in their place on the wall – at the other end of the workshop.

His expression had changed. His mouth was slightly open now, as if he was panting; she could see his tongue, wet and pink, inside. His nostrils flared, his eyes unblinking, staring at her, coming closer.

Her heart thumped hard inside her chest, confirming the message from her brain, goose-bumps breaking out all over her body. She pulled her coat tighter round her, trying to find a little warmth, reassurance.

Pancart's mouth curved into a hideous smile as he advanced, flexing his fingers greedily round the throbbing jigsaw, its blade vibrating menacingly, and her fear deepened, realising she was going to have to fight for her life. Abruptly, although she was already shivering with cold and apprehension, she slipped the coat off her shoulders and held it in her hands. 'What do you want?' – shouting over the monstrous noise of the screaming machine.

He stopped, surprised by the question, then the slanting eyes became no more than slits. 'You! I've been dreaming of this for days.'

He was close. The acrid smell of sweat was repulsive but she stood her ground. He wasn't close enough.

Two more steps.

Lifting her chin, she took a deep breath and yelled, 'Come and get me then!'

As he reached out to grab her hand, her arms jerked up, opening the coat, flinging it at his head. The jigsaw fell to the ground, grazing her leg, but for a moment he was blinded, giving her a second to push past and escape.

He was quicker than she'd expected. Swiping the coat off, he snatched at her arm and dragged her to him. 'I like a woman with spirit!'

She almost groaned at the hissed cliché. 'I've got plenty of that!' and she brought her knee up sharply, jabbing him viciously in the groin.

He doubled up, but didn't let go.

Her feet lashed out, aiming for his shins. It made no difference, the grip on her arms tightened, digging into her flesh.

He hit her. Her face ricocheted off his savage hand, her cheek stinging as if it had been scorched, and for a brief moment they stood looking at each other. Then his right hand slid down to her wrist and, watching her face hungrily, he brushed the bulge in his trousers with her fingertips.

She recoiled, twisting suddenly, and was startled to find she'd managed to wrench herself free. Swinging her fists wildly, Kate caught him on the jaw and retreated. Almost immediately she collided with the metal guide of the shrieking circular saw; she was trapped again, wedged between the sliding surface and the main platform.

He punched her on the side of the skull. She staggered forward almost into his arms, stunned, stumbling over her own feet, unable to stop herself falling. There was a crack as her head hit . . . she didn't know what, and she stared in astonishment at the pain.

Lurching to her knees, still dazed, off balance, she reached for something solid, pulled herself up, reeled back, straight into Jo-Jo.

Slowly, he turned her round, his jaw set, his eyes burning bright, pressing her against the roaring machine, clutching her throat, throttling her, pushing her down, bending her backwards, towards the lethal slicing blade behind, large enough and sharp enough to split tree trunks.

A handful of hair was caught and torn from her scalp, burning sharply as it was ripped out. She struggled frantically, twitching from side to side, but he held her rigid, pushing her head closer to the cutting edge of the saw.

'You're crazy! Leave me alone!'

'I'll leave you alone, when I've finished.' Lifting her slightly, he leaned over her, his breath hot and foul on her face. 'Do you know what I'm going to do to you?'

Kate didn't answer.

He punched her again. Red lights flashed in her brain and as the skin on her spine tore on sharp cast iron corners, she put her hand out to save herself.

The teeth of the whirling saw touched her fingernails, tearing at them. She snatched them back, took a swipe at Jo-Jo, but he caught her arm and dragged her away. 'Are you frightened?'

Her eyes were wide and terrified as she swallowed, trying to find her voice.

'And I haven't even started yet!'

Pel swung round, searching for a solution, his eyes scanning everything in the glittering, frosted yard.

'*Patron*, we're wasting time.'

'Right! Get both main gates open, then spread out!'

No one argued.

As the second gate swung back, Pel was sprinting to his brand new Peugeot. Climbing in, he slotted the key into its ignition. The engine turned over and died. Fucking car!

He screwed up his eyes, willing his thoughts to clear.

Don't think about Kate.

Don't think about Darcy.

This is just another police emergency.

Got it! It's cold, needs choke.

This time the engine fired. He revved it noisily then, clipping himself carefully under the seat-belt, he engaged first gear and manoeuvred his pride and joy gently into the yard.

Nosjean was standing to the right, watching, anxious, waiting.

Misset was pressed up against the wall to the left, looking remarkably intelligent, light bulbs behind his eyeballs.

Pel revved the engine again, his foot pressed down on the clutch, praying his plan would work.

He released the hand-brake, lifting his left foot abruptly. The wheels spun, squealing on the ice-covered cobbles, smoking as the rubber smouldered under the friction, then, just as he thought it was useless, the tyres caught and the car shot forward.

The solid oak doors came hurtling towards him, then, with an almighty bang, the bonnet folded, rippling in front of the wind-screen, and the car stopped dead.

One or two planks were splintered and broken.

Not enough.

And the Butcher would have heard. The element of surprise was lost.

Not entirely. He'd probably be wondering what was going on.

Crashing the gear-box into reverse, he tried to move the car away from the doors. It resisted, struggling back only a bare metre; the wheel arches were bent down into the tyres, working as brakes.

'Pel! Stop!'

Misset appeared out of nowhere, squeezed between the bonnet and the solid wooden barrier, and bending, took hold of the bumper in both hands. For a moment Pel wondered what the hell he was up to.

He could see Misset's teeth, clenched in effort, the veins in his temples standing out, throbbing, looking as if they'd burst. Briefly Misset was as crimson as young Morrison, then with a back-breaking wrench, he jerked upwards, pulling the bumper outwards.

Thumbs-up.

Pel hit the accelerator, twisting urgently to look over his shoulder. The car lurched backwards.

Brake.

First gear.

Accelerate.

Drop the clutch.

The brand new, rather bent Peugeot charged again. Pel kept the pedal pressed determinedly to the floor of the car.

Another ear-splitting collision.

The windscreen shattered into a million tiny cubes.

Regardless, he wrestled with the gear-box and heard the car complain, groaning, agonising, as it was extracted from the hole punched in the thick planks, bumping grudgingly back over the cobbles, the wheels grinding angrily on their axles, the torn coachwork shredding the tyres as it bit into the rubber.

The hole was large enough for a man to slip through.

Nosjean and Misset were inside. Three uniforms followed.

Pel fought with a buckled door frame, forcing his way out of the wreck, ran a few paces, and ducked under the fractured wood.

Georges Pancart was cornered, staring, his hands in the air. Nosjean and Misset faced him, legs bent, arms stretched straight and tense towards him – cover and hold – steadying the automatic pistols, daring him to move a muscle. The gendarmes were either side, completing the circle, making escape impossible. He wouldn't be going anywhere without being cuffed to at least two of them. The huge circular saw went on screaming in thin air.

And just in front of Georges Pancart, almost hidden by hastily kicked wood-shavings, was Kate, her emerald green jumper ripped, a bloody breast exposed.

Pel removed his jacket and dropped it over her then crouched down to feel for her pulse. As he did so, he noticed his hand was shaking, he was reliving the day Darcy died.

Blinking back the image of violent death, of his despair at the waste of an excellent officer and a good friend, he looked at Kate's pale face, unsmiling and silent.

Not her as well.

Please God, not that.

Easing his fingers under the tumbling dark hair, Pel swallowed, holding his breath. He closed his eyes, praying he'd find her heart still beating.

'Call an ambulance,' he shouted, 'and someone switch that thing off!'

In the eerie quiet that followed, he stood up slowly and walked towards Jo-Jo Pancart, now trembling with fear.

Pel looked up into the Butcher's eyes, searching to see what went on in the mind of a man who could do what he had done; the College Cadavre was still clear in his memory. He saw nothing he could determine. Was this animal human?

'Tell me,' he said silkily, 'when you were with the woman in the caravan, why did you cut off her finger?'

'I . . . I wanted to test the poultry shears.'

Without realising it, Pel's fist had clenched into a hard ball, his arm swung back, and he smashed it into Pancart's stomach.

The prisoner doubled up, gasping, sobbing, tears in his eyes. 'You can't do that! You bastard, you're not allowed to!'

He was human.

'*Embarquez-le!*'

Geneviève opened the door anxiously as the wailing police car rocked to a halt outside the house and she saw Pel running up the path. 'Get the Twingo started, you've got to take me to the forest. Pujol will need help.'

'Oh *mon dieu*, what's happened?'

'Don't argue. Grab your coat and get going!'

'Madame Routy's still waiting to serve our supper.'

'Damn the woman, she can eat it herself!'

As Geneviève drove, Pel calmly told her of the evening's events. She kept her eyes on the road and changed gear smoothly and efficiently. 'Just one other thing,' he ended, 'I'm afraid I buggered my new car a bit.'

'A bit?'

'Well, quite a lot actually.'

'How much?'

'It's a write-off.'

'Oh, Pel, you've only had it a few hours.' She was disappointed but, compared with everything else, did it really matter? 'Oh well, perhaps the garage'll sell you your old one back.'

The moment Geneviève stopped outside the Darcy house, the front door flew open and Pujol rushed at them.

'Kate . . .?'

'How are the children? What did you tell them?'

'They're fine, I didn't tell them a thing. What about Kate?'

'Let's sort the kids out first, shall we? That's why I brought my wife.'

All four boys were sleeping peacefully under duvets on the sofas. Only Patrick opened an eye as they went in. 'Where's Mum?'

'Don't worry about her,' Geneviève said soothingly. 'We'll tell you all about it tomorrow.'

'But where is she?'

'In hospital, under observation.'

He eased himself out from the covers, carefully wrapping a baby brother back under them. 'Look, Geneviève, I'm thirteen years old and I want to bloody know.'

'You're very like your father, aren't you?' Pel could have bitten his tongue off.

'How do you know? You've never met him.'

'I'm sorry, I meant Darcy.'

232

'Yes, maybe I am. He taught me a lot, and one thing was not to be fobbed off with silly stories or half-truths.'

Pel put an arm round the lean shoulders. 'If you'll help Pujol and me get this little lot upstairs into bed, we'll have a man-to-man directly after they're settled, *d'accord*?'

Watching her husband carry a small sleeping form tenderly up the stairs, Geneviève sighed in amazement. He'd never liked babies, shown absolutely no interest in them at all, always said he didn't regret not having children; in fact, once, shortly after Darcy had been murdered, he'd admitted he was grateful they didn't. But to see him place the slumbering bundle on the mattress, arrange the tiny limbs comfortably, pulling up the covers and tucking them in, brushing the soft curling hair with his fingertips before joining her on the landing, she found it hard to believe her eyes. 'You really –'

'Police business,' he replied seriously, and winked. 'Now, Patrick, tell me, do we leave the landing light on? Bedside lights? What do you reckon?'

Tuesday, 7th December

The door to the sergeants' room slammed open and made the usual collection of mugs on the filing cabinets jingle. 'My wife says you're not an ugly lot, but looking at you this morning, I know she's mistaken! I've just spent half the night sitting in someone else's house and have had very little sleep, so don't start!'

Gilbert dropped his copy of *Lui* on the desk, stood up and shuffled over.

'Especially you!'

Gilbert extended his hand. 'Just wanted to congratulate you, guv. Nice one.'

'Oh, thank you.'

'Lambert's been pestering for you, I told him to stuff off. You'd report in when you were good and ready.'

'*Ah bien.*'

'And seeing as today is going to be back to the old monotonous grind and waiting for Forensics to get its arse in gear, why don't you take it easy?'

'Easy! Good God, Gilbert!'

'Now, now, guv, watch the old blood pressure.'

Pel's blood pressure was near boiling point all day. Leguyder was being his normal aggravating self and refusing to answer questions until he'd finished *all* his analyses of *all* the articles removed from Pancart's apartment. And Lambert had a go at him for not completing the paperwork before moving into 10 avenue St Pourçain.

'If I'd waited for the necessary paperwork, Madame Darcy would be dead, sawn into small pieces, and fed into that monstrous boiler of his! She'd be nothing but a pile of charred bones right now.'

'Even so, Pel, Maître Brisard has pointed out that its absence may prejudice the case when it comes to court.'

'We caught him red-handed! Or should I say, not quite red-handed, he hadn't started jointing her, thank God.'

'Police procedure is not written to be ignored, it should be applied, to the letter, even in the most extreme cases. You were out of order.'

Pel's eyes grew hard. 'Then suspend me.'

It would have given Lambert the greatest of pleasure, but looking at the cantankerous detective standing defiantly in front of him, he had the idea it would give Pel the greatest of pleasure too; particularly when speaking to the journalists already clamouring at the doors for personal interviews with the arresting officer of the hated Burgundy Butcher, and all of whom he'd avoided, so far.

'Not this time, but it's your last chance.'

When Kate opened the door to her house, Pujol was sitting at the kitchen table attempting to feed the twins a late breakfast. Neither of them seemed to want any. Patrick and Jack were grinning at his thwarted attempts. She was very pale, her face was badly bruised where her cheek had caught the side of a machine as she'd fallen in the struggle, her shoulder ached from the terrible fight before she'd finally lost consciousness, and she

234

was wearing a very old-fashioned sweater that didn't suit her. Pujol smiled with relief, and sneezed into a poised handkerchief: she was still beautiful. 'How do you feel?'

'Shaky and ancient. How are you? Your cold's worse.'

'Fair's fair, we take it in turns at headquarters. Jack reckons that with a nose this red I stand a good chance of being elected to lead Papa Noel's sleigh on Christmas night.'

She walked round the table kissing her delighted children then stopped beside Pujol, putting chilly scarred hands up to his face. 'That weirdo last night suggested you were only being kind to me because . . .'

'Because what?'

She looked deep into his eyes. There was no malice, no lust, just simple uncomplicated friendship. 'It doesn't matter. He was wrong.' She put her lips to his cheek. 'Thanks for looking after them. They're all I've got left.'

Wednesday, 8th December

Leguyder finally phoned through at midday. 'Nothing,' he said. 'The clothes you gave me are clean.'

'He must've burnt the bloody ones in his ruddy boiler. What about his shoes?'

'Also clean.'

'They can't be!'

'Not a speck of blood anywhere.'

'But you said the caravan would've been swimming in it.'

'I did. The only hypothesis I can put forward is that he and his victim were naked when he killed her, that he remained naked while he was dissecting the body, and only redressed afterwards, perhaps even after washing, putting his shoes on as he left the caravan to throw the bags in the river. Or, as you suggest, he burnt the lot. Unfortunately, there's no proof. The cinders I've examined are just that, nothing but wood ash.'

'What about particles of earth from the campsite?'

'You've got a hope with the weather we've had. The soles of his shoes, and the stitching, revealed nothing but rainwater, sawdust and mud, and that's not the right sort.'

'So you can't prove he was ever at Larroque.'

'No. But I can prove he was in the caravan. His fingerprints match one on the door, his feet match some on the wall by the bed.'

'It's not enough! Not for a conviction of murder. Without something more he'll get off with the attempted murder of Darcy's wife, and if he's got a clever lawyer, it'll be no more than assault.'

'I thought he admitted testing the poultry shears on the finger I found?'

'And has since denied it. You know we need more than that. This is his first recorded offence, he might not even go to prison!'

'I do know,' Leguyder replied calmly. 'That's why I spent all sodding night in the lab when I should've been at home in bed. I've got the most dreadful headache this morning.'

'Take an aspirin,' Pel said unsympathetically. 'What took all night?'

'He had a knife on him. I dismantled it, piece by piece.'

'What knife?'

'A large pocket knife attached to a chain, clipped to the waistband of his trousers.'

'Yes?'

'It's got his fingerprints all over it and . . .' Leguyder sneezed. 'Excuse me.'

'And?'

'And this is what's taken so much time, determining the substance clogged into the joint. It was obviously recently washed because some of that substance was detergent, but once I'd finished taking it apart, we found what we were looking for round the rivet that held it together. I've subsequently been able to extract a DNA profile of it. It was blood.'

'And . . .'

'It matches the College Cadavre.'

'Bingo!'

'But . . .'

'What?'

'Nothing, Pel. Congratulations, you saved Kate Darcy's life and you've caught the Butcher.' The scientist sneezed again.

236

'Sorry, I think I've caught a cold somewhere, I'm feeling distinctly ropy today. By the way, who was the victim in the caravan?'
'We still don't know.'

In the next-door office, Lambert was frowning as he spoke quietly into the phone. 'Brisard, at last! It's all gone wrong.'
'What's all gone wrong?'
'Pel and Gilbert are getting on like a house on fire!'
'They can't be! We chose Gilbert with Pel specifically in mind.'
'I'm telling you! I've just had Gilbert in here and asked his opinion of his commanding officer. He said, and I quote, 'Pel's a bleeding stickler for equality amongst men, particularly his men, including the women, even the kid with the big tits that fielded phone calls for a few days. Sometimes he's a bit of a fucking bore, but aren't we all? Apart from that, yeah, he's okay, glad to be on the team'.
'Impossible'.
'Then I called Pel in and asked him what he thought of Gilbert after partnering him for a week. He was short and to the point: "Can be a bugger but shafting up nicely." '
'What did he mean by that?'
'It was a slip of the tongue, he meant shaping up nicely.'
'Oh dear, I think we've lost Round One'.
'Better luck next time?'